All's ___ ___ngle Valley

A Novel

Martha Reynolds

For Judy—
Thank you—
Enjoy this—
love Martha

Other Books by Martha Reynolds

The Swiss Chocolate Series
Chocolate for Breakfast
Chocolate Fondue
Bittersweet Chocolate

Bits of Broken Glass

Best Seller

A Winding Stream

Villa del Sol

The Happy Ever After Series
A Jingle Valley ~~Wedding~~
April in Galway

All's Well in Jingle Valley

Copyright ©2019 by Martha Reynolds

Cover art copyright ©2019 by Heather McCoubrey & Carol Wise (Wise Element)

ISBN-13: 9781691821280

ONE

Julie Tate forced herself to think happy thoughts before dialing Freddy's number. *Smile, dammit. He can always tell.*

She knew someone had picked up, but there was nothing, only dead air.

"Freddy?" Julie called into her phone. She pressed a button to put it on speaker and continued to fold laundry.

"Hang on, doll, Val just threw his sippy cup on the floor." Julie listened as Freddy cooed in the background. There was that all-too-familiar pull on her heart. She folded a pale blue hand towel and touched it to her cheek.

"You can call me back."

"Nope, all set. He's fine. I should've worn a bib! Right, Val?" Freddy chuckled. "What's up?"

Julie tossed a pillowcase on top of the other linens and held the phone to her ear. "April Tweed and her fiancé are coming up for the Columbus Day holiday weekend. I want to put them in the wedding suite."

"Isn't that bad luck or something? I mean, fine by me. It's not booked. And it's April Tweed! Jules, I'm still pinching myself. I love her."

Julie smiled. She had been thrilled when April reached out, pleased that her old friend from Manhattan remembered their venture. Freddy's marketing ideas had worked, apparently—a holiday photo card in December, another in the summer. April wasn't an online subscriber to their quarterly newsletter, but Freddy was diligent—make that obsessive—about keeping addresses and emails on file for every single person either of them had ever met. "Someday it'll pay off," she remembered him telling her.

"Well, don't forget what happened the last time we were counting on a society name from New York. What was that girl's name again?"

"Margot Dexheimer," Freddy said without hesitation. "I can't believe you'd ever forget."

"I only forgot her name. I remember everything else about that cursed booking." Margot Dexheimer, the emotionally stunted only child of Manhattan real estate mogul Morton Dexheimer and his Botoxed X-ray wife Emily. Margot's ill-fated betrothal to a young Russian (*what was his name?*) who was arrested for participating in a huge Medicare fraud scheme. Julie wondered if Margot had found someone new, or if she made weekly visits to Rikers Island. *Forget about Margot Dexheimer*, she told herself.

"Anyway, April Tweed is no Margot Dexheimer. This could be really great for business, Freddy. I just wish they were giving us more time. The first of December is in less than two months. Do you think they'll have a big wedding?"

"Probably not with such short notice, but it doesn't matter. We've done big and small weddings before. I've got some paperwork to finish up while Val is sleeping. How about I stop by in an hour or so?"

Julie smiled. "Give Valentino a big smooch from his Auntie Julie." She disconnected and finished folding laundry, trying not to think about sippy cups.

TWO

While she waited for Bill to arrive home from the school where he taught, April Tweed used her time to pack their bags for the long weekend away. Jingle Valley looked charming, according to Julie's website. And there was a photo of her standing next to her business partner, Fred Campion, surrounded by green grass and tall sunflowers. Julie looked exactly the same, April thought, absentmindedly touching her hair. She'd met Julie Tate at a spin class five years ago and the two had been comfortable with each other from the start. Maybe it was that Julie hadn't ever watched *Echo Falls*. Or maybe because she hadn't fallen all over herself when April mentioned that she appeared on a daytime series. They'd begun a tradition of going for coffee on Wednesday mornings after spin class, and had become good friends, even if April would say she didn't have any close friends. When Julie had made her decision to move from Manhattan and start a new life and a business in her hometown of Dalton, Massachusetts, she'd called April to discuss it. But April, who had just been killed off the show in a most undignified way, had been on vacation and didn't return the call until Julie was already gone, off to her new life on a farm in the Berkshire foothills. April had sent her a Japanese maple for good luck.

She and Bill walked in comfortable silence past the

loungey café on Seventh Avenue, the one that served the roast beef sandwich Bill liked so much. The car rental place was in Columbus Circle, and April enjoyed being under a warm sun. She turned her face up to a cloudless blue sky. The sun was setting earlier as late summer dissolved into autumn, and she was grateful for the time outside. Bill slipped his free hand into hers as they strolled past a middle-aged couple arguing in front of Duane Reade Pharmacy. A young woman in oversized sunglasses swerved around them, never looking up from her phone.

She told Bill she didn't want to drive. "It's been years, Billy. I will if I have to, but I'd rather not kill us both."

"Are you nervous, love?" He squeezed her hand before letting it go to open the door of the rental agency.

"I don't think so," she said, pausing in front of the open door. "I'm looking forward to seeing the place." She dismissed her own thought with a shrug. "I just hope it's as nice as it looks on their website. It would be hard to turn it down now that I've asked for the date. And we're spending the weekend there."

"It'll be fine. Believe! Come on, let's get the car. We might get out of the city ahead of the mass exodus." He took April's small bag from her hand and secured it on top of the big rolling bag he'd pulled behind him, a double-decker of luggage for their weekend away.

Thirty minutes later, Bill had snaked his way out of the city and was driving north, parallel to the Hudson River, past Peekskill and Mahopac, Fishkill and Poughkeepsie.

"It would be great to visit Hyde Park one day," April murmured.

"We will," he replied. She noted that he drove with concentration, eyes on the road, hands at ten and two, the way her father had taught her when she was sixteen. April smiled and relaxed in her seat.

Continuing north, she observed exit signs for towns that were likely named by German and Dutch settlers—Staatsburg, Rhinebeck, Germantown. Bill pulled the car off the highway and meandered into town.

"Germantown! We're still in New York, aren't we?" April pulled her seat back to an upright position.

"Yeah, but I could use a break. This place looks good." He drove into a small parking lot on the side of a homey-looking café. "Could you eat?"

"Sure," she said, glancing at her watch. "We'll be early-bird diners. I know this is more your style."

Bill laughed. "Think of it as a late lunch, then."

**

When they reached the Massachusetts Turnpike, the GPS voice directed Bill not onto the Pike, as April assumed, but put him on a secondary road heading east into Massachusetts. Now with the sun behind them, Bill drove into an approaching dusk. He flipped on his headlights and stared hard at the road ahead.

"You okay, honey?"

"Yep. Just not used to this—you know, driving at night, on an unfamiliar road."

"I know you wanted to leave in the morning. I'm sorry, I shouldn't have pushed for going tonight."

"It'll be fine," he muttered. "I just have to pay attention."

After a few minutes, Bill stopped again and April knew they weren't at the farm yet.

"Everything okay?" She squinted out the window into total blackness. So unlike her city of constant light. "Where are we, Billy?"

His hands still gripped the steering wheel, even though the car was in park. "I just need to stop for a minute, Bren. I'm as tight as a cork in a bottle." He opened his door and stepped outside, lifting his arms over his head, twisting his torso from side to side.

Poor Billy, she thought. He's tense from driving. And I was so insistent about leaving tonight. She opened her door and got out of the car.

"It's cold out! We must be close. Right?"

"Right. We're just outside of Pittsfield, and Dalton's another ten to fifteen minutes down the road," he said.

Bill flexed his shoulders, then opened April's door before jogging around to his side. The GPS pointed him east and Bill looked determined as he stepped on the gas and headed down the road.

Even with his high beams on, he still missed the entrance to Jingle Valley. Cursing under his breath, he turned the car around and headed back. He drove up a long driveway and parked the car next to a silver Prius.

"We're here," he said. "Finally." He exhaled and raked his fingers through his hair, from his forehead to his neck. "Okay, let's do this."

April fidgeted next to him. She flipped the sun visor down and slid the lighted mirror on so she could reapply lipstick. As Bill turned off the ignition, he took her chin in his hand and turned her face to him. "You are gorgeous, my love. And this weekend is going to be wonderful." He stopped short of kissing her freshly colored lips, giving her a chaste peck on the cheek instead.

"Hope so." She opened the car door and stepped out, her heel sinking into the gravel of the driveway.

**

Julie greeted them outside as they walked toward the door of a house.

"Welcome to Jingle Valley!" She held out her arms to embrace April first, then Bill. "I'm so happy to see you both. April, you are ageless. What has it been, three years?"

"Probably four since we last saw each other. Thanks, you're sweet. This is your place!" April squinted in the near-darkness. Dim outdoor lights were charming but ineffective. All she could make out was a looming structure yards away she assumed was the barn. The three were standing in front of a house, Julie's residence, April assumed, an old white farmhouse that looked to be in need of a paint job. A yellow-lighted lantern hung on either side of the front door, and solar lights marked a pathway to the barn. Two large pumpkins slumped on the front step, and there were those dead cornstalks tied to the posts of the carport. *October in New England*, April thought, smiling.

As if reading April's mind, Julie said, "I didn't put on any of the really bright lights, because they can be harsh, but you'll be able to see everything better tomorrow in the daylight. How was the drive?"

"Fine, fine," Bill said, and April was grateful that he fibbed. "You have a lot of land. That's the barn, where the weddings are held?"

Julie nodded. "Yes, and your room is on the second floor in the back. I'll take you there. I was hoping Freddy could join me for the grand tour, but his babysitter cancelled at the last minute."

"Oh! And his wife…?" Bill asked.

"His *husband* Bob manages a bank in the next town, and they have a little boy. He's beautiful." Julie gave them both a bright toothy smile.

"And what about you, Julie? I remember a conversation where we spoke about children. Do you have any?"

"I'm an aunt to Val—that's Freddy and Bob's boy—and I couldn't be happier! Now, let's get you settled in. I want you to stay in our wedding suite, see how you like it, because it'll be yours again in eight weeks!"

She paused, and tapped her index finger against her chin. "Oh! Hang on just a sec," she called before racing into the house. The area was suddenly floodlit and April blinked against the stark brightness. When Julie emerged from the house, she explained. "I know it's dim without these lights. Can't have any of our guests falling down in the dark! But you can understand why I didn't want you blinded."

Julie led the way around the outside of the barn, past rows of decorative cabbage and chrysanthemums in orange and russet, where a well-lighted, covered staircase led to the second floor. "Let's get you settled first. I know the drive from the city can be exhausting."

She climbed the back stairs and led Bill and April down a carpeted hallway to their suite. Soft light from wall sconces cast gentle shadows on their feet. "Since we first opened, we've added three extra rooms on this floor. It wasn't enough to just have the suite. Now, if you want any of your guests to be closer than the hotel in Pittsfield, there's plenty of room. But here's the suite." She pushed open double doors and stepped to the side. April walked into the room.

Three large windows looked out into a dark night. April stared into the blackness, imagining the landscape outside, seeing her reflection in the window. There was a polished wood floor and a couple of small tasteful rugs in shades of beige, and two large mirrors on the inside walls that she imagined reflected daylight. She moved into the bedroom, where a king-sized bed stood high off the floor, covered in shades of blue and violet. April counted eight pillows at the head of the bed, all in the same rich colors.

Julie stood waiting as Bill and April emerged from the bedroom and wandered around the living room. A small kitchenette stood along the far wall and April spied a Keurig coffeemaker. *Perfection.*

"I hope it's okay," Julie said finally.

"It's wonderful," Bill gushed. "Sweetheart?"

April turned to face Julie. "It's really magnificent, Julie. I didn't know what to expect, but if the barn looks anything like this, I think we've found an ideal spot for our wedding. And I'm looking forward to seeing the views!"

Julie mimed wiping sweat from her forehead. "I'm so glad! I mean, April, I'm sure you've stayed in the best hotels."

April tilted her head at Julie but said nothing in reply.

"Sorry, I don't know why I said that. I guess I'm just nervous that Jingle Valley measures up to your standards."

"We both love it," Bill offered.

"Do you want to see the barn tonight? Or it can wait until tomorrow if you're tired."

"How about we meet you down there in about fifteen minutes?" April asked.

"Great. And, by the way, everything will look different tomorrow in the daytime. It's supposed to be a sunny day." Julie beamed at them before handing the key to Bill and closing the double doors quietly behind her.

"I think she was afraid we wouldn't like it," Bill chuckled, as he poked his head into the spacious bathroom. "Great shower," he murmured.

"It really is nice, isn't it? Honestly, Billy, I had my doubts, but this room is as good as any I've stayed in."

"Better than the Hotel Meyrick in Galway?"

"Well, you weren't in it with me, were you?"

He shook his head. "No, my little room was nothing like this."

THREE

Julie hurried downstairs to the barn and surveyed the large room. Strings of tiny white lights were suspended from the beamed ceiling to the walls, and votive candles flickered along the sideboards and on one of the tables. Until she knew what April wanted, Julie held back from doing too much decorating. The important thing was that April and Bill liked the venue and booked their wedding there.

She pulled out her phone and sent a text to Freddy.

They're here. They love the suite and are coming to the barn in a minute or so. Any chance you can get here?

She kept one eye on the door and another on her phone. Freddy replied.

Bob just walked in the door. Give me ten minutes and I'll be there.

Great. Freddy was better at schmoozing customers, even though Julie was the one who knew April. Well, she didn't really know April that well. They'd ridden bicycles next to each other in spin class and gone out a half dozen times for coffee. April didn't talk a lot about herself, and Julie was careful not to ask questions. She imagined April had put up with enough of the limelight. It was just around the time that Julie had decided to pack it in and move to Dalton that April was killed off the series. She remembered not seeing her at the gym for two weeks in a row, and then hearing about the demise from Freddy. She'd called him one afternoon and he had sounded irritated.

"What's wrong?" she recalled asking.

"I'm watching my soap, Jules. And they just killed off the main character."

"How did I not know you watch a soap opera? Are you for real, Freddy?"

"Shush. There's a commercial on now. I've been hooked on *Echo Falls* for years. I tape it when I'm not home. Don't judge me."

Julie laughed. "Wait. Which show do you watch?"

"Echo Falls. Why?"

"Oh! The woman on that show, she's my friend from spin class. I don't know who she plays, but her name is April-"

"April TWEED? You're friends with April TWEED? Why did you never tell me? Hold on, I have to record the rest." Julie waited while he hit buttons. *So that's why she wasn't in class? Because she lost her job? Poor April.*

"Julie, tell me again how you're friends with April Tweed. I cannot believe this."

"We take spin class together. I knew she acted on a soap, sorry, on a *daytime series*, but I never asked her about it. I think she was glad to be somewhat anonymous with me. But she hasn't been in class lately."

"They killed her off! She was devoured by a mountain lion! Stop laughing, Julie, it was very tragic. And I just read in *People* that her husband left her for a model." He paused. "Oh, sorry, babe, that cuts close."

"Just because Christopher married a model doesn't mean I can't handle it. Honestly, what the hell difference would that make? Didn't I tell you that April and I took spin class together?"

"Um, no. I definitely would've remembered that."

"Well, now you know. Wow, I'm sorry she lost her job. I want to tell her about our move to Dalton."

"Maybe she won't want to hear it, Jules. I mean, she got killed off the series, and now you're moving away. Although I *would* like to meet her. Maybe you could invite her to lunch and I could just happen to be there."

"She just wanted to be treated normally, Freddy. And I did. Treat her normally."

"You should have let me know that you knew her," he pouted.

"Yeah, sorry. But I feel so bad for her! Should I send her a text?"

"You seriously have her phone number???"

"Of course I do. And no, you can't have it. But should I send her a note? I thought maybe I'd see her before we left. Now I'm not so sure."

Julie had called and then sent April a text, but she never heard back, and then it was time to leave Manhattan. After she and Freddy were situated at Jingle Valley, she sent a mini-spa basket to April and invited her up to the farm anytime. She did receive a lovely thank-you note for the basket, which she still had tucked away somewhere, and April had a Japanese maple tree shipped to the farm, but they hadn't kept in close touch. The tree was about two feet tall when it arrived, and it now stood majestically at over ten feet high. Julie made a mental note to show it to April when she came.

A noise at the door brought Julie back to reality. Bill and April entered the barn and paused. Julie hurried over to meet them.

"Wow," April whispered. "It's stunning."

"It is," Bill said, his arm around April's shoulders. "This is perfect, isn't it? It's exactly what we'd talked about."

Julie brought the palms of her hands together in a prayer of thanksgiving, just as Freddy strode in.

"Hello! Pardon my lateness." He paused at the sight of April and Julie thought he actually quivered. She tried not to roll her eyes. With a sharp intake of breath, he said,

"Miss Tweed, it's an honor." Freddy, cool, suave Freddy, looked like a twelve-year-old in the presence of Miss America. Or Cher. Julie half-expected him to curtsy.

April smiled coolly, a look Julie imagined she'd perfected after years of fans clamoring for an autograph. "It's April, please. I hear you're a new father."

Freddy beamed at Julie and turned back to April. "Yes! His name is Valentino, but we call him Val. He's thirteen months tomorrow." Freddy sighed and stared at April as if she was his own darling boy Val.

"Hi, I'm Bill Flanagan. April's fiancé." Bill stepped into Freddy's line of vision, breaking the spell.

"Oh! I'm so sorry. Fred Campion."

"It's okay, I'm used to being in the shadows."

Freddy cleared his throat and glanced at Julie before speaking. "Well. We're certainly looking forward to hosting your wedding on the first of December. Tomorrow we can tour the grounds, look over menus, talk about music and flowers." At the mention of flowers, Julie turned her head away and fussed with a perfect display of seasonal decorations on a side table. "Have you eaten? Can I have the kitchen make you something?" He turned toward Julie. "Jules, the kitchen is open, yes?"

"Um, sure," she said. "What would you like? Salad?

Sandwich?"

"Prime rib? Just kidding, we don't have prime rib." Freddy waited for a smile from April. And waited.

"We ate earlier," April said, stifling a yawn. "Billy, you want something?"

"Well, I wouldn't say no to a sandwich. Nothing fancy."

"Turkey okay?"

"Turkey is fine. Little bit of mayo."

"Coming right up," Freddy said. "Please sit. Relax. April, can I get you a glass of wine? Bill?"

April nodded her assent to wine. "Red if you have it."

"Just a glass of water for me," Bill said.

"You got it. Julie, come give me a hand, will you?" Without waiting, he grabbed her hand and pulled her away into the kitchen.

"We'll be right back," she called over her shoulder.

**

"You're a nervous wreck, Freddy! What has gotten into you, anyway?"

"Excuse me, but this is April Tweed. I've followed her career since she first appeared on *Echo Falls*. God, she was gorgeous back then. I mean, she still is. All right, I need to make a turkey sandwich for *Billy*. Did you catch that? She calls him *Billy*. How cute!"

"I'll get the drinks. Hey, they seem to really appreciate the place. At first I wasn't sure."

"I think they do, too. You said they liked the suite."

Julie retrieved a bottle of water from the refrigerator and filled a tall glass, then found an unopened bottle of Malbec and half-filled a stemmed glass. "This should be okay, right? We have plenty more at the bar. I'll bring this and ask. Hey, I was thinking tomorrow I'd take April around, show her the menus, ask about music. I imagine you and Bill can talk business?"

"*Billy*." Freddy made a face. "Don't worry, I won't call him Billy. But don't assume he's going to handle the business end. She's the one with the money."

"You don't know that."

"I googled him. He's a math teacher. Used to work at a private school in Connecticut, but now he's at a public school in the Bronx. The Bronx, Jules."

"Still…"

Freddy cut the sandwich on the diagonal and set one half to rest atop the other, then pulled a small bag of chips from a deep drawer. "Pickle? No pickle?"

"Ugh. No pickle." Julie picked up the glasses and turned to head out of the kitchen, but Freddy stopped her with a gentle touch to her arm.

"Honey, I'll deal with the flowers, all right? You don't have to talk to Luke."

Julie pressed her lips together. On her way out of the kitchen, she said over her shoulder, "Whatever. I don't care about him, anyway."

She was through the door and back into the barn when Freddy muttered, "Like hell you don't."

FOUR

April was groggily aware of Bill getting out of bed, but she turned over, away from the dim light that escaped between linen curtains at the bedroom window, and tried to go back to sleep. It had taken Bill close to two weeks to develop a normal sleeping habit after he'd moved in with April, and in spite of the wedding suite's mattress being just the right firmness, the sheets and blankets luxurious, the pillow perfect, she had felt him flip his pillow several times during the night. Opening one eye, she glanced at the clock next to the bed. It wasn't even six o'clock! She heard him close the bedroom door softly, but seconds later, there was a crash from the living room.

Throwing off the Egyptian cotton sheet and cashmere blanket, April swung her legs over the side of the bed and pulled on her silk robe. In bare feet, she padded across the thick bedroom carpet and opened the door.

"Are you all right?" she asked, her voice still full of sleep.

"Sorry, honey. I banged into this table and almost knocked the lamp over. I didn't mean to wake you."

No getting back to sleep now, she said to herself. *Oh, well.* "Are you making coffee?"

He pulled a large white mug from the Keurig and glided to her, his arm outstretched. "This one's for you."

April accepted the coffee and took a sip. "Good," she murmured. "Still too early." She pushed aside a curtain at one of the big windows. "It's still dark out there." Letting the curtain drop, she took another sip as Bill joined her.

"You didn't sleep well last night," she mentioned.

"Did I keep you up? I guess I'm just not used to that bed."

"It's a great bed, though, Billy. Are you still having nightmares? Flashbacks?"

"Not too much," he said, but he kept his eyes on his mug.

"Have you talked to your therapist about it? About the nightmares?"

Bill nodded. "We're working through it." He pulled a cord that separated the drapes. "Look, there's the beginning of daylight. We must be facing east."

April gazed out the window. True, there was a soft gray light that just outlined the landscape. He leaned against her to look to the right. "Can you see? I think that's October Mountain to the south."

"How did you know that?" She set down her mug to wrap her arms around his chest.

"Google maps. More coffee?"

In the small kitchen area, he placed another pod in the machine and refilled April's mug.

"You know, it hasn't even been a year, Bren, and in less than two months, we'll be married."

"I know. But you don't think we rushed into it, do you?"

"Of course not! I had to wait this long for you. Wait, do *you* think we rushed it?"

April shook her head, her dark hair catching the light from the room's lamps. "No, Billy. I'm happy. Happy to be here with you, ecstatic to be marrying you."

He settled next to her on the sofa and together they lifted their bare feet to a marble-topped coffee table.

"I had a great idea for our honeymoon. You said I could plan it, right?" With April's smile, he continued. "I wanted us to go to the Dordogne, in the southwest of France. It looks fantastic, but the problem is, there isn't much to do there in December and January."

"We talked about Paris, too."

"Yep. And Paris at Christmas would be great, unless you think we should wait until the spring to go. My time off at Christmas is limited, and I was hoping we could see London, too, maybe take in a show while we're there."

"Are you telling me all of this so it isn't a surprise? Because it really doesn't matter, Billy."

"But it does. It's our honeymoon. And I want it to be perfect. It's just that if I plan something to surprise you, it might have to be in the spring. Or next summer."

"Okay," April said. "Go ahead and surprise me. I don't mind waiting for the honeymoon of our dreams."

"I agree. So, today we'll take care of wedding details. And we need to finalize a guest list so we can get the invites out."

"I know." She cupped her hands around the mug and brought it to her lips. "So, besides your brother and sister, and her husband and their kids, who else? Folks from school?"

"Yeah, I have the names and addresses. They probably won't make the trip but I think I should ask them anyway. Especially since I'm new and they've been so kind. I know Dan can't perform the service, but I want him to stand up with me."

"What about your kids, Billy?"

"My kids? No, I don't think so," he said with a raw laugh.

"Why not? They'd probably love to come out."

"Bren, I haven't talked to any of them in years. I told you

that." He set his empty cup on the table.

"Well, it just seems that maybe they'd like to see their dad get married."

"They don't think of me as their dad."

"Okay, but you're their biological father. You're related to them by blood."

Bill stood up. "No, honey. No." He bent to kiss the top of her head. "I'm going to shower. Join me?"

"You go ahead. I need one more cup."

"You're missing out, you know," he said, striking a pose.

**

Two hours later, April and Bill descended the polished oak staircase to the barn. It was just as pretty in the daylight, as streams of weak sunshine filtered in through skylights in the roof. April noticed there was room for a small band and dancing. She'd ask Julie about spacing out the tables so that the room still looked full, even if there were only a few dozen guests in attendance. She had no intention of inviting anyone from her days at *Echo Falls*, since no one had bothered to reach out to her. Well, except for Melanie, who had sent a tower of chocolates shortly after April's unfortunate departure from the show. A tower of chocolates, seriously, a gift from the ingenue who'd replaced her. As if she didn't feel old and fat enough already. April had given them to her doorman.

She pulled out her phone and texted Julie that they were in the barn. Almost instantaneously she received a message back to come to the main house.

"Julie wants us to go to the house," April called to Bill, who was inspecting something in a far corner of the barn. "Billy!"

"Coming," he said, and they walked across a gravel pathway to the white clapboard farmhouse that April assumed was Julie's residence. In the morning light, April was able to better appreciate all the autumn trimmings around the barn. Wreaths of bittersweet, ears of dried corn, pumpkins on hay bales. It was both kitschy and adorable. *Did Freddy live there, too? With his husband and their baby?*

Julie opened the door for them. "I thought we could have breakfast in here," she said. "It's just the three of us." She gestured for them to enter, and April and Bill stepped into a spacious bright kitchen. White cabinets and stainless-steel appliances dominated the roomy interior. *What a difference from my tiny kitchenette*, April thought. She could move around this room without bumping into anything.

"It's a beautiful space," she breathed.

Bill agreed. "So big! It reminds me of my old house."

"Did you live in an old house, too, Bill? They don't make them like this anymore. The kitchen in my old apartment was miniscule. Come on, make yourselves comfortable."

Bill pulled out a chair for April, and she smiled at the cheery green and yellow cushion on the chair seat. When she was seated, Bill sat in the chair to her right, and Julie set plates on the table.

"I wasn't sure if you ate breakfast, but I can cook eggs, pancakes, bacon, whatever you want." A large bowl of fruit and a plate of croissants looked tantalizing. The three cups of coffee she'd gulped down earlier sat in April's empty stomach, longing for bread. Julie added a napkin-lined basket of what looked like scones, and she confirmed, "These are spinach and cheddar. I didn't make them, but they're delicious. Coffee?" She filled three yellow mugs, then sat down.

"So! How did you sleep? I want the truth. If there was anything that detracted from your enjoyment, please tell me so I can fix it." With raised eyebrows, Julie held her coffee cup aloft and waited.

"Honestly, I slept great," April said, spooning mixed fruit into a small yellow bowl. She exchanged a glance with Bill, who confirmed that he, too, had slept soundly.

"Oh! I almost forgot." Julie jumped up and retrieved a platter from the refrigerator. "Meats and cheeses." She shrugged her shoulders and grinned at Bill.

"The room is terrific," Bill replied. "Couldn't have been nicer, really." He stared at the selections for a few seconds before plucking a scone from the basket, and using his fork, speared two slices of ham and one of cheddar.

"I'm so glad. We've tried to add as much luxury as we can. Some people still think of barn weddings as overly rustic, but it's just the décor. We want you to remember this experience as the best wedding you could have." She stopped short, and April laughed.

"Don't worry about it. We have three weddings between us already. This will be the fourth, and it *will* be the last one, right, honey?"

Bill nodded, pointing to his full mouth.

"Bill, Fred will be here in about an hour. Today I thought April and I might go around to the cake shop, talk about music. You're welcome to join us unless you want to tour the grounds with Fred. And he's the business guy in this partnership, so you'll deal with him for the deposit."

Bill touched a napkin to his mouth before speaking. "Sure, that's fine. So you're going to handle the cake and the music. And flowers?"

"Julie, let's do the cake and the flowers this morning. But I'd like Billy involved with the music selection." April squeezed Bill's free hand. "We have some songs that are meaningful to us."

"Sure, of course," Julie mumbled.

They ate in satisfied silence. Julie asked, "How's Carlie?"

"Oh, she's great, thanks. She's going to stand up with

me for the service. She's all grown up now, living on her own. Well, with a little help from me, of course. Thank you for remembering her."

"She's a great kid," Bill added. He picked another scone from the basket and split it open.

"And how about you, Bill? Do you have children? Will they be attending?"

April could almost feel him stiffen beside her, and hoped Julie didn't notice. But he carried on as if it was the most normal question in the world, which, April realized, it kind of was. "I have children, yes, but they live out west. They won't be coming to the wedding."

Julie caught April's eye and quickly looked down at her empty plate. Okay, no more talking about kids now, April thought. No one is comfortable with the topic. Except Freddy and me.

At the sound of tires on the gravel driveway, April saw a look of relief pass over Julie's face. "That would be Freddy." She stood. "Can I get you anything else? More coffee?" Both April and Bill shook their heads no, so Julie cleared the table as Fred entered the kitchen. It was as if he brought the sun inside the kitchen, warming away whatever awkwardness had taken root in the room.

"Good morning! How's everyone today?" He bent to kiss April's cheek and she inhaled sharply. He smelled so good! Like the woods and the beach and the sun all rolled up in one. Bill stood to shake his hand, and Julie piled dishes in the sink.

Freddy clapped his hands. "Are we ready for a big day today?"

"We are! But I do hope to see that little boy of yours at some point," April said.

"I thought we'd all have dinner together tonight, here at the house, if that's okay with you," Julie said. "I can guarantee that Val will steal the show until he falls asleep."

"That's great," Bill said.

"Jules, are we doing the flowers?"

"No, of course not," Julie snapped. "April and I will go to the florist's first thing."

What's Julie's problem with flowers, April wondered.

"April, why don't we meet back down here in, say, an hour?"

"Sounds good. Billy, you coming?"

"Is there any more coffee, Jules?" Freddy pulled a mug down from a shelf.

"I'll join you for a cup," Bill said. "You go ahead, Bren. April."

Julie looked from April to Bill. "Is Bren a nickname?"

April cast an intimate glance at Bill before answering. "Sorry. When we were in high school…"

"I know, I know!" Freddy crowed. "Sorry, I'm a big fan, so I know your given name. Brenda Bornstein! Am I right?"

He is so cute, April thought. "You're right. I'm sure it's no secret to some, and usually Billy only calls me Bren or Brenda when we're alone. No one else calls me Brenda." *Well, my mother.*

"I let that slip," Bill said, but grinned as April pressed her lips to his cheek.

Freddy shrugged. "It's a good name, April Tweed."

"Tweed is my middle name," Bill murmured.

"Get out! I did *not* know *that*. You took his middle name as your last name? Wow. So I'm guessing this love goes back to high school then." Freddy leaned forward on his forearms.

April spoke. "We've both always had feelings for each other."

In a quieter voice, Bill added, "Through a very unfortunate set of circumstances, we broke up right after high school. I don't really want to get into it, if you don't mind."

April finished the story. "Suffice it to say, we both went

our separate ways, but neither of us ever forgot about the other. Last year, I had the misfortune to appear on a magazine cover…"

"Oh, that horrible one? The 'Whatever Happened to April Tweed' cover. I remember. I was furious at whoever thought that was a good idea." Freddy's nostrils flared in indignation, as if he were the one whose worst photo ever had appeared on the cover of a weekly gossip rag. Still, April admired him for it.

"Yeah, that one," Bill said. "Anyway, I picked it up. Actually, I bought all of the magazines in the rack because I felt awful that they'd put such an unflattering photo of her on the cover."

"I bought all of them I could find, too! What a crappy thing to do to you, April," Freddy added.

"Anyway, I read the article, and it said she was filming a miniseries in Ireland, in Galway, and, I don't know, the synapses fired and I booked a ticket. I was determined to find her."

"Wow," Julie sighed. "I can't even imagine someone caring so much about me that they'd do that."

"I'd fly to Ireland to find you, Jules."

"Thank you for that, sweetie. So it worked then, Bill? You reconnected in Ireland?"

"Yeah. It was weird at first. Probably weirder for her,

right, honey? And she was in the middle of filming, you know. *And* her co-star was very interested in her at the time. Conor Whelan? Have you ever heard of him?"

Julie shook her head, but somehow April knew Freddy would be familiar with the actor.

"Oh, Conor Whelan. Hunky and smarmy." Freddy shimmied his shoulders. "Is the miniseries going to be shown here in the States?"

April shrugged. "It might be. It did help to revive my career, somewhat. I hope it's picked up, maybe on PBS or Netflix." She waited at the door, her hand on the brass doorknob. "Anyway, I'll meet you down here in a bit, Julie."

"Fred, what time works for you?"

"Anytime is fine. I'm here, so probably find me in the barn."

With a quick goodbye, Bill and April exited the house and made their way to the side of the barn, where the covered staircase led to the second floor of the barn. The sun was shining, and illuminated a bank of oaks and maples that skirted the property in fiery oranges and reds. A tall man was in the garden near the stairs, tending to decorative cabbages and large masses of mums. He straightened up as Bill and April approached.

"Morning," Bill called. The man stood, well over six feet. Straight black hair fell over his eyes, no matter how many times he pushed it back, and his dark eyes jumped from Bill to April. His face was calm, unsmiling, but April was positive his were friendly eyes.

"Morning. I'm Zack." He removed a glove and offered his hand first to Bill, who took it, then to April, whose own hand disappeared in Zack's paw. "You staying upstairs this weekend?"

April nodded. "I'm April, this is Bill. We're getting married on the first of December. Thought we'd come up this weekend to check it out." She gave him her best smile and held his gaze until she saw his lips move upwards.

Zack nodded thoughtfully. "Good choice. Julie and Fred do a great job." He lifted a flannel-covered arm and pointed to a tiny house on the far end of the property. Wisps of smoke rose from the chimney. "Me and my wife Sarah live there. I tend the property and she does a lot of baking."

"Oh! Are you joining us for dinner tonight?" With Zack's blank look, April gave Bill a gentle poke. "Never mind. I probably misunderstood."

Zack regarded him with an impassive face before speaking. "Well, nice to meet you."

They hurried upstairs.

**

April had just stepped out of the shower and stood naked

in the bathroom. She turned slightly and glanced at her backside. *I'm doing everything I can*, she told herself. *The years just keep coming, though.* At the sound of the door opening, she grabbed a towel and wrapped it around herself.

"Hey, you," Bill said, approaching her with his arms open.

"Hey." April turned back to the mirror and dragged a wide-toothed comb through her wet hair.

He let his hands rest on her shoulders as he stood behind her, admiring her reflection. "You are so damned beautiful, you know that?"

I'm glad he thinks so. She turned to face him. "I thought we might have a little extra time together this morning, but then we got talking, and…"

"Honey, we have all weekend. I know they want to get going on the day. And there's a lot to do. Can you pencil me in for later this afternoon? Before dinner maybe?"

April smiled. "Sure. I should get dressed."

"Let me help," he said, as his fingers deftly pulled the towel away from her body.

FIVE

Back in the kitchen, Freddy lingered over the last of his coffee. "They're an interesting couple, don't you think?"

"How so?" Julie asked, her hands in soapy water at the sink.

"I don't know, they seem mismatched in a way. She's so glamorous. He's kind of schlubby."

"Freddy. He's very nice."

"Sure he is. And he's devoted to her, you can see that. Maybe it's what she wants, what she needs. But if you'd ever seen Conor Whelan, Jules. Holy smokes. They call him the George Clooney of Ireland."

"Not for his humanitarian efforts, I presume?"

"Correct. George Clooney of the 80s and 90s, way before Amal. Conor's a real player."

"Maybe April could see through all that. And it is pretty romantic to have your high school sweetheart travel across the ocean to find you and try to win you back."

"Listen, doll, I'm serious. If you want me to take Bill, or April and Bill, to Luke's, I will. I know how to shop for flowers."

Julie leaned against the kitchen counter and wiped her hands on a yellow dishtowel. "No. I have to handle it. It's business. That's the way Luke wants it to be, fine. He's the only florist in town, otherwise I'd have no problem driving into Pittsfield. But then he'd know I did and I can't let him know that I'm afraid to see him." She pulled out a chair, but before she could slump into it, Freddy held her upper arms.

"*Are* you afraid to see him?"

"A little. Maybe not afraid. Just chicken."

"Oh, sweetie." Freddy wrapped Julie in his big embrace. "You're so much better than this." He stroked her hair as she pressed her face against his broad chest. "He's the one who missed out."

"I know," she said, her words muffled against the thick cotton of his shirt. She pulled away reluctantly. "But now I'm thirty-eight. My chances of finding someone— someone normal—are about as good as…as what?"

"About as good as a wax cat in hell?"

"Yeah, that."

"Okay, so go get April Tweed her flowers. By the way, your hair looks fabulous. Sexy messy. Just add a little eyeliner."

Julie rolled her eyes. "I can't. I always ruin it."

He grabbed her hand and walked with her to her bedroom at the rear of the house. "I can do it for you."

"Don't overdo it," she warned.

"Me?"

SIX

Julie drove into town, with April sitting beside her.

"The colors are beautiful here, Julie. Nothing like fall in New England, right?"

"I know. I missed it when I lived in the city, even though we had some color in the park."

"Do you miss the city at all?"

Julie sighed. "Sometimes. I miss the energy. I realize that I derived a lot of my own stamina from it. You know, how the city breathes into you? How you feel invigorated every time you walk outside?"

April nodded. "When I was in Galway earlier this year, I was sometimes reminded of New York. Galway is different from the rest of Ireland. It undulates. Lots of students in the city give it life. From what I've heard, it's really the life force of Ireland."

"Sounds like you enjoyed it," Julie said.

"Galway? I could have given it more of my time. I did a little sightseeing, but mostly I was either on the set or in my hotel room. Carlie loved it, though. Maybe it's meant for a younger person." April kept the rest of it to herself—the times spent with Conor Whelan, his half-drunk marriage proposal, the way it all ended.

Julie stopped at a red light and a woman in the crosswalk waved at her. "Oh, that's Mary Jo. I've known her since I was a kid. Hi!" The light turned green as Mary Jo made a signal with her hand that Julie should call her. Julie tooted her horn lightly and kept going.

"When Bill said he'd traveled all the way to Galway to find you, April, I just found it so romantic."

"That's Billy. After all the years that had passed between us—thirty years! Imagine, he saw this horrible photo of me in a magazine, he read about the filming, and just like that he decided he'd try to find me. I was shocked, really. Billy Flanagan! The boy in high school I was so sure I'd end up with."

"But something happened to break you up." April looked down at her hands in her lap, but didn't respond. "I'm sorry, I shouldn't have mentioned it."

"Oh, that's a story that needs wine. Lots of it. Are we looking at cakes first?"

"No, let's get the florist out of the way," Julie muttered, pulling into an empty parking space.

April laid her hand on Julie's arm. "What's going on? When flowers were mentioned back in your kitchen, you seemed angry. Is this not a good florist?"

"Oh no, no, he's good. He's the best, actually. Really the best." She checked her reflection in the sun visor's mirror.

"Wait." April turned in her seat, her hand still on Julie's arm, willing her to stay. "Your face is flushed. What's going on?"

"I shouldn't have said anything. It's just…well, I was in a relationship with the florist until about a month ago."

"Oh no. Do you want me to go in by myself? I can do that. You can wait here if it's too difficult to see him."

Julie's shoulders sagged. "That's the coward's way out. Plus he'll know. You're my client. We go in together."

"But this is clearly stressing you out, Julie. Would it be better to wait until Freddy can go with me?"

"No," Julie whined. "Because he'll find out you're having the wedding at Jingle Valley and he'll know I'm avoiding him. No wonder I can't keep a guy. I sound like a fifteen-year-old."

"Hey. *Hey.* Stop. You're beautiful and successful. Tell me, who broke it off?"

"He did."

"Did he say why?"

"I know why. I kind of gave him an ultimatum. April,

I'm thirty-eight years old. I can't wait forever if I want a baby. Even now, it's probably too late."

"I'm sure it's not too late, Julie. But that was a deal-breaker for you? He didn't want kids?"

"No, it's not that he doesn't want kids. But time isn't on my side. And he doesn't understand."

"All right." April combed fingers through her dark hair and curled a chunk of it behind her ear. "Well, as you said, this is business. I want the best floral arrangements possible for my December wedding and Luke—what's his last name?"

"Plante."

"Seriously?"

Julie smiled. "Yeah."

"Okay. Luke *Plante* is going to deliver. Today, this is business, Julie, nothing more. You don't ask how he's doing, you don't compliment him, nothing. You're doing great, and we're here for flowers. In fact, once you've introduced us, step outside for some sunshine and fresh air. I will deal with him myself."

"Thank you. You're everything I wish I could be."

"Oh, no I'm not. I don't have anything invested in this transaction, remember that. All I want out of this are flowers. You and I are both strong, independent women.

But matters of the heart are always a different thing. We love what we love."

Julie nodded.

"Come on, let's go." April opened her door and together they stepped into Luke's Flower Shop.

A little bell signaled their entrance. No one else was in the shop at that early hour. April breathed in an intoxicating mash-up aroma of freesia, roses, lilac, jasmine. It was an adorable place, she thought, filled with lush greenery.

A voice called from the back. "Be right with you!" April removed her big dark sunglasses and arched her eyebrows at Julie. "Steady," she whispered.

"Good morning, how can I—?" Luke faltered when his eyes landed on Julie. "Hey, Jules."

April slipped her hand into Julie's and squeezed. "Luke. This is April. She's having her wedding at Jingle Valley on December first and needs to discuss flowers." She gripped April's hand hard, too hard, as April winced.

"Um, sure. Hi, April, I'm Luke." He glanced back at Julie before extending a hand.

Pulling free from Julie, April took a step toward Luke and accepted his handshake, grateful for the brief and gentle grip. "Nice to meet you. I have some ideas. Can we talk about it?" Turning back to Julie, she said, "I could really use a coffee. Would you mind getting one for me, Julie?"

"Oh! Sure. Yes, okay."

"Take your time. Cream only." April waited for Julie to leave before returning to Luke. "Now, you and I are going to figure out the floral arrangements for my wedding, but all you really need to know is that I want white and red. Got it? Good. Now, why did you break up with my friend Julie?"

Luke's lower lip dropped as he stared at April. "Do I know you?"

"Possibly. I'm April Tweed. I used to be on a soap opera until they killed me off. I've done some commercials since then. So yes, Luke, you might know me." She paused, sized him up. *He's sweet, handsome.* "Look, I don't usually get involved, but why did it end with Julie? Hurry up and tell me, she'll be back soon."

He looked down and bounced the toe of his boot against the floor. "I just don't think we were at the same place."

"She wants to be married and she wants to have a baby. She's thirty-eight." April softened her tone. "Was that the problem?"

Luke gulped. "I don't know if I'd be a good father. I love Julie, and I miss being with her. But I own this business, and I work all the time. She owns her business, and she works all the time, too. Who parents a child?"

"You both do. You get help when you need it. You have Freddy and Bob close by, and don't you folks know everyone? It's a small town. Full of good people, I'm sure. You do whatever you have to do."

Luke scraped his thumbnail against the collar of his shirt. "What if it's too late?"

"What do you mean by that? It's never too late."

When he finally looked up and met April's stare, and she saw something painful in his eyes. "My father was forty-four years old when I was born, and he died when I was nine."

"I'm sorry, sweetie. You got cheated on that one. But you and Julie are healthy. People live longer these days. And besides, that's not a reason! Life is short, Luke. I'm going to marry the boy I fell in love with in high school. That was *thirty* years ago! We have a chance to find happiness now, at this late stage, and I'm not going to miss the opportunity." She took Luke's hand in hers and noted its smoothness. "Look, you love her, you want to be with her. If children come, that's wonderful. If not, there's always adoption. And adoption doesn't always mean a newborn, unless Julie has her heart set on it. But you need to *talk* about it. Talk about *all* of it." The tinkling of the bell at the top of the door signaled Julie's return. "Red and white only, got it? I trust you to do the right thing," April whispered.

"Coffee," Julie said, handing a cardboard cup to April. She looked from one to the other. "Are you taking care of things?"

"Yes," they both answered in unison. "Yes," April repeated. "I need to make a call. I'm going to step outside for a minute." Before either of them had a chance to stop her, she left the flower shop. Standing on the sidewalk in the sun, she put on her sunglasses and sipped her coffee. *If I was lucky enough to get back together with Billy, after all this time, then there's hope for those two in there.*

Minutes passed. April strolled down the street, looking in shop windows. Carver Hardware ("Keys made on the premises!"). Hair Design by Antonia ("Be Your Prettiest Self!"). Valeri's Karate Studio ("Your Journey Begins with a Single Step").

"April!" She turned to see Julie waving at her, and headed back to where she stood outside the flower shop.

"Hey, how did it go?"

"I'll tell you in the car. Come on," Julie linked her arm in April's and they walked back to Julie's car. Once inside, Julie turned excitedly to face her friend.

"It was so hard to see him again! Just the sound of his voice, the way he says my name. I kept telling myself that I was there for business and business only, but he stood so close to me. I could smell him, April—clove and cedar. I wanted to breathe it in forever."

"So far, so good, I would say," April said with a smile.

"He asked if we could get together and talk. Just talk. He said he misses me. I almost cried."

"Did you cry?"

"No! I kept telling myself I wouldn't. Besides, I'd ruin my eyeliner. I was actually kind of cold to him at first, telling him we'd said everything we needed to say."

"Oh, Julie. It sounds like he was trying."

"He was. He asked if we could have dinner on Monday evening. He knew you were staying through the weekend."

"Please tell me you said yes."

Julie appeared to glow from within. "His hair is longer than it used to be. He pulls it back now, did you notice? And his eyes, like chocolate with flecks of gold in them. You can only see the gold in the sunlight, but I know it's there. And his hands! He could be a surgeon with those hands!"

"Julie! Did you agree to have dinner with him?"

"Yes, I did. You look relieved, April! Thank you for caring! I don't know if he wants to get back together. Maybe he just wants to apologize. Maybe he wants *closure*. God, I hate that word, but maybe that's what he wants. *Closure*." She wrinkled her nose, like she'd just opened a baby's diaper.

"So, that's good news. Where are you going for dinner?"

"I don't know. I asked if we should meet somewhere, but he wants to pick me up at my house."

"Good. You'll have to let me know how everything goes."

"I will, definitely." Julie grinned. "He was very impressed, you know, that you're having your wedding at Jingle Valley. He said we'd probably get helicopters overhead."

April recoiled. "Good lord, I hope not! We're not looking for a lot of publicity."

"Maybe a little publicity?"

"Good press for Jingle Valley is fine, Julie. If we can bring you some positive press, I'm all for that. Now, let's go sample some cake."

Julie opened the car door. "It's just a short walk down the street."

"Then why did we get in the car?" April asked.

"Because I didn't want to tell you everything outside on the sidewalk! Come on, we're going to Cake Walk, and you're going to love their dark chocolate raspberry and vanilla lavender cakes."

SEVEN

Freddy took Bill through the barn, again in daylight, and pointed out the tiny chapel.

"What kind of a service are you going to have?"

"Not religious," Bill answered quickly. "I mean, I was raised Catholic, but I'm twice-divorced. April doesn't have an affiliation, so we need to find a justice of the peace to perform the ceremony." He grimaced. "See, my brother is a priest, but he can't perform the service because it's not in a church."

Freddy leaned against a rustic oak beam and stroked the stubble on his chin. "Would you want to be married in the church, so that your brother can marry you and April? There's a Catholic church not far from here."

Bill shook his head. "No, it really wouldn't make any sense at this point. My first marriage was annulled so that I could marry my second wife, but we divorced and I figured I was done. You know, it didn't matter. I can't get that marriage annulled now. And besides, April's not Catholic. She'd be shocked if all of a sudden I said I wanted to be married in the church!"

"Okay. Well, we can get you a JP if you want. One less thing for you to worry about. So, should we talk about music? Or wait for April?"

After tentatively agreeing to check out the music of a small trio that Freddy knew for simple music during the ceremony and light swing/jazz at the reception, Freddy cleared his throat.

"So, should I be working directly with you, Bill, regarding payments?"

"Uh, yeah, that's fine. I mean, my money is her money. She's got more than I do, but I should pay for the wedding. Can you give me a ballpark estimate?"

"Let's have a seat so we can go over the numbers. Coffee?" Freddy checked his watch. "It's close enough to noon if you want something stronger."

"Oh, no, thanks. I'm a recovering alcoholic."

"Oh! Sorry, I didn't know. Is this going to be a dry wedding, then?"

"Not at all. Just for me." Bill rolled his eyes.

**

Together, Bill and Freddy compiled a sample menu for April to view. Fred uploaded some of the trio's music so Bill and April could listen to it later. Bill wanted an open bar, but needed to run it past April, since he wouldn't be partaking.

"Listen, it's going to be great," Freddy said. "Add this to

whatever the women pick out for flowers and a cake and you've got yourselves a wedding!"

Bill let his gaze linger on the list of items and their estimated cost. "I can't believe it. Just last year I read about her, decided to try and find her, and now we're getting married."

Freddy threw an arm around Bill's shoulders. "Never too late, my friend. I'm hoping our Julie realizes that."

"What do you mean?"

Freddy stepped back. "Probably shouldn't have said anything. She was involved with the florist until recently. It was a tough breakup. I'm hoping that this wedding—you know, ordering flowers and everything—might make them realize how much they miss each other. I've been trying to work a little magic behind the scenes." He mimicked puppeteering and wiggled his eyebrows.

"Well, Julie seems like she has it all—she's attractive, successful, very sure of herself."

Freddy smiled. "We all do our best."

Pivoting, Bill eyed Freddy's lean physique. "How much weight do you think I could lose between now and the wedding?"

"You want a tip? Okay, you've got six weeks. No bread, no sugar. No alcohol—oops, you've already got that one covered. No eating after six o'clock. What time do you eat dinner?"

"Usually between seven and eight."

"Eat at five. I'm telling you. If you can't eat until seven, then only raw vegetables. Salad, no bottled salad dressing, just a little olive oil and lemon. And you have to walk thirty minutes every day, even if it's pouring rain. No cabs. I lived in the city, I know. Walk everywhere you can."

"Okay. No bread, no sugar."

"Give up carbs completely if you can. Eat chicken and fish and vegetables. It's only six weeks, Bill. You can do that. Come on, we're going to take a nice long walk around the property. Maybe check in with Zack and Sarah." He strode to the door of the barn and all Bill could do was hurry along behind him.

EIGHT

For dinner that night, Julie served penne and meatballs.

"When did you have time to make meatballs, Julie?" April asked as they took seats around the table.

"Before we left. It's not hard, really. I buy a mix of ground beef and ground pork, add a slice of white bread soaked in milk and crumbled into the meat, an egg, and plenty of herbs."

"Then tell them what you do," Freddy prompted.

"I don't want to scare them. Okay, I drop the raw meatballs directly into the tomato sauce, then I let them simmer in the crockpot all day."

"Really? You don't fry them first?" April looked from Julie to Freddy to Freddy's husband Bob in disbelief.

"Nope. I learned this from my friend's grandmother, who always made them this way. The first time I made them, Freddy freaked out about the raw meat thing."

"It's true, I did. So did Bob. And Luke, too."

"But once you ate them, you all groaned with pleasure." Julie folded her arms.

Caesar salad and garlic bread rounded out the meal, and there was plenty of Chianti. April watched Bill. He spooned four meatballs onto his plate, next to a generous helping of salad, but took no bread, no pasta, and drank no wine, asking instead if Julie had any seltzer water.

"Sure, I'll get it for you. It's in the fridge."

Bill stood. "Happy to help myself. Can I get anyone anything while I'm up?"

April excused herself and followed him into the kitchen. "Billy, are you all right?"

"I'm great! But this is day one of my plan for the next six weeks. No bread, no carbs. I want to be svelte on our wedding day!"

"Billy, you're fine the way you are. But it looks a little weird for you to just have meatballs and salad on your plate."

"Then I'll explain. Bren, this is important to me. I'm not drinking wine, either. And I'm happy to explain that as well. Nothing to feel weird about."

April shrugged. "Well, I don't think it's necessary, but whatever." She left him and returned to the noisy dining room.

**

Little Val, at thirteen months, demanded everyone's attention for the first twenty minutes of the meal, but soon he fell asleep on the sofa. Julie had piled cushions around him as a sort of fort, to keep him from rolling off the couch, even though she'd piled even more cushions on the floor. Freddy's husband Bob sat with him until he fell asleep, then rejoined the adults at the table.

"So, how did everything go today? Were you able to tackle all the items on your list?" Bob asked, looking from Bill to April.

"I think we did," Bill replied, using his fork to push croutons away from his salad. He lined them up around the rim of his salad plate. "All April and I need to do as soon as we get back is send out the invitations."

"We'll do that on Monday night," she added, narrowing her eyes at the croutons on his plate. "I think we had a great day, wouldn't you agree, Julie?"

"It was a good day, yes," she said, smiling.

April caught Freddy's eye and he winked at her. *Well, well,* she thought.

"And how many people do you expect at the wedding?" Bob refilled his wine glass and held the bottle aloft as he glanced around the table. He refilled everyone's glass but Bill's, who lifted his seltzer water to his lips.

"I'd say around forty," April said. "Bill's got colleagues at work, and they've all been so kind to him since his accident."

"Accident? What accident?" Freddy asked.

"Oh, I thought you'd probably told him," April whispered to Bill.

Bill shook his head and set his glass next to his empty plate on the white linen tablecloth. "On the first day of school, I was stabbed while walking to work."

Everything stopped as Julie, Freddy, and Bob stared slack-jawed at Bill.

"Are you kidding?"

"Oh my god."

"Are you okay?"

"Just a little stabbing," Bill joked, reaching for April's hand under the table. She squeezed it back. "I'm fine. Still healing, still dealing," he said. His ragged laugh fell flat.

April set her wine on the table. "He was stabbed by two men in a playground on his way to work. Billy teaches at a school in the Bronx. He was very, very lucky," she said, her voice catching as her grip on his hand tightened.

"Wow," Julie said. "I'm so glad you're all right."

The sound of knives banging against forks and forks hitting plates filled the air in the dining room. April chewed her lower lip and tried to come up with a new topic of conversation.

"So, anyway," Bill continued, "between my work friends, some of April's closer friends, and our family members, we don't see out guest list going over forty.

"That's very manageable. We did a wedding last year for three hundred. Remember, Freddy?"

"How could I forget? Bob didn't see me for weeks. I think that's why we adopted Val—so Bob would have someone to talk to."

"Yeah, only Val couldn't talk when we picked him up," Bob replied.

April looked at the two of them, and envied their easy rapport. "How old was Val when you adopted him?"

"Three months. Tiny little thing, he was. From people we spoke with, people who had adopted from other countries, apparently our process wasn't nearly as bad as some of them. We have friends who've adopted from Russia, China, from Guatemala—back when you could—and there were horror stories, believe me. One of our friends traveled to Bulgaria, she had a little girl promised to her, but when she arrived, after nearly a year of paperwork and red tape, the little girl who was promised wasn't there. She'd been adopted by another family! So the agency offered her another child, and it was a decision our friend had to make, right then and there—would she take this other little girl home? Fortunately, there was an American nurse that had accompanied the group, and she was able to assess the little girl."

"What happened?" Bill asked.

"The nurse said the child's cognitive functions were all normal. She wasn't sick, just kind of small. Probably a little malnourished. Our friend brought the child home, and they're doing really well. But it can be scary."

April cast a quick glance at Julie, who was quiet.

"Well, I'm glad it all worked out. And of course for you both as well. Val is a beautiful little boy."

"We're so grateful to have him," Bob said.

"Was he always named Valentino?" Bill asked.

Bob chuckled and pointed his fork at Freddy. "Go ahead, you tell them."

Freddy leaned back in his chair and finished the wine in his glass. As Julie lifted a new bottle to refill his glass, he stopped her with his hand. "I'm done. One of us needs to be a sober parent. It's my turn tonight. Okay, so Valentino. The little darlin' was originally named Gilberto. Gilberto! No son of mine was going to go through life with a name like Gilberto."

Bob interjected, "So my wonderful husband decided that he should go through life instead as *Valentino*."

"Hey, it was good enough for Ricky Martin's kid."

"Right. But you're not Ricky Martin and we live in Dalton. I see home schooling in our future. And martial arts," Bob added, and everyone laughed, even Freddy.

"This has been a wonderful evening," April said. "Julie, Fred, thank you. For everything. We're so looking forward to returning to Jingle Valley for our wedding."

"Thank *you* both for choosing us," Julie replied. "It means the world to us that you want to be married here."

"And April, for me personally, this is like a dream come true, but I'm your number one fan," Freddy said, giving April a crazy-eyes look that made her laugh. "I would like to contact an old friend in Manhattan, if you'd allow it. Her name is Alison and she's in PR. Would you be okay with a little bit of publicity? I mean, you *are* April Tweed."

April shifted in her seat. "I don't know, Fred. I'm not a TV star anymore. They look at me more like a has-been. And you know, the press hasn't been very kind to me in recent years."

Freddy persisted. "Alison would be kind, though. She's a dear friend and she listens to me. I was thinking maybe a spread in a magazine of the wedding."

She regarded him. "You want coverage for your business." At his expression, she grinned. "I'm not against it! Good for you. But tell your friend I want the focus to be on Jingle Valley, not on April Tweed. Billy? Would you be okay with it?"

"Honey, they don't care about me! This should be your call."

April swirled the last of the wine in her glass. "Maybe it would serve them right to see that I've landed on my feet, that I've found happiness after all. And my dress is gorgeous. Give me a day or so to think about it. Can I call you once I'm back home?"

"Of course. Think about it. But I believe it would be great."

"Of course you do," she said with a friendly wink.

NINE

Back home in New York City, April had the invitations printed at one of those quickie printers (no engraved invites needed this time), and she and Billy mailed them out at the end of the day. Thirty-six guests invited, all the singles encouraged to bring someone. April knew they wouldn't all show up.

The following day, while Bill was at school, April watched the clock until it was nearly noon, then she made two phone calls—one to Arizona and one to Minnesota. *He'll be grateful for this* later, she convinced herself. *He won't ask, but I will. And if nothing comes of it, fine. At least I tried.*

Bill's first wife Mary Pat reacted very differently than his second wife Sylvia, which told April a lot about the two women. One had moved on and found happiness with her new husband and the other may have remarried, but still harbored a lot of bitterness.

Mary Pat, in Arizona, said she'd ask the children, Danny and Norah, but Sylvia, in Minnesota, refused, saying that since Bill wasn't there for them, there was no reason for her children to attend the wedding. April thanked them both, and reiterated to Mary Pat that she'd cover the cost of Danny and Norah's airfare and lodging.

"I'm grateful, really. Bill has missed having a relationship with his children, and he's spoken frequently about the fact that you've always provided him with updates. He knows his failings, but I can assure you that he's a different person these days," April said.

"We all change, I know that. I'm not the same as I was at twenty-four, either. But don't expect a miracle. Danny and Norah have been raised by my husband and me. They're both aware that Bill Flanagan fathered them, but they also know very well that he left them. They don't consider him their father at all. They have my husband's last name." April heard Mary Pat blow out a breath and wondered if she was a smoker. "And my kids both work, you know, so if they want to go, they'll have to see if they can get time off."

"I understand. If they can fly out on Thursday night or early Friday, I can get them back on a plane on Sunday. I just think it would do everyone good to meet and reconcile. Hey, it's a trip east for the kids, right?" April tried to laugh, but it really wasn't funny and she knew it.

"Okay, April. Okay. You send the information and my husband and I will talk to the kids. I'm happy for Billy, and I'm glad for you, too. I used to watch you all the time on *Echo Falls*. I hated it when they killed you off."

April smiled. "Yeah, I hated it, too. But it is what it is, right? I'll text the info to you once I get confirmation that your kids want to come." *I hope they will. I really hope they will.*

She should have told Billy, she knew that. She knew they shouldn't keep things from each other. She knew all of it, and yet she didn't tell him, not when he breezed in that afternoon, not over dinner that evening, not in bed before they kissed goodnight. *They probably won't come*, she rationed. *No harm.* It would be a waste of time to upset him. She wanted nothing more than for Billy to have some peace in his life regarding his children. Two of them, anyway.

**

What she did tell Bill over dinner that evening was that they needed to have lunch with her mother. Per his request, she had picked up a roasted chicken at the Peruvian deli on Eighth. Paired with a ready-to-go bag of mixed salad greens, dinner was ready in five minutes. Bill weighed out five ounces of white meat, and it sat on his plate next to his salad, dressed only with a squeeze of lemon. An unopened bottle of fizzy water stood tall next to his plate.

He didn't say anything about lunch with Ellen Bornstein right away, and April knew he was measuring his response.

"Do you have a date in mind?"

She peeled the skin off her chicken breast with a sharp knife and set it on the edge of her plate. "Probably the sooner the better, don't you think? This weekend?"

Bill unscrewed the top of his fizzy water, waited for the

whoosh, filled his glass to half, then took a long drink. He set the glass down and smiled. "Sure, honey. Make the plans with your mom. Whatever you decide will be fine." He looked down at his plate as if calculating the calories.

He ate quickly. *Well, of course,* April rationed, *he's got to be starving.* Bill had cleaned his plate before April had even eaten half. He pushed back in his chair and said, "It got warm today! I'm going to take a quick shower."

April called to his retreating back. "Want company?" but he'd already disappeared into the bedroom. As if he hadn't heard her.

While Bill was showering, April cleared the table. *The way he's eating, this chicken could last for days*, she figured. She picked up her phone and called her mother.

"Hello!" her mother shouted into the receiver.

"Mom, it's me. How are you?"

"Oh, Brenda. I'm so glad you called. What a horrible day it's been."

"Why? What happened?"

"First thing this morning the cable went out. Not just mine, the whole house. I asked Lorna if she paid the bill, because with Lorna, you never know. But she showed me her checkbook. So I called the cable people and I was left on hold for fourteen minutes! Can you believe it?"

"Actually, I-"

"And then, after someone finally came on the line, they gave me what they call a *window*. A window that's three hours! Sometime between ten and one, they said. Well, I didn't trust Lorna to handle it, and Ruth and Emily were taking a ceramics class at the college, so I had to sit around and wait for someone to show up."

"And did someone show up, Mom?"

"Finally. It was nearly noon. I'd just taken my salad out of the refrigerator. It was leftovers from lunch yesterday, and I had to throw the whole thing out. The lettuce had turned and I refused to eat something that could give me food poisoning. Then I had to wait while the guy fixed the cable. I could hardly understand a single word he said, except for 'ma'am.' Oh, Brenda, what an awful morning. I missed *Morning Joe* and I'm exhausted."

She can't see me roll my eyes. "Listen, Mom, the reason I called is I want to invite you to the city this weekend for lunch. Or an early dinner, whichever you prefer."

"Just you and me?" Her voice was suddenly small.

"No, Mother. You and me and Bill. We want to tell you all about the wedding venue. We went to the Berkshires this past weekend to visit and make arrangements."

"So you're going to do it after all. The Berkshires, Brenda? You're expecting everyone to travel to the Berkshires for your wedding? Your second wedding, and his third."

"Yes," April said with a heavy sigh. She's the reason I have to see a colorist every three weeks.

"How am I going to get there? To the Berkshires?"

"Mom. You're going to take the train into the city and drive up with us. Now what about this weekend?"

"Well, let me check. Hang on."

April tapped shiny red fingernails on a speckled granite countertop. She heard the shower shut off.

"Brenda, are you there?"

"Still here, Mom. Saturday at noon?" Bill's PTSD therapy session would be over by then.

"All right, dear. I'll come to the city to have lunch with you."

"And Bill."

"Well, of course 'and Bill.' I heard you the first time."

"Great. See you Saturday, Mom. Love you." April clicked off, knowing her mother would never echo those words back to her. She never had, and she wasn't going to start now.

April padded down the long hallway to their bedroom, just as Bill was zipping up his jeans.

"Hey, handsome."

He smirked. "I'm glad you think so." He tugged a polo shirt over his head and pulled it over his belly.

"I do think so. Saturday at noon? Your therapy is at ten, right?"

Bill rubbed the left side of his head but smiled nonetheless. "Yep. Noon is fine."

She threw her arms around his middle and felt his stomach pressing against hers. "We'll get through it together. And maybe—maybe—we'll laugh about it later that night."

He kissed her forehead, but April looked up into his face, took his chin in her hand and brought his lips down to hers. As she felt him respond, she pressed closer. "I need you."

TEN

By Friday afternoon, Bill's colleagues had received the invitations, and a few remarked that they were looking forward to the wedding. Most probably wouldn't make the trip, he surmised, and was glad that he'd had **No gifts, please!** printed in bold letters at the bottom of the invitation. He didn't want his still-new colleagues to think he, or April, was fishing for checks.

Sondra, who worked in the guidance office, met him in the hall. "I think it's lovely, a wedding in the Berkshires! My husband and I can make it a getaway weekend. Thanks, Bill."

"I'm really glad you can come. You're going to love this place. And we got a special deal on hotel rooms—did you see the insert?"

"I did. We'll book tomorrow. Last time we were up that way was before I had kids. Oh, the freedom was so nice! And you're doing okay?" She peered at him with interest.

"Never better," he chirped.

Bill had invited everyone at the school that he had contact with, knowing that they wouldn't all show up, but not wanting to hurt anyone's feelings. He understood how things worked. Back when he was at Hopkins, one of the teachers had planned a baby shower for one of the other teachers, but a couple of the older women were left off the invitation list. Oh, that was a scene! One of the older women wouldn't speak to the party planner for weeks. *People are so eager to be unhappy*, he thought.

He had been on his practically-no-carbs diet for nearly a week and already he felt better. Giving up sugar had been easier than he expected, after the third day. And April was encouraging, preparing salads and chicken and fish and leaving out the bread and pasta. He planned an hour in the school gym after his last class, hoping for a little strength to face Ellen Bornstein the following day.

Ellen was one of a kind. Tiny, birdlike, with sharp features and a sharper tongue, she had a way with the backhanded insult. Sometimes Bill didn't get the jab until their conversation had moved on and it was too late for rejoinders. He repeatedly told himself that loving April meant getting Ellen, at least until she was dearly departed. And if his own mother were still alive, he couldn't even imagine including her in his relationship with April. So he would put on nice clothes, assist Ellen into the cab, and let her choose the restaurant. He wondered if she was still a vegan.

**

While April headed to the gym for her spin class on Saturday morning, Bill met with his therapist. He had agreed to the therapy sessions, acknowledging that the assault and its trauma could lie buried in his subconscious for long after the physical scars had healed. As a recovering alcoholic, Bill was keenly aware of triggers. *I've faltered, I've made a lot of mistakes. But here is my chance for lasting happiness, with the woman I was always meant to be with.* He was determined not to screw it up.

**

Bill didn't know who was more nervous about lunch with April's mother, but he felt he was way ahead of April at the moment.

"Do I need to wear a tie?"

"Absolutely not! We're not going high-end, honey."

"You never know with your mother. She might suggest Gramercy."

"She might. We can walk in to the tavern, but probably not the dining room. Then again, she might still be on her vegan kick." She sighed. "I could really go for a burger today."

"Okay, no tie." He turned and stood in front of April, imagining he looked like a law professor with his tweedy jacket and brown oxford shoes. "*You* look gorgeous," he added, "and you make it effortless."

"Stop," she murmured, turning away, but not before he saw her wide smile. Bill knew she appreciated the compliments, and they weren't gratuitous. April wore a dark green wraparound dress and knee-high black boots.

A faux shearling black leather jacket completed the look.

"You belong on the catwalk, you know."

"My mother will find fault with it, so thank you for the compliment in advance," she said.

He gathered her in his arms. "It doesn't matter what she says. We both know Ellen. She has to snipe, it's just part of her DNA. Thankfully, you didn't inherit it." With a kiss on her cheek to avoid smearing her freshly applied red lipstick, he led the way out of the house.

They walked hand in hand to the train station and awaited Ellen Bornstein's arrival on the 11:52 train. Bill spotted her first.

"There she is," he whispered, pointing to a tiny woman with darting eyes just feet away. Her hair, now nearly all white with flecks of dark gray, was cropped close to her small head. He was reminded of an old seagull on the beach.

"I see where you got your fashion sense," he whispered, as he felt a nervous stomach rumble in response to her nearing presence. April broke free and strode toward her mother.

"Hey, Mom," she said, bending to kiss her mother on the cheek as Bill caught up. He stood behind Ellen, where she couldn't see him.

"Brenda," Ellen replied, craning her neck to look up at

her daughter. "Where is he, then? Did he disappear?"

April laughed, but to Bill it sounded more like a hurt puppy's yelp. "Don't be silly. He's right here," she said, turning toward Bill, who stepped around to stand directly in Ellen's vision. He took small steps, as if there might be hidden mines beneath his feet. As he stretched out his hand, Bill hoped it was as dry as his mouth.

"Ellen, good to see you." *We've never met*, he said to himself with incredulity. *We've actually never met!* Of course, he'd seen photos, and they'd talked on the telephone, but Bill Flanagan and Ellen Bornstein, his soon-to-be mother-in-law, had never stood in front of each other until that moment. Bill silently thanked April for not seizing upon the moment to take a photo on her phone.

Ellen regarded him with her sharp little eyes, looking him over as if he were a fat and juicy earthworm who'd just dared to stick his head out of the ground. Finally her lips turned upwards. "I was hoping we'd meet before the wedding. And here we are." She looked to April. "We're having lunch?"

"Of course, Mom! Would you like to choose the place?"

With a wave of her bony hand, she said, "Oh, it doesn't matter. Any old place is fine."

"Italian? Sushi? Billy, what would you like?"

Bill opened his mouth to suggest sushi, in keeping with

his diet, but before he could get one word out, Ellen interrupted.

"Oh, not sushi, puh-lease."

"Why don't we go back to that place we like, honey? In the hotel? They're serving brunch until three." She pulled out her phone. "You get us a cab and I'll call." The taxi was important, but April didn't need to call their favorite brunch spot. She was still remembered by some people in the city, and the manager of Jay's was one of her fans. He always had a table for them.

**

Twenty minutes later they were seated at a table by a floor-to-ceiling window. Ellen looked even tinier when seated in her chair, as if she was a six-year-old girl at the adults' table. Bill thought she could use a booster seat, or a telephone book, if they even existed anymore, and he smiled at the thought of asking the waiter for one. He perused the menu and kept one hand on his fiancée's thigh.

"I already ate breakfast," Ellen muttered, scowling at the menu.

"They make a great burger here, Mom. Or are you still vegan?"

Ellen regarded her daughter with a withering expression. "No, dear, there was no point to it. Veganism is for those who can't handle daily living. That's never been me."

Both April and Bill suppressed smiles as they bent their heads into the menus. "Well, I said I wanted a burger and that's what I'm going to have," she pronounced, setting her menu on the table.

Bill made a point of asking for no potatoes or toast with his omelet, and Ellen picked up immediately. "Why are you against toast and potatoes? They're perfectly acceptable accompaniments to eggs."

He chuckled. "I'm all for them, Ellen, but I'm trying to lose a few pounds before the wedding." He winked at April.

With another once-over, Ellen said, "Well, I can understand that. And my Brenda, she's very picky, you know. After her husband left her for that underwear model, she starved herself for months."

"Mother."

"It's true? What, I can't speak the truth?"

"That was a very long time ago." April smiled, baring her teeth. "I happen to think Bill looks fine as he is, but I'm completely supportive of him, whatever he does."

"Yes, of course you are. So, why December? What's the rush?"

"We're not rushing, Ellen, but Bren- April and I were apart for a long time. The fact that we've been able to reconnect is such a blessing, such a wonderful gift, that we don't want to wait until spring or summer. We want to be married before the year is up."

"Ah, tax benefit?"

"Good lord, Mom."

"What, I can't ask?"

April looked down at her place setting and Bill knew she was either praying for patience or imagining ways to silence her mother, legally, of course. She squeezed Bill's hand under the table and gently removed it from her leg.

"We're so glad you'll be able to come to the wedding, Ellen," Bill said. *Lame* and *a lie.*

"Well, you're getting married." Ellen was about to say something else, but stopped, pressing her lips together. "Brenda, we should have a champagne toast." Ellen raised a bony hand to signal their server, who hurried over.

"Mother."

"It's okay, Bren. Ellen, I don't drink. But please, go ahead and order champagne." He turned to the server. "Bring champagne for the ladies, please, and a club soda for me."

Ellen Bornstein narrowed her eyes and cocked her head, assessing him with her bird-like eyes.

"Is this part of your diet plan, too? No bread, no potatoes, and no champagne?"

Bill lifted his chin and clasped his hands in his lap. This time he felt April hand on his thigh. "No, Ellen. I'm an alcoholic. I don't drink at all." He stared at her hard. He'd read somewhere that giving a gull a hard stare would make it back off.

Ellen blinked. "Well, there's nothing wrong with that, dear. We all have our failings. How long have you not been drinking?"

"Eight years, eight months, and two weeks," he replied.

Ellen leaned back in her chair and sucked in her cheeks, making her look even more gaunt. Finally she spoke. "That's impressive. I'm very impressed. Well done. Well done, Bill." As Bill unclasped his hands and felt his heartbeat return to a normal rhythm, Ellen added, "No drinking, no carbs. I hope you're at least having a lot of good sex."

ELEVEN

"Have you spoken to Dan?" April stood in their tiny kitchen and Bill was all the way down the long hallway in their bedroom; she had to raise her voice. When he didn't answer, April rinsed her hands in the sink and walked to him. She asked him again, through the slightly ajar bathroom door.

"Have you talked to Dan?"

"Not yet," he said. "I'll call him this morning."

"You just want that nailed down."

"Yep."

Okay then, April thought. *It's up to him*. But she didn't know who else he would ask to stand up with him if it wasn't Dan. She sensed that there had been tension between the brothers ever since Bill's accident and Bill and April's sudden engagement. Did Dan disapprove? Was it because Bill had been married twice? And the last marriage wasn't annulled? *It's not as if we'd get married in a church anyway*, April reasoned, but she liked Fr. Dan and hoped there was nothing between the brothers that couldn't be repaired. *Stay out of it now. He said he'll call him.*

April kept track of wedding replies, and there weren't many. She could understand—traveling to Dalton for the weekend probably wasn't practical for some of Billy's colleagues. A few of her friends had said yes, but more than a few had simply returned the card with regrets— often without even a short note wishing them well. *Is that how things are done these days?* Julie kept telling her not to worry—that she and Freddy had dealt with recalcitrant RSVPs many times and always planned for plenty of food. Seating wouldn't be a problem—there was room enough for two hundred, but again Julie had told her they'd simply reconfigure the space so it wouldn't look cavernous and empty. April hoped so. She was beginning to think they should have simply flown to Paris and gotten married there. But even as it was, they'd chosen to delay their honeymoon. As much as she had her heart set on Paris, she'd reasoned with Bill that spending Christmas break there wouldn't be her first choice. They'd planned instead to go in the springtime.

April stood in front of her window and looked out over midtown Manhattan. She loved the city, loved its vibrancy, but she had to admit, the weekend they'd spent in the Berkshires was delightful. She envied Julie for being bold enough to make the move, but April knew in her heart that she could never leave the city she loved, the place she'd called home for nearly thirty years.

"I'm going to run some errands," she called to Bill. Coffee with Carlie, dry cleaning, pick up something for dinner. "Be back in a few hours. Good luck with Dan!" She closed the door behind her and felt her heart lift. It wasn't that she needed to be away from Bill, necessarily, but having been without a man for so long, his constant presence sometimes crowded her. *Does he feel the same way?* And she worried about him—the stabbing had been only weeks previous, and although he saw his counselor regularly, he didn't discuss the incident or the therapy sessions with her. April didn't ask, figuring it was better for Bill to let it all out with his therapist, but the fact that they never spoke about it left her uneasy. *Is he really okay?* He seemed fine, day to day. He demonstrated his love to her in a normal fashion, on a regular basis. She knew he didn't sleep through the night, but wasn't that the way it was for men? As far as she knew, he hadn't even wanted to drink. *Are things too perfect?*

The sky was a soft gray, backlit by the sun on a quiet October morning. April had a charity event coming up in the middle of November—just one Saturday evening, and it wouldn't interfere with the wedding plans. Bill said he'd join her, and they'd rented a tuxedo for him. "You know, you can buy this one if you like it. There might be more black-tie events in our future."

He'd bitten his lower lip, a sign she knew meant he was weighing his response, choosing his words. "This isn't really my thing, you know. I mean, I don't mind going with you when you need me there…"

"I know. And I do need you there. Once in a while, I have to appear at these events, but don't worry, they don't call me much anymore. I was just thinking it might be more practical to buy the tux."

He stood in front of a mirror, letting the tailor mark where alterations needed to be made. "Besides, Bren, I still want to lose more weight. Let's hold off on buying."

"Sure." April had dozens of gowns, but for the charity event she'd be wearing a dress lent to her by one of the newer designer houses. And Bill wouldn't need a tuxedo for the wedding—they'd already decided to keep it more casual—Bill in his charcoal gray suit, April in her Grace Kelly *High Society* dress. After all, they were getting married in a barn.

She stepped into CoffeeX, Carlie's favorite place these days, and looked around for her daughter. A rail-thin girl with bleached white hair and dark-rimmed eyes stood behind the counter, waiting on customers and looking as if she'd rather be anywhere else than there. April slipped into a chair at the far end of the café and waited. Carlie had texted that she had news.

Her daughter entered and April smiled broadly. Carlie looked every bit the New Yorker, fashionable and apathetic, in an indigo wrap jumpsuit and snakeskin-embossed ankle boots. She said something to the white-haired girl at the counter, then jogged across the airy café to greet her mother.

"Have you been waiting?"

"Not at all, I just got here and grabbed this table." April looked around. "I like it. It's bright. Usually coffee shops are darker, tighter."

"I know. I like it, too. But there's another reason I come here all the time." Carlie turned her head as a good-looking, dark man approached. He wiped his hand on his apron before offering it to April.

"Hi, I'm Axel." His handshake was strong but not bone-crushing. Skin the color of a cappuccino, dark hair like a well-groomed poodle, and a self-assured, sexy smile.

"Oh, you work here, Axel?"

"I work here a lot. This is my café." He radiated confidence and, April noted reluctantly, a little arrogance. *He's just proud of himself. Nothing wrong with that.*

She tried not to stare. He was gorgeous, she thought, with those black molten eyes. "Nice to meet you, Axel." With a glance at Carlie, she asked, "How long...um, how long have you had this place?" *How long have you been seeing my daughter?*

"A little over three years now. It started out slow, but we do okay, even with the Starbucks on the next corner."

April noticed as Carlie pushed an errant strand of hair away from her face and gazed at Axel. When he turned his eyes on her and smiled, she actually squirmed in her chair. *Oh, dear*, April thought, *she's in deep.*

"What can I get for you today? Carlie, your usual? Ms. Tweed?"

"Call me April, please. And just a coffee. Cream, no sugar."

With a thousand-watt grin, Axel said, "You got it. Be right back." He weaved his way between tables and disappeared in back.

"Carlie! Why didn't you tell me? And, yes, he's dreamy."

"I know, right? I've only just started seeing him, Mom, that's why I didn't say anything. We met at a party last month, but we've only been on, like, two real dates. But we have this connection, you know? There's definitely something cosmic between us."

"I see that! And you're positively glowing." *New love.*

"I'd like to bring him to the wedding, is that okay?"

"Well, I don't see why not. Oh! Wait. I was going to put you and Gran in a room together. There aren't that many rooms on the property." *I can't put my mother in a hotel.*

"We can just get a room at a hotel. There are hotels there, right?" she giggled.

"There are. About a fifteen-minute drive away. So you'd be sharing. It's fine," she rushed to add.

"I know it's fine, Mom! But we haven't slept together yet, in case you were wondering. I'm just thinking that by the time the wedding rolls around, we will be, and I'd like us to have a room."

"Okay. Let me see what I can do. Gran can have her own room and Father Dan might want to be at the hotel. I'll call Julie and find out for sure. I think I counted three in addition to the suite." *If Bill's kids come, I'll need to put them somewhere, too.*

"Thanks, Mom. He makes me feel really special."

"And you look fabulous, honey. Those boots!"

Carlie lifted a shoulder and her wrap jumpsuit slid off a bare shoulder. "They're Chloé. Axel bought them for me."

April knew fashion enough to know that her daughter was wearing fifteen-hundred-dollar ankle boots. Axel must be doing very well, she thought. Or there was another explanation, one she wasn't able to ponder, as Axel reappeared. He placed a frothy coffee in front of Carlie, and another mug in front of April. Then he set down a small plate of pastries.

"You have to have something with coffee, yes?" He bent at the waist to kiss the top of Carlie's head, as if she was a six-year-old. Carlie's father used to do that, and the realization provoked an icy shiver. "I'll see you tonight, baby. April, it was a pleasure to meet you. Please come see me again."

"Of course," she murmured, giving Axel her best smile. Then she picked up a chocolate-filled croissant.

**

April returned to the apartment and found Bill despondent, slouched on the sofa.

"What's wrong?"

"Dan said he won't stand up for me. Well, he said he *can't*. Because we're not having a church ceremony." He drummed his fingertips on his knees.

"What did he say?"

Bill puffed out his cheeks and blew a long breath before speaking. "He's Catholic. You're not. I don't practice. We're not getting married in a church, or in a Catholic ceremony. He asked me what we expected of him then. I couldn't answer."

"But he's your *brother*, Billy."

"He's a priest. Priest outdoes brother in this case. He said he had to decline, and that means standing up with me."

"Will he attend the ceremony anyway?"

Bill lowered his head. "I don't know. We ended the conversation without me asking him." He lifted his eyes to April's. "Actually, I ended the conversation. Badly."

"Oh, Billy."

"I know. I'll call him back to apologize." He rubbed his forehead. "Do we have any aspirin?"

"Of course. Let me get it for you." In the kitchen, April poured water from a pitcher into a glass. *Maybe Julie's friend Freddy would stand up with him.* Bill wasn't close enough to anyone at school—he hadn't been there long enough, and as far as she knew, he didn't maintain friendships with guys from Connecticut. He'd lost a lot of friends when he was drinking, and even though he'd offered apologies, he'd told her that it was too difficult to pick back up. Maybe his brother-in-law? April was shaking her head as she walked back into the living room.

"What is it?"

"I was just thinking. What about your sister's husband?" Bill's groaned reply was enough of an answer. "Okay, then Freddy up at Jingle Valley. I'm sure he'd do it."

"Do I have to have someone?"

"I don't know if you're *required*, Billy, but you should. If you don't want Eileen's husband, then I'll ask Julie if Freddy will do it. It's just standing up next to you during the ceremony."

"Fine," Bill muttered.

"Fine to Robert or fine to Freddy?"

"Whatever, Bren. I don't care." He lifted his feet to the sofa, stretched his body along its length, and closed his eyes.

April returned to the kitchen, poured another glass of water, and took two aspirin out of the bottle on the counter.

TWELVE

Julie hummed to herself as she scrubbed her bathroom floor. She and Luke were trying, and it was the trying that filled her heart. The 'date' was a success, an evening spent laughing and talking and flirting. And they had been honest with each other.

"I know I scared you away when I started talking about marriage," she said.

"I shouldn't have been scared. I want to be married, too."

"But?"

Luke set down his fork. "But we're older, and the idea of having children right away gave me pause."

"But I'm thirty-eight. And you'd said you wanted children. At least one."

"And I do. I still do. It's just that we both work all the time. All the time, Jules! I don't want a baby raised by someone other than us."

Julie gulped ice water. "I feel the same way, I guess." *Just say it.* "I think we could make it work, Luke. Your shop is only open one night a week. Jingle Valley isn't always booked. And we have Bob and Freddy. It takes a village, right?"

"Maybe. I just don't want a child of ours growing up not knowing who his—or her—parents are."

"That wouldn't happen." Julie felt a stirring inside her—as if warm water was coursing through her veins, awakening her senses. She couldn't ignore the tiny spark of hope.

He reached across the table for her hand. "Do you know how much I've missed you? How I've hated being away from you?"

"Are we getting back together?" Underneath the table, she crossed the fingers on her free hand.

"If you'll take me back."

**

From the bathroom floor, Julie moved to dusting, opening a window in her bedroom even though the air outside was frigid. She didn't care. She and Luke were back together. They weren't talking marriage just yet, but both of them knew, they knew. It would happen. Maybe at Christmas, Julie thought. Maybe one day he'd say, "Let's just make it legal." She wished she could be the one to say it, because she would just say it. No elaborate proposal, no prolonged engagement. Let's just do it, she'd tell him, and off they'd trot down to the town hall to make it official. And get started on baby-making.

Why can't I be the one to ask him? Because of tradition?

Luke isn't a guy tied to tradition. Would it offend him, though?

Her phone vibrated in her back pocket. When she pulled it out and looked at the screen, she recognized April's number. Pushing down a tingle of dread (that damned Margot Dexheimer had ruined it), she answered.

"April! Good morning! How are you?" *Please be fine. Please be fine. Please be fine.*

"I'm fine, Julie, thanks. Listen, I have a question for you."

"Anything!" *Thank you for not cancelling.*

"Do you think Freddy might be able to stand up with Bill? At the ceremony? Bill's brother Dan is a priest and he says he's unable to be a part of the ceremony, because it's not Catholic."

"Really? Oh, okay. Well, I'll ask him, but I'm sure he wouldn't mind."

"Oh, thanks. It would be a huge relief. Bill's been pretty down about it ever since he found out."

"Sure, no problem. I'll send Freddy a text and I'll let you know as soon as I hear back, okay?"

"Thanks so much. Oh, and Julie? How many guest rooms do you have upstairs in the barn? The wedding suite, and then are there two more?"

"There are three, but the third room is pretty small. But we're blocking off rooms for you at the hotel. What do you need?"

"I'll need all three. That should be fine. All the guests will be at the hotels, but we'll put my mother in the smaller room. I was going to have my daughter share with her, but now Carlie—my daughter—wants to bring her new boyfriend, so they'll need a room, but they might end up at the hotel. And I wanted to offer the other one to Dan, Bill's brother. Even if he's not a part of the wedding, it would be a nice gesture." *And Bill's kids. Well, I'll deal with that when—if—it happens.*

"Of course, that's no problem. I'm glad we can accommodate. And I'll let you know about Freddy today."

"Great, thanks."

Julie ended the call and slumped to an overstuffed chair in the living room. *I need to stop thinking she's going to cancel. She's not going to cancel.* She sent a text to Freddy.

Would you be willing to stand up with Bill at the wedding? His priest brother said he can't do it because it's not in a church.

Within minutes she had a response.

I'll do it. He doesn't have any other friends?

Guess not. Thanks. I'll let them know. Book club is meeting at 5.

Can you handle it?

Y

The Dalton Library's monthly book club meeting gathered in the barn, and Julie was grateful for the business. It wasn't much, but it had brought additional bookings to the venue. Dotty Kenyon's daughter was married in the barn the previous year, as was Leah Melvin's grandson and Anna Warburton's niece. Leah had her retirement party a couple of months earlier—she had worked forty years as a realtor in the Berkshires and was given a memorable sendoff by her colleagues and many in the real estate industry. The retirement party was the biggest event Jingle Valley had hosted all year, but April Tweed's wedding would likely surpass it. April had champagne taste, and fortunately, a champagne budget to match.

Julie's phone buzzed again and she thought it would be Freddy, adding a witticism he'd just thought of. That was Freddy. But it was Luke.

Are you busy?

Just cleaning. Thx for the interruption!

What do you have going on today?

Book club at 5, nothing else. You?

Can you come to the shop?

Sure. What's the mystery?

You'll see. xxx

Julie smiled at her screen. *What was he up to?* She tamped down fantasies of him whisking her to the marriage license office. *Stop it.* She was acting like a lovesick teenager and she knew it. But she tossed the dust rag into the hamper and hopped in the shower.

**

Forty minutes later, Julie pulled up to the curb a half block down the street from Luke's flower shop. She checked her makeup in the rearview mirror and hurried out, walking quickly to her destination. She opened the door and smiled.

Luke stood alone in the shop, holding an autumn bouquet of dark red and mustard-yellow mums. He extended his arm and she took the flowers. *He's going to propose to me here?* But Luke didn't drop to his knee. Instead, he kissed her cheek and said, "You're going to thank me."

"Am I? Why?" Her heart dropped a couple of inches in her ribcage. *Whatever it is, don't be disappointed. Be nice.*

"I have a client for you."

"Oh! That's…great! Wow!"

"See? She stopped in to ask about wedding flowers, and then told me that she'd had her heart set on having her reception at The Showboat."

"The Showboat? Oh, the place in Lenox that burned down."

Luke nodded. "So I suggested Jingle Valley. She didn't know about it, but she seemed to like the idea of having her wedding reception in a rustic setting. That's how I described it." He handed her a card, the little cardboard card that was usually found in delivered bouquets. "Here's her name and number. You should call her."

"I will," Julie murmured. "Thanks." She continued to stare at the card, blinking back the pressure building behind her eyes. *Do. Not. Cry. Dammit.*

"Everything okay, hon?"

"Absolutely! Thank you so much for this. Well, I should get back home and give her a call before she finds another venue." With a quick kiss, Julie hurried out of the shop, the little bell above the entrance taunting her as she left.

**

Driving back to Jingle Valley, Julie fought back tears. *I hope for it too much. He's not ready. We just got back together.*

"But why? Why wait?" she yelled at the windshield. "If we're supposed to be together, if we want to be together, what the hell is he waiting for?" The windshield didn't answer. With tears blurring her vision, Julie veered into a rutted part of the road and nearly lost a tire. She righted the car quickly and focused. "Get a grip, Jules," she instructed herself. "If I want to propose, I should just do it. I'm acting like a teenager, and Luke doesn't want a teenager." She gripped the steering wheel with both hands and guided it into the long driveway.

Back in her warm kitchen, she put the kettle on for tea and pulled some leftover chicken out of the refrigerator. Then she texted Freddy to let him know about the new client.

I'm two minutes from your front door, he wrote back. Apparently he was closer than that, as he entered the kitchen, with Valentino in his stroller, at that moment.

"Hey, doll," he said, then stopped short. "What is it? Why have you been crying?" He lifted Val from the stroller and dragged an old oak highchair, which had been in the Tate family since Julie's father Ben was a baby, and strapped Val in, then scattered some dry cereal on the tray to keep him occupied.

"It must have been the wind! Brutal out there!" Julie turned off the stove. "Are you hungry? Does Val want something more than Cheerios?"

"Stop it. Yes, I'm hungry. Val has his cereal. He'll throw most of it on the floor. Why were you crying? Don't lie to me."

Julie sat heavily in her chair, ignoring the chicken on the counter, and told Freddy what had just transpired. "I'm an idiot, I know. I thought that when we got back together, we'd be making definite plans, you know?"

Freddy cut pieces of the roasted chicken and put them on a plate. Then he sliced a baguette and tore open a bag of romaine lettuce, filling two bowls. He opened the refrigerator door and found a bottle of salad dressing. "You drinking tea or should we have wine?"

"Don't you have anything to say to me? Like, 'Julie, you're not an idiot,' or 'Give it time and he'll come around?' Anything?"

"Let me fix these plates first. Tea or wine?"

"Tea. If I start with wine, I'll overdo it."

"Me, too." Freddy put tea bags in mugs and set the kettle on the stove. "You need a Keurig, you know." He brought the chicken, bread, and salad to the table. "Val, did you already eat all of your cereal?" He bent over to check the floor. "Nothing on the floor? I guess you liked them."

"Got!"

"Good," Freddy said. "Doesn't your Auntie Julie look awful when she cries? Look how puffy her eyes are?"

Val turned to look at Julie. "Goo."

"That's right, your Auntie Goo."

Julie waited while Freddy poured boiling water over the tea bags and set both mugs on the table. "Okay, I'll admit, I was hoping he had called me down to the shop to propose. Or something."

"Or something? Something *like* a proposal, you mean?"

"Shut up."

"Don't say that in front of my child, please."

"Sorry. See, what I was thinking was, if I were the guy, I'd say, 'Let's just get married now. What are we waiting for?' But I can't say that to him."

"Why not?" Freddy asked, pulling apart a piece of bread. He kept the hard crust and gave Val a couple of pieces of the soft interior.

"Because. Because I already scared him off once."

"But you two cleared the air on that, right?" Julie nodded, her mouth full. "And you both agree that time isn't necessarily on your side as far as waiting, right? What? Come on, Jules, it's the truth. If you want a baby of your own, tick tick tick. But you know how I feel about adoption."

"Oh lord. I'm almost forty. If he waits, it means he doesn't want to try and have a baby."

"It does not."

"Yes, it does. If he wants a baby, with me, we need to get going on it. It doesn't always happen right away, you know."

"I know, sweetie. And it might not happen just because you want it to, or because you go at it like rabbits. You're not twenty-four."

"No kidding."

Freddy filled a sippy cup with whole milk from the quart Julie kept for tea and placed it on Val's tray.

"Let me ask you a question. Would you be willing to live with him? Or to get pregnant—if you can—without being married?"

"I'm not against it, but why shouldn't we get married?"

"I'm just saying."

"I don't see any reason not to get married, and he hasn't given me a *reason* not to get married. He told me what he was worried about regarding having a kid, and I thought we'd cleared it up."

"Do you want me to talk to him?"

"Hell, no! No, Freddy, I do not want you to speak with Luke about this. If he and I can't talk about it and figure things out, then we don't belong together."

"Okay, I was just asking."

"Let's talk about something else. Like the client we might get." Julie wiped her mouth and began to clear the table.

"All right. You make the call while I put Valentino down for a nap. Then I'll join you."

"Great."

THIRTEEN

When April returned home after her meeting with
Carlie—and Carlie's new boyfriend Axel—she found a
note from Bill on the kitchen counter.

Went out for a long walk.

April stared at the note, then stared out at the row of
buildings across the street, pressed together like books in
a library. *No xxx? He always does the xxx thing.* She
knew she worried too much about him, but after all, he
was an alcoholic in recovery, he'd been stabbed not even
three months ago and was still dealing with whatever
PTSD there was associated with it. And his only brother
had opted out of standing next to him at his wedding
because they weren't getting married in a damned
church. She crumpled the note in her fist. Anyone else,
April would have given them their space, let them walk
it off. But she used her phone to send a text to Billy.

Just got home. Are you okay? Do you need me?

She erased the last sentence and replaced it with Can I
meet you somewhere?

After a few minutes and no reply, anxiety crept up from
her gut to her throat. *Come on, Billy, don't put me
through this.* And she stopped herself. *Me? This isn't*

about me.

Her phone pinged, and she grabbed it. But it was a message from Julie, not Bill.

Freddy said he'd be honored to stand up with Bill. Talk soon.

April still had her coat on. She picked up her keys from the table where she'd tossed them, slipped her phone back into her pocket, and headed out in search of her fiancé.

**

She knew she shouldn't have been looking for him in bars, but she couldn't help poking her head into each one she passed on her way down Seventh Avenue. As she crossed West Fifty-fourth Street, she spotted him, exiting a Dunkin' Donuts on her right. She raised her arm.

"Billy!" she shouted, but the noises of the street muffled her voice. Hurrying to catch up with him, she saw him hand money to a homeless guy seated on the sidewalk, wrapped in an old red-and-black-plaid blanket. "Billy!" she yelled again, and he turned. But he didn't break into a smile upon seeing her; instead, he stared. Glared at her.

"I was worried," she gasped. "I was hoping you hadn't gone all the way down to Times Square!" She slipped her arm through his and drew him closer, but he stood stiffly away from her.

"You actually called my ex-wife?" he hissed.

"What?"

"You heard me, Brenda. You called Mary Pat to invite the kids—my kids—to the wedding. After I specifically told you not to." He yanked his arm away and walked away from her, toward Times Square.

Damn these shoes, April thought. "Billy, wait. Let me explain." She reached him and pulled on his jacket, forcing him to turn around again.

He crossed his arms in front of chest and ignored the people hurrying past them. "Go ahead, explain to me here on Seventh Avenue why you intentionally did something I didn't want you to do, after I *said* I didn't want you to do it. Why in the world would you call Mary Pat and invite Danny and Norah to the wedding?"

"Can't we go somewhere and talk about this?" she pleaded. "Look, there's an Irish place across the street. We could have a bite. It's Irish," she said, smiling, but faltered when his eyes stayed flinty and hard.

"Nope. I'm not going anywhere with you until you explain. Because for the life of me, Brenda, I don't get it. So if you want to talk, now's your chance."

April hung her head. She knew she was in trouble. Why she thought her plan would work, without him getting mad, was an unanswerable question. She knew when she called Mary Pat that he'd be mad. Thank goodness Silvia hadn't phoned him, too. At least not yet.

"Okay. I was wrong. *Very* wrong." She peeked up at him but his face was as if carved in stone. Only a muscle in his neck pulsated, raging. "I just thought that it was an opportunity to have your children, your grown children, see you happy. I offered to pay their airfare and hotel."

"For how long?"

"Oh, just for the weekend. Like, they could fly here on a Thursday night or a Friday, fly back on Sunday."

"So, my children, whom I haven't seen in *twenty years*, would fly across the country to see their absent father— correction, their *biological* father—get married to you, a celebrity, chat it up, have a glass of champagne, and then fly back to their lives. And all's well that ends well, right? Are you out of your mind?"

April shrank under his berating. But he was right. What *was* she thinking?

"I kept looking for the right time to tell you. I don't even know if they'll come, and if they weren't coming, then, I thought, no harm. Billy, I'm so sorry." Did she see a tiny softening around his eyes?

"Well, Danny isn't coming. Mary Pat said he can't get off work. Somehow I think he didn't want to come, anyway. But Norah is. Norah is coming to the wedding, Brenda." He uncrossed his arms and they hung limply by his sides. He stood in grim defeat.

"All right. I'll do whatever I can to make her comfortable, Billy. I will. Whatever she needs. Whatever *you* need."

Bill rubbed his eyes, then dragged his hands back over his scalp, making what little hair he had left stand on end. April would have cracked a loving joke then if the circumstances hadn't been so fraught with tension. Instead, she waited.

"I have no idea how this is going to go. But you got all of us into it." He glanced at his watch. "I'm going to a meeting. I need it pretty bad right now. See you at home." And without a peck on the cheek or a touch to her face, Bill Flanagan turned from April Tweed and walked away.

**

April watched Bill walk back up Seventh, in the direction of their home, but then made a left on West Fifty-sixth. April pulled out her phone and called Carlie. But the call went directly to voice mail.

"Hi honey, it's just me. Nothing important. Catch up soon."

She stood on the sidewalk, oblivious to the throngs of people pushing past her. *He didn't call off the wedding, at least.* She thought he might cancel, he was so mad. April didn't pray, ever, but she found herself making a silent imploration that Bill's daughter Norah was a sweet girl who wanted her daddy to be happy. *He's right about all of it. There isn't enough time for them to reconnect, on any level. Unless she's willing to stay longer.* April didn't even know about the flight—did Bill arrange it already? She had offered to cover all of the costs, but she needed to know when Norah would arrive and how long she planned to stay. At the same time, she knew she couldn't call Mary Pat again. Not if Mary Pat was going to tell Billy.

"April Tweed?" A woman's voice jolted her out of her thoughts. April looked at the source of the voice, a middle-aged woman in a dark purple velour tracksuit and sneakers. Her short blond hair was streaked with silver, as if she'd meant it to look that way. April became April Tweed, parting her lips to give the fan a wide smile.

"Hello," she said, taking in the group of three women, apparently all on holiday in the Big Apple.

"I watched *Echo Falls* every single day, well, until they had you eaten by that mountain lion. I was actually the president of the April Tweed Fan Club in Greenville." The woman gestured to her friends. "We're all from North Carolina. It's our first time in New York! And I can't believe I'm standing on the street talking to April Tweed!" She fished around in a canvas bag and pulled out a small camera. "Would you mind? It would make my day!"

Just shoot me, April thought. "Of course!" she said. "What's your name?"

"Oh! I'm Evie, and that's Maxine, and she's Annie.

Maxine and Annie are sisters."

"Nice to meet you all," April said.

"Annie, you take the picture. Take more than one, then I can pick the best one."

April backed up against a building and Evie stood next to her. April posed, as she was so accustomed to doing, even though it seemed like years since she'd last posed for a photo.

"Say 'fried green tomatoes!'"

"What?" April was so surprised so forgot to smile.

Annie laughed loudly. "I knew that would get you!"

"Annie, stop it. Come on now, this is serious," Evie said, inching closer to April.

Once the camera had been clicked four or five times, April stepped forward, ready to say goodbye to the three women.

"And would you mind just taking a picture of the three of us? Because one of us always has to take the picture." April thought none of them understood the concept of the selfie, but agreed anyway. She accepted the camera from Annie.

"Smile!" she said and snapped four photos before handing the camera back to Evie. "It was very nice to meet you all, but I really must be off," she added, already moving away from the group.

"Oh, we would have loved to buy you coffee, or a drink." With a glance to her friends, Evie added, "This was the best part of the whole trip to New York City. We love you, April!"

April raised a black-gloved hand to the trio before hurrying away up Seventh Avenue to her empty home.

FOURTEEN

Freddy bundled little Val into the car seat and slipped behind the wheel.

"Ready to run errands with Daddy, Val?"

"Da!"

"Great! What are we going to listen to today?" Freddy connected his phone and pushed a few buttons. The overture to *Hello, Dolly!* filled the car's interior. "Ooh, Val!"

"Ooh!" Val echoed.

Freddy shifted into reverse and began singing. "Call on Dolly!" he chirped, glancing at Val in the rearview mirror. The little boy listened with a resolute expression, repeating sounds and words when he could. By the time "Ribbons Down my Back" began, Freddy had pulled into the driveway of his friends' house. Val was about to have a play day with Grayson and Brooklynn. Grayson's mom Anya and Brooklynn's mom Paige had invited Freddy and Val to the house, and Freddy had agreed, mentioning the importance of Val's interaction with other children. The words that Bob had made him repeat the previous evening.

"He's fine at home, babe!"

"Fred, he needs to play with other kids his age. He doesn't understand the concept of sharing toys."

"That's ridiculous."

"It's not. Do you want Val to grow up to be a brat? A kid no one wants to play with?"

"Fine," Freddy muttered.

Later that evening, Val was so exhausted from his play day that he didn't even ask for a second story when Freddy and Bob put him down for the night. The couple had gotten used to eating after Val was asleep, and Freddy set leftovers on the table.

"See? He needed to be able to play with others."

"Yeah, yeah. It was okay today, I guess. But it doesn't have to be ongoing. There's time enough for him to play with others. I still love having him all to myself."

"I know you do. But he's developing, and developing social skills is important. You of all people should know that." Bob brushed his hand over Freddy's shoulder as he cleared the dinner plates and brought them to the sink. Freddy cooked, Bob cleaned up—that was the deal, and neither of them complained about the arrangement.

"Our boy will be *very* social, I'll see to it. I just worry. About germs. Not everyone keeps as clean a home as I do. I checked out Paige's bathroom. Ugh."

"But that's the point. He needs to get out of the bubble. All kids encounter germs! We did, and we turned out all right, didn't we?" He accepted the empty salad bowl from Freddy. "And you need to get out, too. Don't you have a big wedding coming up?"

"Actually, we have two big ones coming up. April Tweed on December first and possibly—probably— another one on New Year's Eve. Plus Julie and Luke…" Freddy touched his fingers to his mouth.

"Wait. Did he ask her?"

"Not yet, but he's going to. He told me he wanted to surprise her, but she's going out of her mind waiting. I'm afraid she's going to ask *him* if he doesn't do it soon."

Bob chuckled. "I'd love it if she did ask him. So when is it going to happen? The wedding?"

"Julie's? Probably not until the spring, I'm thinking. She really wants a baby. I'm pressing her to consider adoption. Maybe we could go back to get a little brother or sister for Val."

Bob turned from the soapy water and faced his husband. "We can have as many as you want. Just be sure."

"I'm sure. About everything."

**

Julie had cooked for Luke, and they were relaxing in the living room. No television, no distractions, just the two of them. She'd been turning it over in her mind all day, this idea to ask him about marriage. Would he be offended? Why should he be? Luke was a modern-thinking man, and what difference did it make if she asked him? Still, she was a little peeved that he hadn't asked her yet. Why was he waiting? Was he still harboring doubts? If she asked him, she had to be sure he'd say yes. *This is what guys go through*, she thought. *No one wants to hear 'no' to a marriage proposal.*

"You're quiet, honey. Everything okay?" Luke asked.

"Hmm? Oh, yeah. Everything's good."

Luke rubbed his thumb over the back of her left hand. He rode it in between her fingers, up and down, but when he got to the spot where a ring would be, he paused.

"Jules." He squeezed her hand and forced her to meet his gaze. When she looked at him, she saw an intensity in his eyes that she'd never seen before. His pupils were so big that his eyes looked completely black. She drew in a sharp breath, and at the same time Luke slipped from the couch to the floor in one motion, to rest on one knee.

"Oh! Luke."

"I've thought about it and thought about it, and I waited because I wanted to do something spectacular, something that might match the enormity of love I have for you. But Julie, you know that's not me. That's not

110

us! So instead of just thinking about it and wondering what to do, I'm doing it. Now." He pulled a small box out of his pocket and held it out to her. "Julie Annika Tate, please say yes. Please marry me."

Julie's mouth hung open as she stared at Luke, and the box. She'd never expected it to happen like this, in the living room. But why not? Why not where they were most comfortable? With quivering fingers, she plucked the box from his palm and opened it. On a pale green velvet cushion lay an antique diamond ring, round, Art Deco style.

"Where did you find this?" she breathed. "It's gorgeous."

"I knew you'd like it. I found it in an antique jewelry shop in Stockbridge. I think it'll fit, but we can get it sized if it doesn't."

Julie held the ring up to the lamp to look at its brilliance, then handed it to Luke. "Yes, I'll marry you."

He slipped it on her finger, where it twirled. "Too big," he said, disappointed.

"No, it's fine. My hands are cold."

"No. I want it to fit. Let's take it to get sized. Can you get away tomorrow?"

"I just want to stare at it," she said, then laughed. "We're getting married!" *I don't have to ask him! Whew!*

"But we'll fix the ring. I don't want it to fall off."

"No, you're right." Julie slipped the diamond off her finger and tucked it back into the little box. "Should I call Freddy? Is it too late?"

"It's quarter to ten. What do you think?"

"Let me take a photo of it on my finger and I'll send the picture to him," she giggled.

Luke smiled as Julie took the ring back out, slipped it on her finger and held her fingers close together. She snapped a few shots with her phone, then chose the best one, showing it to Luke, who nodded his approval.

After she sent the photo with no caption, she turned back to her now fiancé.

"I love you."

"I love you, too! When do you want to get married?"

"Tomorrow." When Luke laughed, she added, "I'm only half-kidding."

"Seriously? Jules, don't you want to plan a wedding?"

"I am planning a wedding. Two weddings! We got another booking for New Year's Eve, thanks to you."

"We could wait until spring if you want. It's so pretty here when the flowers come out."

"Spring! Luke, I don't want to wait until spring. I'm nearly thirty-nine years old and I want us to at least try to have a baby."

"Okay, we'll find a justice of the peace tomorrow, when we resize your ring. But we'll have to get licenses and whatever else they require. And wedding bands."

"I know. But as soon as possible!"

"And we can start working on that baby matter tonight," he said, taking her by the hand.

FIFTEEN

The night Bill finally came back home, he hadn't even locked the front door before he'd asked, "Did you contact Sylvia, too?"

April nodded. "She said no, kind of a flat-out no."

"Not surprising. We don't communicate. But you knew that." He hung up his jacket. "So just Norah is coming then."

"I did offer to pay for her airfare and hotel."

"I know, Mary Pat told me. But she took care of it. Norah will arrive in New York a week before the wedding. She has friends there, and she'll take the train up to Albany on Friday the thirtieth, then return to New York on Sunday and fly home…I don't know, whenever. She'll be in Dalton from Friday evening until sometime on Sunday."

"Okay. Hey, Billy…"

He put his hand up. "Don't, Bren. Not now. I'm tired." For a minute they stared at each other, unable to speak. "I may need to attend more meetings as we get closer. Just wanted you to know."

Again April nodded mutely. "Do you want to eat?"

"I ate something while I was out," he replied. "I think I'll just shower and go to bed."

April gripped the counter to support suddenly shaky legs. Still, he hadn't called off the wedding. But going to bed without a kiss goodnight? They never did that. Should she sleep in the living room? There was no extra bed—Carlie had taken hers when she moved. If she slept on the couch, that would be worse, right? They needed to at least sleep together. But it wasn't right to go to bed angry, with unspoken resentment. Still, she couldn't force him to talk more. April imagined he'd have plenty to talk about with his counselor on Wednesday. But it was only Saturday night, and already the day had been one of the longest she'd ever experienced.

She made herself a cup of herbal tea and walked into the dark living room. At the window, she fingered the hanging mobile whose tinkling bells had given her the idea about Jingle Valley. *It had seemed like such a good idea at the time*, she said to herself. She looked down at the lights of the city, her vibrant, humming city, and thought about the farm in Dalton, where she imagined life was peaceful and quiet. *What will our life be like— peaceful? Quiet? Or vibrant and humming?* It was up to them. Up to her.

April placed her empty cup in the sink, turned off the lights in the kitchen, and stepped softly to their bedroom, where she undressed in silence and crawled into bed beside Bill.

**

The following morning when April opened her eyes, Bill was not in bed. She squinted against the soft morning light, trying to remember what day it was. Sunday. Yesterday was Saturday. Did he leave the bed when he realized she was in it? Only once did he stir the previous night as April lay mostly awake, listening to him breathe. Only once during the night did he seem to be in the middle of a deep dream, as his breathing changed and soft, guttural sounds escaped his throat. April had lain under the covers and listened.

As her eyes adjusted and her senses sharpened, she heard light sounds from the kitchen. *He's still here. He hasn't abandoned me.*

Although she would have liked to stay in bed for at least another hour, April rose, pulled on a silk robe, and padded barefoot down the hallway to the kitchen.

"Good morning," she whispered.

He looked up. His face was more serene, she thought, his eyes looked softer. Or was that just wishful thinking?

"Good morning," he said, and April could have sworn she saw the tiniest smile curve his lips upward.

"We didn't kiss goodnight last night," she said, feeling her throat constrict with anxiety, the tell of waiting tears behind her eyes. "That was the first time since we've been back together."

Bill nodded. "I know. That was wrong. I shouldn't have done that."

"Did you sleep?"

Bill poured coffee into two mugs—one with the *Rent* logo on it and another that looked like a New York Times crossword puzzle. As April perched on one of the stools at the counter, Bill slid the crossword mug— April's favorite—to her.

"I had a dream," he said. "I was visited by a woman from my past."

April stiffened. "I see."

He shook his head. "Let me explain. When I was in Galway, I met a young woman on a bus trip. I went to the Cliffs of Moher one day and she was on the bus. Her name was Meg and she had a habit of quoting Pope John Paul and Mother Teresa." Seeing April's confusion, he continued. "Bren, I don't know if she was an angel, but there were times I believed she may have been."

"Oh, you mentioned her a while back. I remember. Something about stepping out."

"Step out fearlessly, yes. Meg was quirky and annoying sometimes, but she made an impression. And I do believe she came into my life for a reason, and to guide us back to each other." He set his mug down on the counter and leaned closer to April. "She stopped me from taking a drink the day I met her. I was ready to drink again, Bren, and it was as if she knew." With his voice thicker, Bill continued. "I never got her full name. She just disappeared. And last night I dreamed about her."

"What happened in the dream?"

"It wasn't long, but I remember. She was in front of me, her wild hair all around her face like wavy straw, and she said, 'Yesterday is gone and tomorrow has not yet come. All you have is today.' Then she grinned and told me Mother Teresa said it. That's all I got."

"Yesterday is gone and tomorrow has not yet come," April repeated.

"All we have is today. Bren, your heart was in the right place when you made those calls. I know that. We'll be okay. Norah will come to the wedding and we'll welcome her. If she thinks she wants to have a relationship with me, I'm open to it. And if she decides she doesn't, I'll accept it."

April exhaled. "Every day you remind me how lucky I am to be with you. I can't wait until we're married, Billy."

"Well, before we get married, we have another celebration. Your birthday is on Tuesday."

April dismissed it with a wave of her hand. "No big deal."

"Of course it's a big deal! But I can't get off work. Would you like to celebrate today? Or next weekend? I mean, we can go out to dinner Tuesday night, or have something here, if you want to invite Carlie over?"

"She's got a new boyfriend, I didn't have a chance to tell you."

"He can come. Is she bringing him to the wedding?" April nodded. "Well, I'll let you figure it out. Birthday girl gets to choose."

I have things to figure out. Like dealing with Billy's daughter. How she's going to get from the train station in Albany to Dalton—are we expected to pick her up? But for now, my forty-ninth birthday on Tuesday. Ugh. I couldn't care less about it. Or how we celebrate.

"I'll talk to Carlie, see if she wants to join us. Maybe we'll wait until the weekend, though, Billy. You've got work, and counseling." She deflected. "It really doesn't matter. We could just get takeout and eat here." Seeing the expression on his face, she added, "Next year we'll do it up big for both of our birthdays."

"Whatever you want is good with me."

"So," April started, tracing her index finger along the rim of her coffee mug, "what do you say about kissing me goodnight now?" When he looked up at her, she trained her eyes down the hallway toward their bedroom.

"Oh! Yes. Indeed."

SIXTEEN

Bob and Freddy invited Julie and Luke to their house for an engagement celebration. Freddy was right, Julie thought, it was easier to keep Val at home. Once he was down for the night, she felt her blood pressure lower. *I'd better get used to it*, she thought, *if this is going to be our future.*

"So! When is this wedding of the century going to occur?" Bob poured wine for everyone and passed around a plate of crudités. She picked up a stalk of celery stuffed with something that she hoped was hummus and handed the plate to Luke, who she knew was ravenous. It was seven-thirty and he'd wanted to eat something as soon as he'd arrived home from work.

"We decided not to have a big wedding," Luke replied. "Julie—and you, too, Fred—have your hands full with April Tweed's wedding and now this other one on New Year's Eve.

"Jules, what's her name again?" Freddy asked.

"You're teasing me because I'm so bad with names. Ha ha, Freddy. Her name is Jane. Jane Nevins. I don't know the name of her fiancé, though. Do I?" she asked Luke, who shook his head.

"Is she local?" Bob inquired.

"She was. Grew up in Becket but moved away after college. She wanted to get married in the Berkshires, decided on The Showboat…"

"The Showboat? That old place? Didn't it burn down?"

Luke smiled. "It did. So when she came into my shop and asked for a recommendation, I suggested Jingle Valley."

"We need to pay you a finder's fee," Freddy said.

"Anyway, we've got April and Bill on the first of December, Jane Nevins and her betrothed on New Year's Eve." Julie shrugged. "We could wait until spring for our wedding, but why?" She squeezed Luke's hand. "I'd marry him tomorrow if the town hall would allow it."

Bob was the only one at the table to take second helpings, and when he stood up after dinner, Julie noticed he'd put on some weight around his middle. *But doesn't that mean he's happy? Will I feel the same way if Luke gains weight? Because I'd expect him to love me the same even if I get fat. Or pregnant.*

"But Jules, I've known you for a long time, and one thing I've always known about you is that you wanted a beautiful wedding. Not a stand-up nothing ceremony in the town hall," Freddy said.

"Is that true, honey? You never said."

Julie crossed her arms over her chest. "Look, that was then. When I was in my twenties, of course I dreamed about my wedding. But it didn't happen. I'm older now, and it's the marriage that's important, not the wedding."

"Still." Freddy stared at her, and Julie looked away, willing her cheeks not to turn pink. She pushed back from the table.

"Dinner was wonderful. Thank you both so much. Freddy, we'll talk soon about Jane Nevins." She kissed his cheek and hugged Bob, wrapping her arms around his middle. "Love to Val."

"Thanks, guys," Luke said, giving that half-hug thing that all men seemed to do.

On the short drive back to the house, Luke asked, "Honey, you'd tell me if you wanted a big wedding, wouldn't you? Because I want you to have what you want."

"Look, my parents are gone, my brothers and sister all live out West, and I wouldn't expect them to fly east anyway. Babe, as long as we get married, I don't care how it happens."

"Okay. As long as you're happy with that."

"Right," she said. *So why have I kept my wedding scrapbook all these years? Out-of-date dresses and themes, stuff I used to dream about, why haven't I ditched it?* Her fingernails dug into her thighs.

**

The following day, Julie snapped at Freddy twice, first because he hadn't done any of the work he'd said he'd do for the Tweed-Flanagan wedding. "How could you not have done it?" she yelled.

"I've been busy, doll. Come on. Val takes up a lot of time! You'll know the feeling soon enough."

She snapped again. "Shut up, Freddy! This is our *business*. You need to find a babysitter for your child. Or go be a full-time dad and leave me the hell alone."

Freddy stopped what he was doing. He leaned back in his office chair and stared at Julie until she looked at him. "What? I'm right, you know."

"No, you were incredibly rude. So I'm going to believe that there's something else going on with you, something besides Val. Because if this argument is going to be about my child, I'll leave this very minute." He rolled his chair away from the long dining room table that they used when they worked together.

Julie set her jaw. "Okay, I'm sorry I was rude. But you can't deny that ever since you and Bob got Val, your time has been taken. You're hardly ever here and when you are, it's as if you're operating on autopilot. Or you bring Val to the house and if he's not sleeping, all of your attention is on him. And then all of *my* attention is on him, too."

"Are you *jealous*, Jules? Is that it?" He was serious. No jokes.

"Of course not! I'm not jealous of a baby!"

"Because I could understand if you were. First it was just you and me, turning a barn into a wedding venue, fretting over our finances. Then we met Bob and Luke and things got really good. Then Bob and I got married. Then Bob and I adopted Val. And you and Luke split up and you were alone. And talking a hell of a lot about your age." He paused, wondering if he'd gone too far. Julie slumped in her chair, arms crossed over her chest, chin lowered. He continued. "But now you and Luke are engaged, doll. You should be deliriously happy about it."

"I am."

"Coulda fooled me." Freddy stood and walked around the table to where Julie sat. He held out his arms. "Come here."

She didn't move.

"Julie Tate. Stand up right now and hug me. I need it."

Reluctantly, Julie got out of her chair and allowed Freddy to hug her, but kept her arms at her side. Freddy held on, enveloping her in his strong arms, rubbing her back in a circular motion. He wouldn't let go.

It worked. She began to cry, but still he held her, letting her work through her emotions, shaking against his strong body.

"I'm sorry," she said in a muffled voice against his chest.

"I know, sweetie. I know." She pulled back, and he pushed her hair away from her face. She looked up at him with wet eyes.

"It's just...I don't know...everything."

"Come with me. I'll make tea." He took her hand in his and led her into the spacious kitchen. Pulling out a wooden chair for her, Freddy gently pushed Julie's shoulders down until she was seated at the kitchen table. He filled the kettle with water from the tap and lit the stove, then pulled his own chair close to hers and sat.

"Tell me one thing that's got you upset. Just one."

Julie heaved a big sigh and let her shoulders sag. Her chin dropped to her chest, but Freddy used his index finger to raise it, until she was forced to look into his kind eyes.

"I don't know," she stammered.

"Just say it, honey. Blurt it out."

"I want a big wedding."

"Okay. That's the Julie I know and love. So, why deny

it? You can have a big, beautiful wedding." He poured hot water from the kettle into two mugs on the counter and brought the steaming cups to the table.

"It's just that we're trying to get April and Bill's wedding ready, and that's important because it's bringing us money. And Jane Nevins is probably even more money."

"Yes, money's important. But so are you. There's money for your wedding, Jules. Whatever kind of wedding you want."

"My brothers and Ella won't fly back for it. Luke doesn't have any family. It doesn't matter."

"Well, you don't know that your brothers and Ella wouldn't fly back for it unless you invite them. And you and Luke both know a lot of people, Julie! You and I have made a ton of connections over the years." He squeezed her hand. "And it *does* matter. This is your only wedding, right?"

She smiled. "Hope so."

"I hope so, too! Luke's a keeper. So make it the wedding you want."

Julie blew across the top of her steaming tea.

"Is it the timing? You don't want to wait until the spring?"

"It's this whole baby thing. If we get married tomorrow, I can start trying. All those years of trying *not* to get pregnant, what if it doesn't happen?" She retrieved milk from the refrigerator and poured a generous amount into her tea.

Freddy softened his voice. "Yes, it might not happen, that's true. You know that. But we've talked about this. And why not start trying now, hmm? You're engaged. You're going to marry this guy. Maybe set the wheels in motion now. No one will think any less of you."

"You mean if I get married with a big belly?"

"What difference does it make? You two can consider yourselves married now. You're not going anywhere, neither is he. Not with that rock on your finger," he said, in an effort to get her to smile. It worked. "And if it doesn't happen, honey, you have other options."

Julie nodded. "I know…"

"And Julie. Look at me, honey. If you're truly bothered that I bring Val to the house…"

"I'm not! Really, Freddy, I'm so sorry about that. I love Val, you know I do."

"I know. But Bob's mentioned it, too. Val needs to socialize more. And I need to find someone I can trust. That's the problem. Now that he's walking, I'm scared to death."

"Yeah. Why can't they just stay in cribs until they go off to college?"

SEVENTEEN

With just four weeks to go until the wedding, April was making lists. Handwritten lists, because she kept everything in a spiral-bound notebook. A list for everything, from guests to food to music. At her count, there were fifty-seven confirmed guests, including family members. Freddy had agreed to stand up next to Bill, after Fr. Dan had said he couldn't. Bill and Dan had apparently worked things out, at least that was what Bill told her. April hadn't spoken to Dan in weeks.

Carlie was still bringing her new boyfriend, and April had a room for them, upstairs, next to the wedding suite. Dan would be one room down, and April wanted her mother in the small room at the end of the corridor. Her mother had said she didn't want to go shopping with her, stating that she had plenty of clothes to choose from and would wear "something very suitable" to her daughter's "second wedding."

"Mom, please stop calling it my 'second wedding' and Bill's 'third wedding.' We're all aware."

"Well, it's not the same, Brenda. I remember your first wedding, quite an elaborate affair, and your father paid a lot of money for something that didn't even last ten years."

"Twelve years, thank you, and I know that Dad spent a lot. I believe I thanked both of you at the time."

"Well. The second wedding is supposed to be muted, low-key. From what you've told me, this one doesn't sound muted and low-key."

"Mom, I can't help some of it. There's going to be publicity, and it's good for the venue. Julie and Freddy have worked hard to turn Jingle Valley into a lovely place for weddings. They deserve the publicity."

"And you're okay with the publicity, too, aren't you?"

"I accept it, Mother."

"Of course you do, honey. Now, you said Carlie and I will be sharing a room there? Does she know I'm a night owl?"

"Oh. Forgot to tell you. Actually, Mom, you'll have your own room. Carlie and her boyfriend will have a room of their own."

April listened to the silence on the other end of the phone and tried to guess what her mother's first line would be. *Is that so? Well, well, well. I've never met this boyfriend.* Or, the best one—*what's his last name?*

"This is news to me. Since when has Carlie had a boyfriend important enough to bring to your second wedding and important enough to share a room with?"

"She's been seeing him for a while now," April replied, deliberately vague. None of her mother's business. "His name is Axel and he owns a coffee shop in the city."

"Oh, good grief. What kind of a name is Axel? What's his last name?"

"You know, Mom, I can't remember. Anyway, you'll have a room of your own. Sorry you don't want to go shopping with Carlie and me."

"Wait now. I didn't know Carlie was going, too. I'd love to see my granddaughter."

"Of course you would. Fine. Do not pester her with questions. She's a grown woman and can do whatever she wants. Come up Saturday morning on the train and we'll all go together."

**

Bill met with his counselor every Wednesday afternoon, after his classes had ended. His counselor, a thirtysomething beanpole of a man with thinning blond hair and the palest blue eyes Bill had ever seen, came to the school, then they walked together past the playground to a coffee shop near the train station. Bill knew why Anders came to the school. The second time he'd arrived to meet him, Bill had told him he was perfectly capable of walking by himself past the playground to the station.

"I understand," Anders had said, in a voice both soft and

clipped. Bill thought he'd heard a trace of a Norwegian accent. He'd have to ask him about it, he thought.

"So next week I'll just meet you at Starbucks," Bill had said.

"Is it an imposition that I come to your school so we can walk together?"

"No, not at all. I just don't want you to think that I can't handle it." In a more subdued tone, he added, "I'm able to walk by the scene of the crime without freaking out."

"Of course," Anders replied. "And if you'd rather not have my company, I'll simply meet you there."

"It's fine. You can come to the school." It was, actually, fine.

At Starbucks, Bill always ordered a decaf—after all, it was three in the afternoon—and Anders always asked for hot green tea.

By November, Bill began to wonder if he needed a counseling session every Wednesday afternoon. This was in addition to seeing Anders on Saturday mornings in the city.

"Do you think I still need these two sessions a week?" he asked, stirring artificial sweetener into his coffee. His attempts at drinking black coffee had failed. He could skip the cream, but not the Splenda.

"Well, Bill, posttraumatic symptoms can wax and wane, if you will. At times there may be no stress at all. This is good, yes. How are the flashbacks?"

"Only at night, and not all the time. I'm pretty focused during the day, with school, and April. The wedding coming up next month."

"You went back to school quite quickly after the event."

"It's not that I went back. It happened on my first day."

"Yes, I realize that. But you returned to school, to the place where the stabbing happened, very soon after it occurred. We've talked about your burying the trauma from the event, in order for you to not lose your job. You'd made so many changes to your life—selling your house, moving from Connecticut, moving in with April…"

Bill nodded. All of it was true. "Yes. I wanted to put the stabbing behind me as soon as possible."

"Is April aware of your sleeplessness?"

"No, I don't think so. She knows I get up at night sometimes. I'm always up and about before she wakes. I've just told her that I don't need much sleep. I do get enough sleep, Anders. I never feel depleted throughout the day."

"And exercise? How are you doing with that?"

"Better," Bill said, thinking about how much he wanted a brownie. "I'm laying off the sugars and bad carbs, trying to get in shape for the wedding. I'm down sixteen pounds so far."

"Good for you," Anders said. *You have literally no idea*, Bill thought, looking at the lanky man on the opposite side of the table. "Do you have a chance to get physical exercise, though? Walking, stair-climbing, perhaps? Do you belong to a gym?"

"April belongs to a gym. I didn't really want to join. That's her time, you know?"

"But what about *your* time?"

Bill looked at Anders. "I'm Irish, I've got one coping mechanism—repression." He was unable to get a smile from Anders, so he added, "I guess I hadn't thought about it."

Anders held his cardboard cup aloft before swallowing down the rest of his tea. "Think about it. There's a lot going on in your life right now, and I want you to carve out some time for yourself. It's important, Bill, and vital to your physical and mental health. You can go to April's gym at your own time, or do different things while you're there together. Or you can join a different gym. For now, I believe we should continue with Wednesdays and Saturdays. This is a nice and relaxed atmosphere, don't you agree? Saturdays are in the office, but I like coming out here to meet you and spend a little time. Just to chat."

"Okay. Well, then, since we're chatting, I'll tell you about something that really made me mad last weekend. Something April did."

"I'm listening."

EIGHTEEN

Julie and Freddy had a meeting with Jane Nevins. Jane's fiancé, an executive who worked in data security, traveled a lot, she said, and was presently in Hong Kong.

"How exciting!" Freddy chirped.

"You'd think," said Jane, rolling her eyes. "He's away *a lot*, but I made him promise to stay home more once we're married."

Julie shot Freddy a quick look that said, *Good luck with that*, and Freddy's look said the same. She loved how they could communicate without even speaking.

"So, that means that today, you get to make all the decisions!" Julie said, smiling brightly.

"I was going to choose everything anyway," Jane said. "It's my wedding," she added. Her eyes glittered like the three-carat diamond on her finger.

They were seated at a table in the barn. Freddy had paperwork spread out in front of him, forms for Jane to sign. She'd given them a hefty deposit, twenty per cent more than what was required, and she was paying extra to have Julie and Freddy coordinate services. With close to three hundred guests invited, the barn would be filled to capacity, leaving less room for the band.

"This doesn't give us much of a dance floor," she complained, then sat back in her chair and waited.

"Um…" Julie started, then glanced at Freddy, who sat up straight and took over.

"Here's an idea, Jane. You've got eight guests per table, which is lovely. But we could seat ten to a table and you'd free up space that way. Your guests won't mind— it's really just for eating. You'd cut back by eight tables, giving you plenty of extra room for dancing. And once dinner's over, our staff can move a few tables farther away to make more room on the dance floor."

Jane laid her hand on Freddy's forearm. "You're a doll," she said, batting her fake eyelashes at him.

Oh good lord. Here we go again. Freddy had that effect on women, many of whom couldn't tell right away that he was gay. But he was wearing a wedding band, for crying out loud!

Julie pushed back in her chair. "Freddy, I'm just going to check on Val. Your son," she added. As she was leaving the room to check on Valentino, who was sleeping in the tiny chapel, she heard Jane say, "Oh, I bet you're the *best* father!"

Julie knew that Freddy was smart. He'd hook Jane, this well-to-do client, and if she wanted to flirt with him, Freddy wasn't going to give her any reason not to. Jane's wedding, set for New Year's Eve, was much bigger than April Tweed's, and Julie knew they'd finish out the year well in the black.

She tiptoed into the darkened chapel, where Val lay on his back under the altar. His eyes were open and they drifted over to Julie as she approached him.

"Hey, sleepyhead," she whispered, lowering herself to the carpeted floor. Val turned to his side on the air mattress and reached an arm out.

"Ooh-lee," he said, his voice like the softest cotton puffs. Julie edged closer and Val put his hand in her hair. His eyes, like small honeydrops, latched on and wouldn't let go.

"I adore you, Valentino. I'd like to have a little boy exactly like you. And if I can't do it the natural way, then maybe your Uncle Luke and I will go to Colombia and find a boy like you. A little cousin. Boy or girl, it really doesn't matter." She blinked rapidly, lost now in the wonder of this tiny person, oblivious to Jane Nevins and her very expensive wedding being planned in the barn.

**

Freddy's voice roused her from her reverie.

"Hey!" he said, walking into the chapel. From her perspective, all Julie saw was his long denim-covered legs and Timberland boots. He sat on one of the benches and looked down on them. "Did you forget about Jane?"

"I guess I did. I enjoyed being down here with Val," she said.

"Well, she likes me better, anyway."

"Is she gone?"

"Yeah. She's fine. Luke's doing her flowers, Cake Walk's got the cake. I suggested a few bands, but I think she wants the Boston Symphony." He smiled. "He's like a little magnet, isn't he?"

"He is," she said dreamily. "I want one."

"Da," Val said. "Up."

"Up indeed," Freddy replied, hoisting his son high into his arms. As he balanced Val on his narrow hip, he reached his free arm down to Julie and helped her stand.

"Oh, I'm stiff. That floor is hard!"

"Of course it is. It's cement. You remember, you were there."

Julie let the air out of Val's mattress, stepping on it with shoeless feet to flatten it, then folded it up and stored it out of sight.

As she and Freddy and Val strolled out of the chapel and back into the barn, Freddy asked, "Did you have the talk with Luke?"

"Not yet. Waiting for the right time."

"Now is the right time, Jules. Come on, you have to do this. I can't stand it when you're miserable. And you're not pretty when you cry. Some women look pretty—not you."

She pushed his shoulder and he set Val on the floor. The little boy took a few steps and walked directly into a table, bumping his head. Looking bewildered at first, he took a beat, then began wailing.

"Well, that's my cue," Freddy stated. He kissed Julie on the cheek. "Bye, love."

"Bye." She watched them leave, Freddy cradling Val in his arms, kissing his forehead. Then she turned off the lights and lowered the heat before returning to her house. Freddy was right, she needed to talk with Luke. Tell him that she did, in fact, want a traditional wedding. She wanted her family there. She hoped he'd be happy about it.

NINETEEN

On Saturday morning, April and Carlie met April's mother at Penn Station.

"Gran!" Carlie called, waving her arm. April watched as Ellen Bornstein looked around, then caught sight of her granddaughter and smiled. Carlie always made her smile. *I'd have given her more grandchildren if I could have*, April said to herself. But once Tony left, she was grateful to have only Carlie to care for.

She stood and watched as her daughter linked her arm into Ellen's elbow and walk carefully with her toward the middle of the station where April was rooted in place. *My mother is aging. She's more frail. Why haven't I seen it until today?* Ellen was still sharp, of mind and tongue. *Maybe that's why*, she thought.

"Hi, Mom," she said, bending to kiss Ellen's powdery cheek. "Nice to see you."

"Well, it hasn't been that long, Brenda," Ellen retorted, always using April's given name. She refused to call her daughter April, and the only other person who called her Brenda was Bill. April wished it was just a Bill thing. The fact that her mother also called her Brenda kind of tarnished Bill's using it. But, whatever. "Here, this is for you." Ellen fished around in her red Birkin bag and pulled out an envelope. She never gave birthday cards, so April knew it was a check. Like she was nineteen, not forty-nine. "Next year you'll be fifty," she said.

And you'll be seventy-eight, April didn't say.

"Gran, do you want to get coffee first?"

"No, no. We should shop while our stomachs are empty, then we'll eat. Now, what are you planning to wear to your mother's second wedding? A dress? Will you wear stockings? You girls today, none of you wears stockings. It could be freezing out and still you insist on bare legs. And let me tell you, some of you girls should not ever bare your legs."

Carlie laughed. *I wouldn't have laughed*, April thought. *I'd have taken offense. Carlie is so easy.*

"I'm looking for a long dress, Gran. That way no one will know." She linked her other arm through her mother's and the three of them walked through Penn Station as if they were in *The Wizard of Oz*.

"Then I assume your dress is floor-length as well, Brenda?"

"You assume correctly, Mom. It's an early evening wedding, so we chose floor-length. I already have my dress."

Her mother stopped walking and leaned around Carlie to stare at April. "What color is it?"

April scowled. "Mom. It's a lovely wintry white, almost silvery. You'll approve."

"Hmmph."

"Gran, it's gorgeous. Mom looks like a movie star, you know, old-time. Which one was it you said, Mom?"

April smiled. "Mother, remember Grace Kelly in *High Society*? The movie with Frank Sinatra?"

"Of course I remember. I loved Grace Kelly."

"Well, if you remember the dress she wore, I found a dressmaker who replicated it pretty well. It's beautiful."

Ellen's beady eyes traveled up and down her daughter's features, and she raised and lowered her sharp chin to survey the area. They were still standing in the middle of Penn Station. "I don't know if it'll be right for you, but I'd like to see it."

"Here, I have a picture of it on my phone," Carlie said.

"Bah! I don't want to see a photograph on a phone! No, I want to see the dress. On you, Brenda."

April shifted her weight and checked her wristwatch. Bill had counseling until eleven. It was only nine-forty. "Okay, let's go to the apartment for a quick peek. Then it's back out again."

As they walked out of the train station, April whispered

in Carlie's ear. "We have to be quick about it. I don't want Bill coming home after his session and finding us all clucking about in the house. And I do not want him to see the dress yet!"

Carlie grinned at her mother. "It's a deal!" she whispered back. April flagged a taxi.

**

An hour later, Ellen was still in the apartment, reluctant to leave. She'd seen the dress on the hanger in Carlie's old closet, she'd fingered the fine silk and lace. She'd been as complimentary as Ellen Bornstein was able to be about anything in her daughter's life. And now it was time to go.

Giving Carlie pointed looks, April said, "I think it's best to head out. Carlie wants to find a pair of shoes. And I'm getting hungry."

"Come on, Gran," Carlie chimed in, offering a hand to her grandmother.

"Trying to get me out of the apartment before your Bill comes back? Is that it?"

"No, Mother," April said with a tight smile. "Bill hasn't seen my dress yet and I want to keep it that way. I'd like it to be a surprise."

"Oh, Brenda, that's what first-time brides do. This is your second time around."

April slammed her hand down on the table so hard, it made Carlie gasp and Ellen flinch. "Enough, Mom! Okay? It's *enough*! You've made it abundantly clear that this is my second wedding and Bill's third wedding. You mention it every goddam chance you get. I've had enough! Do you want to come to our wedding or not? Because if you don't want to be there, fine. You can stay in New Jersey."

There was silence in the apartment, the only sound a muted jingle of bells from the wind chime. Ellen stood up shakily and reached for her coat. "I apologize, Brenda. I would very much like to come to your....*wedding*."

"Great. Then let's go." She was the first one to the door. She opened it wide and stepped to the side, gesturing for her mother and her daughter to exit the apartment. Carlie patted her mother on the shoulder as they all stepped into the hallway.

TWENTY

Julie decided to make Luke's favorite meal, spaghetti carbonara. She'd pay a price for it, she knew, as she wasn't planning to make any adjustments to the rich, creamy sauce. For balance, she tossed a green salad and put it back in the refrigerator to chill. A bottle of Pinot Grigio lay on its side next to the salad bowl, chilling.

She had no idea how he'd react to her news about their wedding, but Freddy had seemed very confident when he said not to worry. Really? She wasn't so worried about Luke's reaction to her request for a more traditional wedding than she was at the fact that she'd not been honest, with him or with herself. Why couldn't she have been truthful with him—truthful with herself, for that matter?

She showered and changed into her best jeans (jeans that would certainly be tight after their decadent supper) and a soft pink sweater that she knew he liked. She glanced down at the antique engagement ring on her left hand, admiring the cut of the diamond. *They don't make them like this anymore*, she thought, smiling. *I wouldn't trade this for Jane Nevins's rock, no way.*

Luke arrived on time, of course, and brought flowers, of course. A large bouquet of orange lilies and yellow carnations, with delicate white baby's breath, brought life and color to the kitchen, and Julie placed the stems in a large glass vase that she set in the middle of the farmhouse table.

"I thought I'd make spaghetti carbonara," she said, with her back to Luke.

"Really? That's my favorite."

"I know that."

He placed his hands on her waist, pivoting her around to face him. "I know you know. Thank you." He leaned in to kiss her, then pulled her close to his body, the length of his pressed against the length of hers. At the same height, Julie loved that their mouths were level. No one had to bend or reach. No neck strain.

"Are you hungry now? Should I start it?"

"Sure. How about some wine first? And can I help?"

"Salad's made. Wine's in the fridge. You can open it if you like." Julie hesitated. Should they have a glass of wine first? Should she do this now? Or wait until they'd eaten? If what she had to say annoyed him, she'd ruin dinner by telling him before they ate.

They moved around the kitchen, a two-step here, a glissade there, but always in harmony.

Julie cooked pancetta in butter in a skillet while spaghetti boiled in a big pot on the stove. While Luke poured wine and set the table, she turned down the heat, and, using tongs, pulled the al dente pasta from the pot and put it in the skillet. Then she removed the pan from the heat and added beaten eggs and pecorino cheese. She shook the skillet lightly to combine everything, careful not to scramble the eggs.

"Can you bring the bowls back?" she asked Luke, who had warmed the pasta bowls with hot water. He held them out as Julie used the tongs to serve. She gave Luke a sizeable portion, keeping the equivalent of just one cup for herself. *What do I figure? Six hundred calories? My entire day's worth of fat grams? I'll just squeeze lemon on my salad. And then the wine. Oh, hell, who's counting tonight?*

They seated themselves and dug in. Luke made noises in his throat not unlike the noises he made in bed. Julie smiled. She took a gulp of wine.

"Hey," she began. Luke looked so satisfied, so…happy. "Can I ask you something?"

"Anything. I'm in heaven right now. You could tell me the house is burning down and I'd take two things with me as I ran from the building—your hand and this bowl."

"Ha! No, really. I want to ask you something."

"Mmm," he moaned. "What's up?"

Julie looked down at the pasta on her plate and gently pushed it aside, while at the same time gripping her wineglass.

"I've been thinking about our wedding. And if I'm being honest—with myself—I would like us to have a traditional wedding. I want to invite my brothers, and my sister, and their family members, and people we know. And I want to wear a wedding gown and a veil on my head and I want you in a tuxedo and I want us to have a first dance together. And all of it."

Luke sat chewing, then swallowed. He reached for his glass of wine and lifted it to his lips, then swallowed.

"That's cool. I always said, whatever you want, babe."

"But, but. I had told you I didn't want a big wedding."

He sloshed vinaigrette into his salad bowl and speared two leaves of Romaine on his fork. "So you changed your mind. You're entitled." His eyes danced and he stuffed lettuce into his mouth.

"So you're okay with it? With not running down to the town hall and having a JP do the ceremony?"

"Sure. You want a regular wedding. Why shouldn't you?" He placed his hand over Julie's. "So we get married in a few months. Right? Are you thinking spring? Because I know you have two big weddings coming up. Unless you think we can pull it off in a month."

"No, spring is what I was thinking, too. I just wasn't sure

how you'd react to it."

"Honey, you thought about it and realized you want something different from what you said. It's fine!"

Was it the carbonara? Did it have magical powers? Or had I really just worried about nothing? Whatever it was, Julie knew enough to accept it.

"How does June first sound?" He'd be busy with floral arrangements—proms, graduations, weddings.

Luke looked up from his beloved carbonara. "It sounds perfect to me."

"You won't be too busy at that time of year?"

He laughed. "I'll be swamped! But I'll hire an assistant. You remember the girl who worked for me last summer? Libby? She's going to help out over the holidays, and I'm sure she'll be around in June."

He's so calm, Julie thought. *Maybe some of that will rub off on me after we're married.*

TWENTY-ONE

On Saturday night, Bill took April to dinner at one of the places that recognized her name and accepted a last-minute reservation. Carlie and Axel were going to a friend's house for dinner but said they'd try to stop by at some point.

The morning and early afternoon had been tense, with Ellen Bornstein dominating the day. From her insistence on seeing April's wedding dress and overstaying her time in April's apartment, to Carlie's frustration at not being able to find a suitable dress ("Why did you wait so long?" "It's not like I have all this free time, Mom"), to their indecision at eating lunch and where ("I don't care" "Gran, help us out here" "I can go back home and heat up a can of soup if it's too much trouble"), April's headache was the size of Staten Island by the time she and Bill hailed a taxi. Add to that the fact that they were still walking on eggshells due to the Norah situation ("I haven't talked to Mary Pat" "But we need to make arrangements"), and the last thing April felt like doing that evening was celebrating her birthday. Staying home in her pajamas would have been preferable to this. But she went along. For Bill. Because this was the first birthday they'd been able to celebrate together since they were in high school.

She slipped her hand into Bill's as the cab lurched its

way through Saturday-evening traffic in Manhattan. The three-mile drive down Ninth Avenue took over forty minutes. *Under better circumstances, we'd have acted like teenagers in the back of this cab*, April thought. But neither of them made a move. Instead, they just sat next to each other, holding hands. As chaste as the first winter snowfall. *Like we're seventy*, she thought.

Impulsively, April turned in her seat, gently placed her palms on either side of Bill's face, and brought his mouth to hers. She kissed him, softly at first, but as he reacted, her passion grew, as did his, and for the last four minutes of their cab ride, April and Billy were those seventeen-year-old kids, eager and unbridled.

She reapplied lipstick as Bill paid the driver, then let herself be led out of the taxi as he pulled her hand. "I was hoping for more traffic," he said.

"So was I."

"Come on, birthday girl."

**

Over gnocchi and salmon, April and Bill healed the fissures that had marked the past week.

"I talked to Mary Pat again. They're not letting us pay for her flight. Now Norah's flying into JFK the Monday before the wedding. She'll stay with her friend, or friends, I don't know, then take the train to Albany on Friday. She'll text us so we know when she gets in, and we'll pick her up."

"You think it'll be early enough on Friday?"

"Not sure, but she's got both of our cells, so she'll let us know."

"Okay. And I've got a room for her upstairs. Carlie said she and Axel would rather stay at the hotel. There are three rooms besides ours, and I need one for my mother. Dan should have one, and if he doesn't want it, we should pay for his hotel room. Then Norah can have the third one."

"I'll call Dan to find out where he wants to stay."

"Is everything okay between you two?"

Bill touched his fingertips to his forehead. As a waiter approached their table to clear the plates, they both paused until the server was gone.

"He could call me, too, you know. But I'll be the guy who calls."

"Family," April murmured. "What are you going to do?"

"So…Carlie is with this guy Axel. She's still standing up with you?"

April nodded. "And Freddy is happy to stand up with you. We've got the judge to do the ceremony, Freddy's got the band, we've ordered the flowers, the food.

Rooms for my mother, for Norah, and Dan. Your sister will handle her own arrangements, right?"

"Of course. But Bren, can I be honest? I can't wait for this to be over and we're married."

"I know. But it's a process." She lifted her hand as she spotted Carlie and Axel walking into the restaurant.

"Here they are," she sang, rising from her chair. Bill joined her, shaking Axel's hand and introducing himself as Carlie kissed her mother.

"Happy birthday, Mommy!" She held tight to Axel's hand, April noticed.

"Happy birthday, April." Axel turned on the charm, and he had plenty of it in supply. She liked him well enough, and he was definitely cute. She just didn't like seeing her daughter so...clingy.

"I'm so glad you could come!"

"Come on, I wudden gonna mish your birthday," Carlie said. She was slurry in her speech and April imagined she'd had more than a couple of margaritas, her favorite.

"April tells me you're a business owner," Bill said, turning to Axel. "How long have you had your coffee shop?"

"A few years now," he replied. "We do okay, but it's a struggle at times. The Starbucks on the corner does probably five times the business I do. And the city has changed, from small businesses like mine, little shops and family-owned restaurants, to chain stores."

"But that's been going on for years now, hasn't it?"

"Sure," Axel replied. "Neighborhoods have been gentrified, rents have skyrocketed. That includes my rent. Small businesses should have rent control, too." He cut his eyes to April, who looked back. *I have no control over that*, she thought.

"Is there any chance it will happen?" she asked.

Axel lifted a shoulder. "There's a lot of support in the city council, but it's been kicked around for decades. Meanwhile, the city becomes more and more cookie cutter. "My lease runs for another three years. If the rent control bill isn't enacted, I can't see myself staying where I am. But hey, Starbucks isn't going anywhere." April could see anger and frustration in those dark eyes.

Axel was about to say something more but was interrupted by a procession of three servers. The first carried an elaborate birthday cake topped with a sparkler, and the two that followed carried coffee and champagne.

"Happy birthday, Ms. Tweed," the first waiter said. "We couldn't be happier to have you celebrate with us." In a lowered voice, he added, "I'm such a fan!"

"Thank you, thank you so much," she replied. "I don't

blow this out, do I?"

"No, honey, I'll take it," Bill said, pulling the sparkler out of the cake and handing it to the server. One of the others poured coffee and the third popped the cork on a bottle of champagne, then filled four tall flutes before Bill could stop him from filling one for him. Then they retreated together.

With a glance at Carlie and Axel, Bill spoke. "Happy birthday to the love of my life. Brenda, April, you were my girl when we were seventeen. To know you're my girl again—can I say that? Can I say you're my girl? Well, you are. You're everything to me. I can't wait to be married to you next month. Happy birthday, my love."

"Happy birthday!" Three flutes and one coffee cup were raised together.

"Who wants cake?"

As if on cue, the first waiter reappeared with a knife and expertly cut four thin slices of cake.

"Will you box up the rest of it so we can bring it home?" April asked. "Actually, two boxes. Divide it up, please." She winked at Carlie.

"Of course, Ms. Tweed. It will be my pleasure."

TWENTY-TWO

Jane Nevins was proving to be the most high-maintenance client Julie had ever known. Yes, Margot Dexheimer had been a handful, but that marriage never happened, after her Russian fiancé was arrested in a federal sweep of Medicare fraud. Julie imagined Margot could have given Jane a real run for her money.

She and Freddy had yet to meet, or even speak with, Jane's fiancé, Edward Ridgewell Lackshaft. "Lordy, I do hope he is not defined by that name, if you know what I mean," Freddy quipped.

"I know exactly what you mean, and I understand why Jane Nevins will continue to be known as Jane Nevins. Here, read her latest email," Julie said, handing her phone to Freddy.

He pulled reading glasses from his shirt pocket.

"Oh, my word, when did you get those?"

He sighed dramatically. "I hate that I need them. Hate it! But how do I look?"

"Like a smarmy professor."

"What do I teach?" he asked, raising his eyebrows

behind tortoise-shell frames.

"Um, medieval Italian art."

"Ooh, good one," he said, squinting at her phone. "Oh, puh-lease. All phones and cameras must be dropped off with the phone attendant prior to the ceremony. Phone attendant?"

"Keep reading," Julie said, rolling her eyes.

"Seat cushions—lavender satin!—will be provided by the venue. Oh, so their bony asses don't get tired?"

"There's more."

"Of course there is. Wait, what? We're supposed to *build* a floral arch for her entry, but only she can enter through it?"

"That would be Zack building a floral arch, and Luke doing the festooning of flowers."

"I'll have Zack charge a fortune for his work. Luke should, too."

"Apparently money's no object with ol' Jane."

"Good!" Freddy took off his glasses and slipped them back into his shirt pocket. "Then ol' Jane can have everything she wants. For the right price."

"That's your area, my friend. Will you respond?"

"My pleasure. I'll send this email to my own account." He touched the screen and handed her phone back. "Lovely. And how's everything with our other couple?"

"Luke and me?" Julie asked, batting her eyelashes.

"No, April and Bill. How is it going with them?"

"Much better than with Jane and Edward. I'll send April a note this afternoon to check in. She asked for a simple dinner the evening of the rehearsal, so that's not a problem. Most of the guests are staying in Pittsfield. The other three rooms upstairs are all spoken for. We'll put the usual comfort items in them. I'll offer a Sunday brunch, she'll probably just want family for that."

"They're getting married at five, right?"

"Yes. And you need to be around for the rehearsal, too, Mr. Best Man."

Freddy nodded. "Got it. Glad they're making it easy for us."

"I know. We get them hitched, give them a beautiful party, get some exposure in the magazine, and move on to Jane Nevins. Your friend Alison came through on the publicity?"

"All set. It's going to be a spread about the trendiness of rustic weddings, because destination nuptials are soooo 2012, don't you know. April and Bill will be mentioned, but the focus is really on Jingle Valley. Alison loves me."

"Everyone loves you, Freddy."

"And once we've got Jane Nevins and Lord Lack-a-shaft married, we're going to concentrate on you!"

"Yeah, yeah," Julie said, feeling her cheeks grow warm.

"What? Why are you blushing?"

"I don't know." She peeked up at him through her eyelashes. "He's moving in tomorrow."

Freddy clapped a hand over his mouth. "No! My little Julie is moving a boy into her house? What would your mother say? Something about a cow and free milk?"

"Shut up. It makes sense, he's here every night anyway. And he can rent out the apartment upstairs from his shop. We might as well get used to being together all the time," she added, busying herself with papers.

Freddy moved closer to her. "You okay about all this?"

"Yeah, of course I am. I mean, it's normal, right? No turning back!"

Freddy sat back. "Julie Tate. Is this bothering you? What's going on?"

"Nothing. I mean, I want him here. It's just..."

"What?"

She shrugged. "Maybe it's the finality of it. I've been so accustomed to having a place of my own, doing my own thing."

"Is Luke a slob?"

"No! Well, not really. I mean, we all have our quirks, right?"

Freddy leaned forward on his forearms, like a little boy anticipating a big piece of cake. "Like what? Tell me one of his quirks. I mean it, let's talk about this."

"Okay. Well, for instance, he uses a bath towel once and throws it in the hamper. He's clean when he gets out of the shower, he doesn't need a new towel every time!"

"And who does the laundry?"

"What do you mean? I do it."

"Okay. So going forward, you share. If he's piling up laundry with relatively clean towels, he can do a load of laundry. What else does he do?"

Julie stared at Freddy.

"Is that it? The towel thing?"

"No. And the towel thing isn't nothing."

"I didn't say it was nothing. I just gave you a way to keep from getting mad about it. What else?"

Julie shifted in her chair and fiddled with a delicate gold chain around her neck.

"He sings. Badly."

Freddy laughed out loud. "Are you're just discovering this now?"

"Yes! And don't laugh. He thinks he can sing, but he can't. And he sings *all* the time."

"How did you not know this before?"

"I guess I did, but I didn't pay attention. Now that he's in the house a lot more, I hear it. And it's driving me crazy. I want to throttle him! Or scream at him to shut up. But of course I can't."

"No, of course you can't, Jules. He'd call off the wedding if you screamed at him."

"Stop being a jerk. It would get on your nerves, too."

Freddy rested his chiseled chin in his hand. He stared at Julie, who sank lower in her chair.

Suddenly he slammed his palm on the table.

"What the hell, Freddy!"

"Good. I have your attention. Now listen to me, Julie Annika Tate. This is *minutiae*! Do you hear me? Look, there are more towels to wash. He sings because he's deliriously happy to be in your presence! Try playing a symphony on the CD player—do you still have one? Of course you do, you probably still have your parents' hi-fi. Play classical music, he can't sing along to Mozart. Now, is that all there is?"

"I can't think of anything else right now," she mumbled.

"Okay. Well, I'm going to tell you something that Bob does. Are you ready?"

Julie sat up straighter. "What?"

"He squeezes the toothpaste from the middle of the tube. Don't roll your eyes at me. You know how I am! It makes me nuts, it always has, from the first night we spent together. And he used to leave gobs of toothpaste in the sink! Can you imagine? I mean, can you imagine that we haven't split up over this?"

Julie smiled.

"If I had let that *quirk* derail us that first night, I wouldn't be married to the best guy around, and we wouldn't have little Val, because I wasn't about to adopt a baby by myself. Listen, sweetheart, what I'm saying is that it's *all* minutiae. Every little quirky thing. And you know damned well that there's at least one thing you do that drives dear sweet Luke up the ivy-covered wall. If you want, I'll find out what it is.'

"No! No, I don't want to know."

"See?"

"Yeah, I see. Smartypants."

"That's my middle name. Better than Lack-a-shaft. Come on, let's do some work."

TWENTY-THREE

Bill Flanagan sat alone in a coffee shop, idly dragging a spoon through his coffee. Oblivious to the noises surrounding him, he conjured up an image of Meg, with her wild halo of straw-like hair and a face like an angel. *I need some guidance from you, dear Meg. I wish you had a quote for me today.*

He'd stepped out fearlessly, winning back the girl he'd loved from the beginning. They were going to be married in ten days. It was Wednesday, the day before Thanksgiving, and Bill was trying hard to be thankful. Instead, dark thoughts clouded his consciousness.

I said I'd forgiven April for what she did, so why am I still resentful? She never should have invited my kids to our wedding, after I'd told her not to. And now Norah is coming. Norah, who I haven't seen since she was two years old. Twenty years ago. What kind of a woman will she be? The fact that she wanted to come east to attend his wedding was, he hoped, a positive sign. Maybe she wanted to have a relationship with him. *But how can we bridge twenty years in a weekend? A busy weekend at that? And then she flies back to Arizona?* Bill let out a long audible sigh.

He'd lived his adult life in quotes. "One day at a time." "If we were to live, we had to be free of anger." (*Good one, Bill*, he said to himself.)

He had called Mary Pat the previous afternoon, after school let out for the Thanksgiving holiday. She confirmed that Norah was still flying to New York, but cautioned him not to expect too much.

"What does that mean? I'm not expecting a Hollywood ending, you know."

"I know that. But she's…she's her own person. Norah does what Norah wants."

"You're not making sense. Send me a photo or something. I haven't seen a picture of her since that Christmas card you sent last year. And I need to have an approximate time of arrival when she gets to Albany. It's an hour's drive from Dalton to the train station."

"I know, I know. I've been trying to pin her down. I'm sending you a photo. Try not to be shocked. Bye, Bill."

She disconnected the call and Bill felt a shiver scurry down the back of his neck. In less than a minute, he received a text with a photo of his daughter. He recognized the round face of his daughter, but she had black-as-ink hair that was shaved on one side and chin-length on the other, and way too much black eyeliner. A sliver of a silver ring surrounded one nostril, and she glared at whoever had taken the photo. *Norah?* His mind went back to a photo of her at eight, one that Mary Pat had sent at Christmas, understanding that Bill had the right to at least see how his kids were growing, even if he had given up all parental rights. This angry woman staring at him, daring him, didn't look anything like the eight-year-old with strawberry blonde curls and freckles. It didn't even resemble the photo he'd received a year earlier, where her hair was all the same length and not dyed black. *Try not to be shocked,* she'd written. *Too late*, he thought. And his resentment toward April grew. *I told her not to, but she did it, anyway. Maybe she should go pick up Norah at the train station. They could have a pleasant hour's drive back to Dalton.*

His counseling session with Anders was off, since Anders was flying back to Wisconsin for Thanksgiving. April was filming a commercial for the New York tourism council, out on Long Island. She wouldn't be back until early evening.

Thanksgiving, their first together, was going to be at some fancy restaurant off Central Park. April had decided, and Carlie and Axel (who apparently had nowhere to go for Thanksgiving) were joining them. Thankfully, April's mother Ellen had declined, citing a tradition she and her housemates (he'd started calling them "the golden girls") had that involved Chinese food in Upper Montclair. Bill would have preferred to stay home, even if the food was brought in. Going out just felt weird, although he had to admit that his past Thanksgivings weren't anything to crow about, mostly depressing days at his sister Eileen's house, where everyone pretended to be cheery, his mother complained, Eileen's kids were more interested in their electronic devices than their grandmother or uncle, Dan wisely stayed in Boston, and Bill couldn't wait to leave. So this year of course would be better.

A group of loud, giggly schoolgirls caught his attention. He should have planned a quiet getaway for the two of them, somewhere in the Adirondacks, or in Vermont at a little inn, but with the wedding so close, it hadn't crossed his mind. April wasn't due home until six. He rolled his shoulders in an effort to loosen up the stiffness, but it didn't help. Maybe instead of a meeting, he should treat himself to a massage. He looked in his phone for a place within walking distance, and called for a walk-in appointment. *Better than an AA meeting*, he thought, as he strode away from the giggly girls.

**

As his back, neck, and shoulders were wrapped in moist heat packs, Bill felt cool peppermint on his legs and feet. He relaxed into the massage and felt his worries melt away under the warmth. *I should do this every week*, he thought. *Time for me.* Soft instrumental music and light aromatherapy added to the overall experience, and Bill was disappointed when it ended.

"Would you like to book your next appointment, sir?" the receptionist asked as he paid.

"Absolutely. Next Thursday, four o'clock?"

He left the spa with a spring in his step, and stopped to pick up flowers for April. All of the resentment and worry that had plagued him earlier was gone. *It is what it is*, he thought. *We'll handle it.* He would be polite and loving toward his daughter—she should have no less— but the main event was his marriage to April. Norah was certainly welcome and would be warmly embraced by everyone there, but the day, the weekend was not about Norah, who was not even Norah Flanagan, but Norah Bonetti.

He asked for orange stargazer lilies and yellow Gerbera daisies, and the florist added ferns and baby's breath, then wrapped everything in green tissue and clear plastic. Bill exited the flower shop and bounced back to his apartment.

TWENTY-FOUR

There were just five of them for Thanksgiving in Jingle Valley—Julie and Luke, Bob and Freddy and little Val. Julie was aware that Bob, whose family lived in Pennsylvania, had little to do with him since he and Freddy got married.

"You can't choose your family," Bob had said at the time. "They're conservative and think I'm bound for hell, anyway." Still.

She and Luke decorated the dining room with succulents and greenery, and Julie had put a twenty-four-pound bird in the oven at five in the morning. Zack and Sarah, who were always invited to dine with them, had politely declined. Julie knew it was because they were vegans, and although she'd reiterated that she'd make plenty of vegan options for them, she assumed that the sight of a cooked turkey would offend them too much. She asked them to come at three for dessert, if they wanted, and they'd left it open. But she didn't expect them to show. Zack and Sarah were contentedly private people who were probably going to spend the day hiking Mount Greylock.

There was enough food to feed extra people, and she and Luke decided to package up whatever was remaining and bring it to the local shelter. Funny, she thought,

Thanksgiving is the time when we all think of feeding others, but they really need it in the months after Thanksgiving, when it's cold and folks need to pay for heat. She made a mental note to bring food weekly. *Easy enough to pick up extra at the market.*

Much of the conversation was about the two upcoming weddings—April and Bill's in just nine days, and Jane and Edward's on New Year's Eve. Eventually, Bob asked Julie and Luke about their own plans.

"I really haven't been able to think about it much, what with these two big weddings we've got on the calendar."

"But you are going to sit down with me, soon, and put your ideas on paper," Freddy said.

"Of course." Julie ate the European way, with her fork in her left hand. After spearing a piece of turkey, she pushed mashed potato onto the back of her fork, then topped it with a bit of butternut squash. She brought the fork to her mouth just as Val let out a wail.

"What happened?"

"He probably doesn't approve of the way you eat," Freddy deadpanned. "We're going to teach him to eat like a regular person. You're just confusing him."

"Stop it. He probably needs a change," Bob answered. He pushed back from the table. "It'll only take a sec." He lifted Val from his high chair and carried him off to Julie's bedroom.

Freddy sank his chin into his open palm. "Isn't he the best? Luke, I hope you're up for the challenge of stinky diapers."

"Not here! Come on, I'd like to enjoy this meal."

"Hey, baby shit happens."

Luke turned his wineglass stem toward the ceiling and drained the pinot that was in his glass. "We don't know whether there'll be kids." With a glance at Julie, he added, "We're hopeful, of course."

"Well, get to work! She's got the ring now."

Julie slapped his arm. "You know, Freddy? Some things don't need to be discussed all the time. Can't we just enjoy this meal that I so lovingly prepared for you?"

"No problem. Let's talk politics."

**

With the Tweed-Flanagan wedding less than a week away, Julie didn't know who was more nervous—she or Freddy. Luke, true to form, was as calm as Pontoosuc Lake on a hot summer day.

"I just want this one to be perfect," Freddy told her on the last Wednesday of November. "Did you see the weather forecast? Possibility of snow on Friday night."

"I saw it. They'll all be here by Friday for the rehearsal, and we can deal with snow. I don't think anyone's talking blizzard." She blew out a breath. "But I still don't know about Bill's daughter. April told me she's taking the train up from the city on Saturday morning."

"Who's picking her up?" Freddy asked. "Is that something we're supposed to do? Should I ask Zack? Would he scare her? He's so big."

Julie shook her head. "No, she said her daughter Carlie would do it. Do you know Carlie's boyfriend's name? I want to have it so we can do a welcome basket for their room." She looked down at her tablet. "I've got Ellen Bornstein—that's April's mother—in the end room. And Bill's daughter—her name is Norah with an 'h'—I'm going to put her in the northern room, next to the staircase. Did they decide who's taking the third room? Is it Bill's brother, the priest? Or Carlie and her boyfriend?"

Freddy clicked his tongue and scrolled through his own tablet. "I think they wanted to give the room to Fr. Dan, and Carlie and—hang on, I have it here somewhere— Carlie and Axel are going to stay at the hotel."

The silence that passed, probably only ten seconds or so, was enough to make Freddy lift his head. "What's the matter, sweetie? You look like the air's been sucked out of you."

Julie cocked her head to the side, as if shifting the words inside her head might bring her some clarity. "What's Carlie's boyfriend's name again?"

Freddy had to look down at his tablet. "Axel. A-x-e-l. I don't have a last name here. Why?"

Julie set her device on the table and sat back in her chair. "Do you remember a guy from the city, years back, before we moved here? He ran a coffee shop and I was smitten with him? We were supposed to spend New Year's Eve together?"

"I don't know, Jules. You had so many men back then. Ow! That actually hurt!"

"Shut up. Do you remember?"

Freddy smiled at his friend. "Not really, honey. Did you end up spending New Year's Eve together?"

"No. I met him to tell him I was resigning from my job and moving here, and I went on and on about how it wouldn't be fair to him to start something, and he told me it was all good because he had a girlfriend anyway—I think she was in Spain or something—but anyway, he never showed."

"Which party was that? I can't remember."

Julie stared at him. "I wore my dove-gray maxidress and red boots."

"Oh! Of course. Coffee Boy. Oh!" He clapped his hand over his mouth. "You think April's daughter is seeing Coffee Boy?"

Julie shrugged. "Unless it's an incredible coincidence. Are there that many Axels in Manhattan who run a coffee shop?"

Freddy rubbed his hands together. "This is going to be the best wedding ever."

TWENTY-FIVE

April's agent phoned her early in the morning. Bill was gone, off to school, but April was still in bed when her phone rang. Pushing her hair back, she answered in a rusty voice.

"Karen, hi."

"Are you sick, April? You sound awful. Tell me you're not sick."

"I'm not sick," she said, swinging her legs off the bed and standing. "This is what I sound like before I've had my coffee."

"Oh! Did I wake you?" Karen was an early riser. She'd told April numerous times that she rose every day at four, worked out in her home gym for a minimum of an hour, took a five-minute shower, dried her hair, put on her makeup, and was at work by six. Every day except Sunday.

"It's not even seven o'clock, Karen, of course you woke me." April walked barefoot down the long hallway and into the kitchen, where she set her phone on the counter and put Karen on speaker. "What's up?"

"Get your coffee and hang on. I've got some great news

for you."

April felt warm anticipation as she placed a coffee pod in the machine and waited for the rich brown liquid to drip drip drip into her coffee cup. "Should I be sitting down?"

"If you want," Karen teased.

"Okay, tell me." April was pouring cream into her coffee, still standing, when Karen's news almost knocked her off her feet.

"There's a new daytime series in development as we speak," Karen said breathlessly. "And the producers mentioned you for one of the leads."

"Are you serious?"

"I am! It's called Star Factory, and it's set in Hollywood. You would be playing the part of Lacey Rogers, a former A-list movie star who mentors young hopefuls."

"What do you have for me?"

"The usual—I'll messenger the script over. Call me when you've had a chance to look through it. But April, this part is made for you! Listen, gotta run, but I'll see you on Saturday!"

April said goodbye and finally, she sat down. Holding her still-warm coffee mug in her hand, she turned over the brief conversation in her head. *I never thought I'd have a chance to work like this again. Not at my age.* And what about Billy? When they reconnected earlier in the year, she was doing the miniseries in Ireland, hardly the same as working full-time on a new series, one where she undoubtedly would have a lead role.

Still, it was real work, not the Weight Watchers commercials or public television cameos she'd had for the past few years. A real role, something she could delve into, even if it was just a daytime series. *Karen knows I need to stay in New York, right? Right?* She and her boyfriend were coming to the wedding. *And what about Billy? I need to tell him about this opportunity.*

He'll support me, won't he? Isn't that what he's supposed to do? But it lingered in her mind long after the coffee cup was washed and left to dry on the rack in the sink, long after she'd showered and dressed. She was still thinking about the possibilities as she entered Central Park at West Drive.

Their wedding was just days away. *Maybe I shouldn't mention it until after the wedding,* she told herself. *Maybe it'll upset him, and he's got enough to worry about, with Norah flying in to see him after nearly twenty years.* That was it. *I'll call Karen and tell her I can't think about anything until after the wedding.*

Karen said she was looking forward to the wedding. She was bringing her partner, a curious fellow named Abner, who went by the name Rocket and got nasty if you called him Abner by mistake. *Okay,* April mused silently as she passed over Greyshot Arch. With mild weather for late

November, she wasn't alone. Bikers, runners, and rollerbladers whirled past her. She veered off to the right and found a quieter spot, away from the main path.

April flopped down on a bench and tilted her head back, closing her eyes against the sun. Temperatures in the upper fifties suited her just fine. There might even be snow in Dalton, she reasoned, but once they were settled at Jingle Valley, it really didn't matter. They'd be there from Friday through Sunday, so snowfall wouldn't make a difference. *It might even add a bit of magic.*

Then she thought about Norah, and her shoulders sagged. *Norah. Me and my bright ideas.* The photo Bill had shown her left her unsettled. In the weeks since April had so brazenly invited Norah, and her brother Danny, and even tried to invite Bill's other children to the wedding, Norah hadn't reached out once. No call, no email, no text to Bill. No indication that she was looking forward to seeing him. *It's not normal*, she thought. *Why bother coming, then?*

"Mind if I sit here?" A middle-aged woman dressed in stretchy pants and a navy cable-knit sweater stood before her. She was shaped like a Bartlett pear and her face was pink and shiny with perspiration.

"No, of course not," April replied, scooting to one end of the bench.

"Thanks. It's a lot of walking here in New York City," the woman said, waving her hand in front of her face. April smiled as she surveyed the woman who was seated next to her. She was clearly overheated in that sweater, and used a brochure to fan her face. She put a red-and-blue zippered tote bag on the bench between them. "I suppose if I walked everywhere like a New Yorker, I wouldn't be so out of shape." She giggled. "You're slim. You must live here."

"I do," April said. "I don't really think about it, the walking, I mean. And it's a nice day today." *Poor thing. She looks miserable.* "Are you here by yourself?"

"Oh, no! I couldn't even contemplate coming to this city by myself. No, the hubby's got a conference at the Marriott, and he's tied up all day. I thought I should take a walk through Central Park. Isn't that what everyone does?"

"And now you have," April said.

"I've only walked a little. I just get so tired. Let me tell you something, forty's no picnic!" The woman laughed at her own joke as April stared. *She's only forty?* April made a mental promise not to complain about her age ever again.

"Can you walk a little farther?" April asked. "I'd like to show you something. By the way, I'm April."

"Oh, isn't that a pretty name!" The woman offered a moist hand. "And I'm Brenda. Brenda Fischer. Nice to meet you, April."

Brenda! April almost told her that her real name was

180

Brenda, but stopped. The other Brenda didn't need the explanation that would be expected to accompany her admission.

Instead, April kept pace with the slower Brenda Fischer and walked her back out to the entrance, where the horse-drawn carriages waited. Asking Brenda to wait just a minute, April walked up to one of the operators and spoke with him, then handed him her credit card.

"April, what is this? Are we taking a carriage ride?"

"*You* are, Brenda! I'm sorry I can't join you, I have an appointment. But please allow me to do this for you. Think of it as a welcome to the city. Do you have an hour available for the tour?"

"Oh my, yes! I've got the whole day. But you don't have to do this."

April patted her arm. "I'm happy to. I want you to relax and enjoy the scenery." She leaned in close to Brenda. "And I already tipped the driver, so just keep your purse closed."

Brenda impulsively hugged her new friend. "Whoever said New Yorkers are rude never met you! I can't wait to tell all my friends back home about this!"

April waved goodbye as Brenda, with the help of a stepstool, hoisted herself into the carriage.

I believe in karma. Maybe this little gesture will bring

me luck when I tell Billy about the new series.

TWENTY-SIX

Jane Nevins called twice a day, and she usually phoned Luke once a day as well. Julie had told Freddy to handle her, because it was obvious that Jane preferred dealing with Freddy. Besides, Julie was concentrating on April and Bill. They'd be arriving at Jingle Valley the following afternoon. Now it was time to shift into high gear. Jane Nevins would have to chill out.

"She wants to see the venue again. This weekend." Freddy rolled his eyes as he disconnected the call.

"Tough for Jane. We're booked."

"As I told her, in no uncertain terms. But there was something in her voice that put me on alert, like she might show up anyway."

"Good lord, Freddy. That woman is a true Bridezilla."

"I know, and I can ask Zack to run interference. We'll be up to our eyeballs and I do not want Jane making demands. We'll have no time for her this weekend."

Julie rubbed her temples. "Why are we in this business again?"

"Because we love it! Because we're making soooo much

money! Because we're crazy!"

"There you go. That last answer," she said.

"Don't worry about it. I'll go talk to Zack. Have you seen him?"

Julie shook her head. "I haven't seen him *or* Sarah. Might be a good idea to check up on them. Sarah's been busy baking, I know that." She put down her pen and looked up at Freddy, who stood staring out the window, his lean silhouette framed perfectly in front of the tall window. "Fred. Have you figured out what to do with Val this weekend?"

"Anya is more than happy to take him. But Val's never slept away from us." He rubbed his knuckles over his stubbly chin.

"He wouldn't be far away."

"Yeah, but still. I told her she could have him on Friday, but even though it'll be late, I'm going to bring him home Friday night and bring him back to her on Saturday morning."

"And again Saturday night and Sunday morning?"

"Yeah." Freddy turned to her. "Am I right? Or am I just nuts?"

Julie hesitated for only a second. "I understand. I don't blame you, Freddy. Val's still so little."

"He'll probably be asleep when I pick him up at night."

"Probably."

"He'd probably be fine staying with Anya for the weekend."

"Probably."

"But I want my kid to sleep in his crib."

"Of course you do."

"So I'm not nuts?"

"Well, you are, but not on this subject."

"I'm going out to find Zack."

**

When Julie decided it was time for a tea break, she stepped into the kitchen and gasped when she saw someone sitting in the chair at the table.

"Sarah! Sorry, I didn't hear you come in."

"I knocked, but you didn't answer. You always said it was okay to just come in."

"I didn't hear you. It's okay." The woman was so tiny that Julie imagined her knock sounded more like a hummingbird's wings. "Do you need anything?"

Sarah was swallowed up by the heavy wooden chair at the farm table. Her feet didn't even reach the floor, and she swung her legs as she sipped tea. "Do you have any walnuts?"

"I think so. Did you look?" Julie opened a cupboard door and fished around inside until she found an unopened bag of chopped walnuts. Handing the bag to Sarah, she said, "You know you can always take what you need. What are you making?"

Sarah used her fingers to curl a thin strand of honey-blonde hair behind her child-sized ear. When she spoke, it was as if a sprite was talking. Julie imagined sparkles of fairy dust dancing in the air around her.

"Walnut biscuits? With cinnamon? Shaped like hearts?"

"Wonderful! Is that for the Sunday breakfast?"

"Yes, but I need to make a test batch first. Thanks, Julie!" Grabbing the bag of nuts, Sarah hopped down from the chair and slipped out the door before Julie could say another word.

Every time I try to make conversation with her, she leaves. Julie smiled and shook her head. Sarah was an odd girl with a heart of gold. She loved Zack and seemed to be content living in the tiny house at the edge of the property. *We all find our own way to what makes us happy*, she reasoned.

**

Freddy searched the fallow, dormant grounds between the barn and the little house where Zack and Sarah lived. He waved to Sarah as she floated toward Julie's house, but she was too far away to see him.

He arrived at the little house and knocked on the door. With no answer, he continued around to the back of the house and found Zack splitting logs on a stump. Freddy watched in awe as the big man lifted a long, yellow-handled axe and brought it down fast, neatly dividing the log. *Whack!*

"Wow, you're good," Freddy said. Zack turned and removed safety goggles. "That axe has a really long handle."

"It's a maul, not an axe." Zack was a man of few words, Freddy thought.

"Ah. I learned something new today."

As Zack approached him, Freddy felt smaller than his six feet. Zack had a good five inches on him. "See the head? It's a wedge. A wedge is less likely to get stuck in the log." Zack handed the maul to Freddy.

"Heavy," Freddy quipped as Zack nodded solemnly. "Can I watch you do another?" He handed the maul back to Zack.

Zack didn't respond, but turned back to the pile of logs and placed one, about a foot or so in length, on the tree stump. Freddy guessed the log to be about ten inches in diameter.

"Come look at this."

"Don't I need safety glasses, too?"

Zack stared at him. "No. I want to show you where the cracks are. That's where I aim to hit."

"Oh. Okay. I see."

Zack held the maul horizontally in front of his body. One of his giant hands held the handle at its base, the other was up near the maul's head. As he swung back, he lifted up on his toes and brought the maul down hard on the log, splitting it in half. The two halves fell to the ground, and Zack picked one up, set it vertically on the stump, and split that one in half. Then he paused.

"Want to try this one?" he asked, holding the maul out to Freddy.

"Me? Oh, this isn't really my thing," Freddy said, laughing.

"I don't believe you," Zack replied, his dark face set, his eyes never leaving Freddy. "Didn't you used to work in construction?"

"Well, yes. But I did architectural millwork. Here I'm a little out of my comfort zone."

"All the more reason to give it a try. Come on." He

removed his safety glasses and offered them to Freddy.

Oh, man. Freddy, who had worked in remodeling for years before partnering up with Julie to run Jingle Valley, knew he shouldn't be intimidated by Zack. He knew he was capable. Physical labor never daunted him.

"Fine," he said, stepping forward. "It's just a stupid log." He bit back a comment about wearing plaid flannel, knowing it would likely fall flat. He picked up the maul as Zack moved behind him, like a golf pro would do for a student. With his big arms, he guided Freddy's hands to where they should be placed.

"Now. Swing back, use your body for lift, and bring it down right in the center." Zack stepped back.

Freddy took a deep breath and did it. He hit his mark, and although he didn't split the log in the middle, he figured 70/30 wasn't too bad for a first effort, either. He handed the maul back to Zack.

"Great, now I can cross *that* off my bucket list. Zack, the reason I stopped by is I have a favor to ask." He proceeded to fill in the details about Jane Nevins and her stated desire to crash the Tweed-Flanagan nuptials.

"You want me to keep her away from the wedding this weekend."

"She's...difficult. Very high-maintenance. Julie and I are going to be flat out this weekend. I'm standing up with the groom, Julie has to do everything else. And we're nervous that Jane might take it upon herself to show up, intrude, you know." Freddy lifted his shoulders. "She can be...troublesome."

"I'll help you out. You got a picture of her?"

Freddy had visions of meeting with a hitman as he pulled out his phone and searched online for a photo of Jane. Turning the phone to Zack, he said, "Here she is."

Zack nodded. "Okay, I saw her at the house. I got it. She's the one who wants the seven-foot arch built. I'll keep her from even coming down the driveway." He clapped Freddy on the shoulder, a rare sign of comradery from the big man.

TWENTY-SEVEN

It was Friday, the last day of November. When April rose, Bill was already gone. Tentatively, she made her way to the kitchen, half-expecting a note from him telling her he'd fled the country. *Get a grip, April! He's not going to flee. If he didn't leave after he found out you'd invited his kids, he's not going anywhere.* She read the scribbled note: *Gone out for a shave and a haircut. Back soon xxx*

April ran her hand through her own hair. Her roots had been touched up the previous afternoon, and Carlie would be able to fix a style that was simple yet elegant. Nothing fancy, April had warned. She glanced down at her nails, tipped in a soft buttery white. The wedding clothes were already packed. Bill had said he wanted to leave by ten, and had arranged for the car rental company to drop off the car by nine-thirty. The clock on the microwave in the kitchen read eight-twenty.

"Coffee," she muttered. "There's still time for coffee." She'd just poured a bit of cream into her mug when Bill burst through the door.

"You look good," she said, smiling. He did. His healthy eating plan had resulted in an eighteen-pound loss, and her guy looked fit and trim.

Bill set a bakery box on the table, then seeing her scowl, said, "I haven't had anything in six weeks! So today we splurge a little. I won't gain it all back this weekend." He held up crossed fingers, then leaned toward her. "Feel my cheek."

April raised her hand, then lowered it, instead pressing her lips to his smoother-than-a-baby's-bottom cheek. "Wow, that's a good shave."

"We have time for a little breakfast, right?" Bill checked the same clock on the microwave. "That was smart, packing up last night."

"Are you ready for this?"

"For the wedding? Honey, I've been ready for thirty years."

"No, I mean, all the stuff. You know, Norah. My mother. Dan. Eileen."

Bill made a cup of coffee and took two small plates from a cupboard next to the sink. He brought everything to the table and opened the bakery box, placing a cinnamon scone on April's plate and one with cranberries and orange on his own. "I'm okay. Really. It's surprising, for me, but I'm feeling very zen about the weekend. Some things will be out of our control, I know that. I'm trying to let those things just happen."

"I'm so proud of you, Billy. And no urges to drink?"

"Well, I always want to. But I'm tying in to my feelings when the urge hits. Am I nervous? Scared? Pissed off?" April cringed. "No, babe, not at you. I'm okay with all of it. Like we said, we'll be welcoming to Norah, try to ensure she's treated well and has a good time. But I can't make up for twenty years this weekend, and I don't think she's expecting me to, anyway."

I hope you're right, April prayed silently as she bit into her scone.

**

By eleven, they were on their way to Dalton. The sky grew bigger as they left Manhattan behind, and wispy clouds stretched across a pale blue sky, from the west to the east. Bill headed out West Fifty-seventh to the Hutchinson River Parkway.

"I looked at our options, and I think crossing Connecticut makes more sense," he said.

"Whatever you think is best, honey." April gazed out the window as Manhattan fell behind them. She noted exits for the chic town of Bronxville, charming Tuckahoe, the more urban Eastchester. Straddling the New York/Connecticut border, they drove past White Plains and Armonk.

An hour in, April felt herself nodding off when Bill spoke. "Let me know if you need to stop."

That probably means he needs to stop, she thought.

"You've been driving for an hour. Why don't we take a break so you can stretch your legs?"

Bill smiled. "You know me too well."

"I should. We're about to get married."

Bill pulled the car into a commuter lot, shifted into park, and turned to face her. "Married? I never agreed to that!"

"Haha. You're not as funny as you think you are."

"Yeah, I know." He slid out of the car and raised his arms high above his head. April liked the warmth of the car, but she got out, anyway, joining Bill for a quick stretch.

"Should I have stopped at a coffee place? Or do you need a bathroom?"

"I'm good for now."

"I can stop again before we get to the farm. We should probably have lunch somewhere before we arrive. I doubt they plan on feeding us until tonight." Bill opened April's car door for her.

They headed back out to the interstate, driving past Danbury, Connecticut.

"I know a few things about Danbury," Bill said.

"Really? Well, regale me with your knowledge."

"Okay. Danbury was well known for its hat making

industry. In fact, you probably didn't know this, but mercury was used extensively in hat making, and a lot of the workers were poisoned as a result. That's where the term 'mad hatter' came from."

"That's awful, Billy!"

"I know. The factory owners didn't really care, and they treated the workers terribly, but the workers unionized for better conditions."

"Did it help?"

Bill shrugged as he kept his eyes on the road. "Management locked the workers out, brought in nonunionized workers. That was in the late 1800s. By the 1920s, hat manufacturing had declined."

April sighed. "And now?"

"Now it's an hour away from the city by train, more affordable than places like Greenwich and New Rochelle. Like any other city, it's got its problems."

"And where did you teach again?"

"New Haven."

"Near Yale."

Bill laughed. "Yes, honey."

They passed a sign for Newtown and April shivered, remembering the awful day in December years earlier, when she'd heard about the mass shooting at the elementary school. Carlie was already in her teens, but April couldn't get the images of those precious children out of her mind.

Bill, sensing her unease, patted her hand. "I remember it, too, honey. What an awful day that was." He didn't mention how much he'd had to drink that night, trying desperately to obliterate the news.

Shortly after noon, Bill asked April to look on her phone for a restaurant nearby. "I need to eat. We need to take a break."

April found a place and let the phone direct Bill to an Italian restaurant on Main Street.

"Looks nice."

"Let's find out!" They exited the rental car and entered the 'ristorante.'

** **

Forty-five minutes later, two satisfied diners got back into the car for the final leg to Dalton.

"Can you even imagine if my mother had been with us?" April asked, laughing.

"Can you even imagine what the journey with Carlie and Axel will be like?"

"Hey, Carlie offered. I wasn't about to turn *that* down.

But something tells me I'll be indebted to her for a long time. I'll suggest this place for them, but I'm sure my mother will find something wrong with it."

They continued on Route 8 as it crossed from Connecticut into Massachusetts. At one point they passed under the Massachusetts Turnpike, then drove straight through the small towns of Becket, Washington, and Hinsdale.

"After Hinsdale is Dalton," Bill said. "We're almost there."

April was tense with expectancy. Although she used her relaxation techniques and nasal-in-mouth-out breathing, when she pressed her thumb to the inside of her wrist, she could feel her pulse racing. She stole a glance at Bill, who was smiling as he drove merrily along the two-lane road that led to Jingle Valley.

"Okay, babe?" Bill took his right hand away from the steering wheel to grasp her left.

"Absolutely!" she said in her brightest voice.

TWENTY-EIGHT

"They're here," Julie said into her phone.

"I still need ten minutes," Freddy whispered back.

"All right. I've got this." Julie ended the call, slipped her phone into her back pocket, and pulled on her jacket to greet April and Bill. She stood on her front step and watched the dark sedan navigate its way up the long gravel driveway, then she pointed to the open car stall. She strode toward the car and greeted April as she exited.

"Welcome back! I'm so happy to see you both again." Julie held her arms out to April, and embraced her like a sister.

"Oh! Nice to see you, too, Julie. We're not too early?"

"Not at all. How was the drive?"

Not bad," Bill said. "It's always longer than you think."

"Did you take the Taconic or 84?"

"Eighty-four, through Connecticut. They both looked about the same. Maybe the other way would have been faster?"

"Nah. You did fine. I remember the first time Freddy and I drove up here together, when we left New York. We took that route, and to me it seemed like forever. But you should have seen him, he was like a fish out of water once he left the city."

Bill had opened the car's trunk to reach for garment bags. Julie stopped him. "Bill, Freddy will be here any minute. He'll take care of that for you."

"We can do it together." He turned, smiling, as a big man approached behind him. "Hey, Fred- oh, Zack! We've met. How're you doing?"

"I've got these," the dark giant said.

"Hey, Zack," Julie said. "So you've met Bill and April?"

"We met briefly when we here in October," April replied. "Nice to see you again."

Zack nodded but instead of extending a hand, he grabbed both garment bags, folded them over his massive arm, and had a piece of luggage in each hand. "I'll bring these up to your room," he said, walking toward the barn's outside staircase.

Julie smiled at April and Bill and said, "He's really great. Doesn't talk much, but he and his wife Sarah are sweet, and we couldn't function without them. Zack will get you settled, and then Freddy and I will meet you downstairs in the barn, okay?"

"Sure. So we should follow him?"

"Yes! Or you can use the stairs inside the barn if you want." Her phone rang and she frowned at it, then waved to Bill and April before turning back toward her own house.

**

April began unpacking immediately. She found that focusing on a task helped her stay focused, and calmed her nerves, though she still couldn't understand why she should be nervous. *It must be because of Norah*, she thought.

"What can I do to help?" Bill asked, nuzzling her neck.

"You can take care of your own bag, babe. There's plenty of storage space." She hung up his suit and her dress, still encased in an opaque bag, in the spacious closet.

"Oh, look! A bottle of sparkling non-alcoholic wine. Very thoughtful. Shall I open it?"

I want the real thing. "Sure, that's great." She set her cosmetics on the wide counter in the huge bathroom.

"Beautiful view, hon. Look." Bill poured the 'wine' into tall goblets and stood in front of the big picture window, then pulled April by the hand until she stood next to him. It was a pretty view, she had to admit. Even at the end of November, with a dusting of snow over the fields and up into the powdery pines. The hills beyond the property rose solemn and sharp, a timeless portrait in shades of green and white against a slate-colored sky. She wanted to fly up into the mountains.

She swallowed what was left in her glass and set it on a mirrored tray. "I'll let Julie know we're ready," she said, pulling out her phone. The spacious suite felt too small. She needed to be in the barn.

"Are you okay spending tonight together?"

"Of course. Aren't you?"

"I know it's tradition for the bride and groom to be apart the night before the wedding."

"Oh, that's just stupid, Billy. We've been together for months now. Wouldn't it be dumb to be apart tonight?"

"Sure." He gathered her in his arms and squeezed the air out of her lungs. At least that was how it felt.

**

By the time April and Bill walked hand-in-hand down to the barn, Carlie and Axel had arrived, with Ellen Bornstein in tow.

"Julie must still be in her house," April whispered to Bill.

As Ellen turned to assess the décor, her bird-like eyes surveyed every inch of the barn.

"This is very interesting," Ellen said. "Not at all what I

was expecting."

"What were you expecting, Mom? Cows and pigs?" April asked with a laugh. "You knew we were getting married here!"

"Yes," she said slowly, as if it was forty years ago and April was six-year-old Brenda. "But I guess I didn't expect a *barn*." Ellen stepped away from the group as April rolled her eyes at Bill.

She ignored her mother and turned to Carlie. "Are you two going to stay here until the rehearsal dinner, or are you leaving and then coming back?"

"Axel's going back to the hotel, to check us in. I'll hang around with you, Mom, and then he'll come back for the dinner later."

"Axel, you can stay, you know. It's a small group. Don't feel as though you need to leave," April said, taking his hand. "At least stick around to meet our hosts." She turned as Julie entered the barn. "Julie! Come here, I want to introduce you!" April waved her over and watched Julie step forward as if her feet were encased in cement blocks.

"Are you all right? Did you hurt your leg?"

"No, no. I'm fine," Julie said, her eyes darting back and forth between Carlie and Axel.

"This is my daughter Carlie," April chirped. Carlie

grabbed Julie's hand, momentarily breaking the spell that had Julie struck dumb.

"So nice to meet you! You have a beautiful place," Carlie said. With nothing but a glassy-eyed smile from Julie, Carlie continued. "This is my boyfriend, Axel."

Axel turned to shake her hand. "Have we met before?" he asked.

Julie tilted her head and glanced at Carlie, then at April. "Not that I know of, but it's nice to meet you." When she caught April's eye again, April gave her a quizzical look. *What's going on with Julie?* she thought.

"Axel will be joining us for the rehearsal dinner. That's not a problem, is it?"

"Of course not," Julie crooned. "Luke—my *fiancé*—will be joining us, too. We'll be ten in all. Let me go tell Sarah." Julie, her feet and legs no longer hampering her stride, practically ran out of the barn toward the main house.

"Well, I'll go check us in at the hotel and come right back," Axel said, giving Carlie a quick kiss. "Just want to be sure our room is there!" He jogged to the main door.

April watched Axel hurry out of the barn and narrowed her eyes. "Be right back, hon," she said to Carlie, before leaving the barn as well.

Outside, April watched Axel catch up to Julie in front of her house, and, unseen by either of them, crept closer to the side of the house where she could eavesdrop.

"Julie." He grabbed her by the wrist, but gently. Julie whirled around to face him. "Of course I remember you."

Julie stood in her place but didn't pull her hand away. "I didn't want to make it awkward for you."

"I appreciate that," he chuckled. "Maybe it shouldn't be, though. It shouldn't be awkward."

"Still…it was a long time ago."

"It's good to see you again."

"You too. Later." She pulled her wrist away and let herself into her house.

Holy shit! April thought. She slipped back into the barn unnoticed.

TWENTY-NINE

With the simple rehearsal and dinner over, the Justice of the Peace had walked home, up the hill to his house next to the church. Axel and Carlie had driven away, to their hotel ten minutes down the road. Ellen was in her room, probably playing Sudoku. April and Bill, Julie and Luke, and Freddy and Bill sat around the big table in Julie's house as a couple of candles burned down. Little Valentino lay sleeping in Julie and Luke's room, exhausted after staying up too late.

"That went well, don't you think?" Freddy asked, looking directly at Bill.

"Nothing to it." Bill lifted a cup of decaf to his lips. He was exhausted, too, just like Val, and couldn't wait to go to bed. He and April weren't getting married until five o'clock the following afternoon, and there was plenty to do the next day. After sending three messages to Norah asking about her arrival time, she had texted back that she'd catch a morning train from New York and should be in Albany by noon. He couldn't dwell on that. Julie promised that someone would pick her up from the station.

"I remember the rehearsal dinner for my first wedding," April said. *She's sounding a little drunk,* Bill thought, *and she's referring to her first wedding. Good thing*

Ellen isn't around to hear it.

"Was it a big deal?" Julie asked. She, too, looked tired, Bill thought. In fact, everyone at the table except April looked ready to pack it in. April was the only one at the table who was wide awake.

"Yes, it was. My parents were determined to marry me off in style. We had about forty people at the rehearsal dinner, most of them I didn't even know. Friends of my father and mother."

No one said anything. *Yikes*, Bill thought, glancing at the others. *I'm going to have to call it.*

"And how many were at your wedding?" Julie asked.

"Oh, over three hundred. This time it'll be a little different." As April looked around the table, Bill squeezed her hand, then leaned in close and pressed his lips to her ear.

"I think it's time to say goodnight, honey."

With a dip of her chin, April cleared her throat. "Anyway, this has been lovely. But I can see we're all tired. Thank you again, Julie. Freddy." She blew him a kiss, which he caught mid-air and slapped on his cheek.

"It was our pleasure," Julie said as she pushed back from the big table, and Bill jumped to his feet. He steadied April as she rose from her chair.

"Everyone get a good night's sleep tonight," Freddy said. He shook Bill's hand and gave him that half a hug thing, then did the same with Luke. April teetered but made sure she kissed everyone, stopping when she got to Bill.

"I'll kiss you in private," she slurred.

"Come on, angel. Let's get you to bed." Bill slipped his arm around her slim waist and walked her through the kitchen.

"Are you okay to drive?" Julie asked Freddy.

"No, not at all. But Bob is. One of us has to stay sober for the kid. Oh! Val!" He turned to Bob. "We almost forgot our son." Freddy turned his face to the ceiling as Bob walked back through the house to retrieve Val. "I love him. I love them both." Bob reappeared, carrying Val, who looked sleepily at Julie and Luke, then ducked his head back into Bob's shoulder.

Bill opened the door to the outside, and a blast of cold night air blew into the kitchen.

"Good night, everyone," he whispered, leading the way outside, holding onto April.

"What time issit?" April slurred.

"It's nearly two," Bill whispered back as they climbed the stairs to the second floor at the back of the barn. "They were probably wondering when we'd leave."

"It's our wedding day," she mumbled.

"Yes, it is, Bren. Lots to do. Let's get to bed."

**

Saturday dawned just hours later and Bill was awake as April slept deeply. *Today I marry this girl*, he said to himself. Even the thought of it made him grin like a teenager. *Finally.*

He'd dreamed about Meg again, but couldn't remember much of the dream, only that she was back at the Cliffs of Moher, ready to fly into the sky. He tried to stop her but she had waved at him and taken off anyway, using large, diaphanous wings to lift off from Hag's Head and soar over the Atlantic. She didn't say anything to him during the dream, not that he could remember.

As April snored lightly, Bill slipped out of bed, pulled on a tee shirt, and raised the heat on the thermostat. There looked to be fresh snow on the ground. *The first of December*, he thought, *covered in snow*. A good omen, he was sure.

Bill checked his phone for any late messages from Norah. Nothing. It was too early to text her. He was sure that she, like most people her age, slept with her phone, unlike Bill, who was happy to turn the damned thing off and leave it far from his bed. But he needed to know her estimated time of arrival. If she took a morning train, even a late morning train, she'd be in Albany by early afternoon. But after that, she'd be cutting it close. And putting them all in an uneasy situation.

Carlie and Axel had offered to pick her up at the station and drive her to Jingle Valley. At first, Bill thought he should be the one to pick up his own daughter, but maybe it was better to stay with April. He couldn't imagine the hour's drive back with Norah—what the heck would they talk about?

Screw it, he thought, and started typing into his phone.

Hi Norah—pls let me know what train you're taking so I can arrange to have you picked up in Albany. It's at least an hour's drive to the farm. Thanks, Bill

Bill stared at the message for a full minute before hitting send. Then he slipped his phone into his bathrobe pocket and made coffee.

**

He heard her moving in the bedroom before she spoke. In the hour and a half since he'd arisen, Bill had enjoyed a sunrise over the hills and two cups of coffee.

"Billy? Are you there?"

He brought coffee to her in bed. "Happy wedding day, my love." He placed the white mug on her bedside table and leaned in to kiss her.

"I have morning breath," she said, covering her mouth. He pulled her hand away.

"You're sweet, at any time of the day."

She sat up in bed and took her first sip. "Oh, isn't that good," she murmured. "I think I overdid it last night. Did I say anything awful?"

"Of course not. You were charmingly tipsy."

"Oh boy. How did *you* sleep?"

"I slept great. I must have zonked out soon after my head hit the pillow. I have to say, this is a great bed."

"It is. Have you heard anything more from Norah?"

Bill took a long swig and sat down on the bed next to April. "No. I sent her a text this morning. I know it's early, but we really need to know exactly when she's arriving. We can't have anyone hanging around the station waiting for her. Carlie and Axel offered to pick her up, but Carlie needs to be here with you."

April sat forward. "That reminds me. I have something to tell you about Axel. He and Julie apparently had a thing going."

"What?"

"Yesterday. When they were introduced? I thought I saw a look pass between them. There was definitely something. So when Julie left the barn, and then Axel all of a sudden left too, I excused myself and crept out, and I saw them."

"Brenda! You spied on them?"

"I guess I did. They definitely knew each other, probably back when Julie was in the city. I meant to ask Julie about it, but I guess I forgot."

"Are you going to tell Carlie?"

"What would I say?"

"Yeah, I guess. But he should at least tell Carlie that he knew Julie. Why hide it?"

"Exactly." April contemplated the scenarios. Maybe better to just leave it alone. "Anyway, enough about them. I know you're thinking about Norah. And I'm so sorry, Billy. I never wanted this to cause any worry or stress."

"I'm fine. Look, today is our wedding day! Nothing— and I mean *nothing*—is going to get in the way of this day."

April's phone vibrated on the table next to her bed. She wrinkled her nose and picked it up.

"Oh, it's from Carlie. Oh. How sweet." She turned her face to Bill. "She wants us to have massages at the hotel. And she said someone there will do my hair and makeup." April hesitated. "I wasn't planning to go all out, but I guess my daughter thinks I should."

"Wedding's not until five. You should do it," Bill said.

April agreed and typed a response to Carlie. "Great. She'll pick me up at ten. What time is it?"

"Seven-thirty."

"Want to start the honeymoon early?"

THIRTY

Of course, Carlie had invited Ellen as well. "Mom, I couldn't just leave her!" she whispered.

"I know. You're a good girl."

Ellen Bornstein surveyed the lobby of the hotel's day spa, and when a bouncy young woman with a high ponytail greeted them, Ellen paused, then eyed her up and down, as if sizing up a chubby worm.

"Good morning! Who's the bride?" The woman looked directly at Carlie, who blushed and gently pushed her mother to the front.

"This is my mom, April."

The young woman's thick, shaped eyebrows rose just slightly. "Wonderful!"

"Nice to meet you. This is my mother, Ellen, and my daughter, Carlie."

"Oh, what fun!" she chirped as Ellen snorted. "Okay, so, I have you all booked for massages, and April—the bride!—I have you down for hair and makeup as well."

"Hair and makeup for me, too," Carlie said. "Gran?"

"What do you think, dear? My hair doesn't need anything and I can very well do my own makeup."

"Would you like a facial, ma'am?"

Ellen lifted her chin and stared down the receptionist until the young woman trembled.

"Okay, then, please follow me!" She bounced her way down a short hallway to the massage room.

**

Four hours later, after a light lunch and a glass of champagne, the three women emerged from the hotel, glowing and coiffed, except for Ellen, whose face was unusually red and blotchy.

"I never should have agreed to that facial! It feels like my skin has been sandblasted."

"Mom, you look fine. You're rosy. By five, everything will be perfect."

"Hmmf."

April checked her phone, which she had stowed away during the spa experience.

Hi honey. Call when you can. No emergencies. xxx

Carlie slipped behind the wheel of their rental car and April asked to sit in the back seat. She dialed Bill's number and drummed her lacquered nails on the seat beside her.

"Hi, babe. What's up?" Bill's voice was unusually bright. April thought it might be better for the others not to listen in.

"Hard to hear you, honey. I'm going to text." She disconnected before he could say anything, then began typing.

I don't want Carlie or my mother to hear. What's going on with Norah?

She stared hard at her phone, willing him to type fast.

I texted her at eleven. She said she's driving up with a friend.

WHAT?

I know. I tried calling her twice but it went to voicemail. So I messaged her that the wedding is at five.

What friend?

No idea, honey.

I'll let Julie know that there will be a plus-one for Norah. OK, we're almost there. See you soon.

April caught Carlie glancing at her in the rearview mirror and she shook her head. She blinked fast, not wanting to ruin her mascara, even if the technician had said it would withstand a driving rainstorm. *This is all my fault*, she told herself. A tempest swirled inside her.

Carlie pulled into the long driveway that led to the house and barn.

"Gran, do you need help getting upstairs?" Carlie took her grandmother's arm in hers.

"No, of course not, dear, but why don't you come with me, anyway? I'll show you my tiny room."

Raising her hands in an *I-give-up* gesture, Carlie followed her grandmother toward the barn. April knocked on the door of Julie's house. With no answer, she assumed Julie must be in the barn, readying the venue for the late afternoon wedding. She stepped carefully across the gravel to the barn entrance.

The sight was breathtaking. Strings of white lights dropped from the rafters to the walls, creating a starlit canopy. The flower arrangements were exquisite— creamy roses in red and white, feathery greenery and baby's breath dotted the tables and sideboards. It smelled like a first snowfall—pure and light and full of promise, and April beamed. *Everything is going to be fine.*

"April, hi!" Julie saw her and waved, and left whatever she had been doing at the far end of the barn to greet her. "You look gorgeous. I love your hair."

April raised a hand to her head. Carlie had convinced her to go for an upswept style. *My smart daughter.*

"Thanks. It was Carlie's idea. I hope I don't wreck it before the ceremony! Actually, I'm looking for Bill."

"Oh! I think he's at Freddy's place. We wanted to keep him occupied today." Julie winked. "You want the number?"

Maybe she should just leave them alone. "I don't know," she sighed, sinking into a nearby chair.

Julie joined her. "Everything okay?"

April filled her in about Bill's daughter Norah, and the text message she'd received on her way back to Jingle Valley.

"Well, adding one more person isn't a problem. We've got plenty of room, plenty of food."

"No, I know. It's just, well, I'm the one who thought it would be a good idea to invite his children. He didn't think it was a good idea, and it looks like he was right."

"You know what, April? Everything will be okay. I'll let Freddy know, and we'll be watching. If they're late, they can just slip in. I don't want either of you to worry about this. Now, can I get you anything? Would you like tea? Something stronger?"

April nodded. "Tea would be nice, thanks. I'm afraid to drink right now."

"I hear you. Come back to the house with me."

"Can I ask you something first?" She locked eyes with Julie, and Julie sat down next to her.

"What is it?"

"You and Axel. Is there something between you two?"

Julie looked down. "Not really."

"That's not really an answer. Julie. He's with my daughter."

Julie hesitated, as if searching for the right words. "I knew him back in the city, yes. But it never went anywhere. He was involved with someone else at the time." She shrugged away the memories. "That's all it was."

"Okay. Thanks for letting me know."

"I don't know if he's told Carlie, but it isn't my place, April."

"I understand. But nothing happened."

"Nothing happened. And then I moved away."

April nodded, then cast her eyes around the barn. "Your Luke did a beautiful job with the flowers."

"He did. I'm so glad you like them. I might have the same thing for our wedding in June."

THIRTY-ONE

Bill had a view of the field if he leaned to the right. By four-thirty, guests were arriving at the farm. Zack stood in the middle of the long driveway like a traffic cop and directed cars to the left, where the frozen ground provided plenty of space for the dozens of vehicles.

Bill peered down and saw his brother Dan step out of a behemoth SUV, followed by his sister Eileen, her husband Robert, their two grown children, and two more miniatures, each holding the hand of a parent. *My family is all here*, he said to himself. He tried not to think too much about Norah.

Dan wore business clothes, not the traditional brown hooded robe of the Franciscan order. He looked like any of the other guests, and Bill smiled, knowing his brother would not have wanted to bring undue attention to himself. "He's still a Franciscan through and through," he said aloud, but April was in the bedroom and couldn't hear him.

By the set of his sister Eileen's shoulders, Bill could tell she was out of her comfort zone. Of course she wouldn't approve of his getting married here, on a farm, in a barn. Anything short of the cathedral would be wrong, he surmised. But at least she had shown up.

Bill watched Eileen stand straighter as she engaged in conversation with Dan. He imagined his sister, with her snippy remarks, so like their mother, and Dan being the kinder sibling, perhaps issuing a mild rebuke. As Eileen's husband Robert laid a hand on her shoulder, they all moved as a herd toward the barn and out of Bill's sight.

Only Dan remained, standing by himself in the space between the house and the barn. As he raised his face to the windows of the suite, Bill lifted a hand. But Dan must not have seen him. He walked toward the barn and out of Bill's sight. Bill watched for another minute, as cars made the long drive from the road to the farm, and parked as directed.

**

They dressed together in their suite, and few words were spoken as they put on their fancy clothes. "You didn't want me to see your dress before the ceremony," he said. "I think we'll be okay," she answered. Bill assisted April with her zipper, and April helped Bill straighten his tie. Neither of them knew if Norah had arrived. They'd already said it all in their conversation an hour earlier.

"Does she even know how long it takes to drive up here from the city?"

"Maybe. Maybe not," Bill replied, keeping the tone of his voice even and soft, belying the dread he felt. "But we're getting married at five, whether she's here or not."

At April's pained expression, he struck a Tin Man pose. "If I only had a scotch," he sang.

"Oh, honey," she said. "We'll get through this together."

"Without alcohol." *Although I wish I had a stiff drink myself right now.* He glanced at his reflection in the mirror.

"Hey, how's Dan? Did you speak with him?"

"I just saw him out the window. They're all here. And Dan and I had a good talk earlier, before he left the hotel. He sounds great, and was very appreciative of the room we offered, but Eileen and Robert had already gotten him a room at the hotel. He said the hotel's nice, even Eileen seemed to approve."

"Well, if she approves, that's saying a lot! So Dan's room down the hall isn't being used, the room I set aside for Carlie and Axel isn't being used, and we don't know if Norah and her friend want one of the rooms. If my mother finds out, she'll want to move to something bigger." April turned her gaze out the bedroom window, and Bill looked, too, at the sky tinged with ribbons of yellow and magenta, at clouds that looked like ducks and swans and fairytale castles. "I remember how upset Eileen was when you were in the hospital. She couldn't bear the place."

"Eileen's had a very…privileged life. She's rarely known difficulty, or sacrifice, and I guess that's good, for her. But it's not reality."

"No, it's not reality. But it's what she knows."

April rested her hands on his shoulders. "You look gorgeous, honey. And I'm not making an entrance. Should we just go down and mingle?"

"Sure. Come on, my bride, let's go get hitched."

**

April tried to keep Bill close and focused, but she knew he was searching the room. He made small talk, was introduced to April's old colleagues and current friends that he hadn't met before, and smiled through it all. He took sips from a glass of club soda with lime, and when he switched the glass to his other hand, April felt the cold condensation of the glass on Bill's palm. Norah wasn't in the barn.

"Five bucks says she doesn't show," he whispered close to April's ear.

April pressed her lips as close to Bill's ear as she could without leaving lipstick on them. "I'm not a betting girl. Let's go find the JP."

She led him to the small area that served as a chapel. "We're ready when you are, Judge."

The JP checked his watch gave a curt nod. "Fine. Let's go up front as we rehearsed." With a hand signal to Freddy, Bill followed April to the far end of the barn. Freddy jogged up to them, then checked a microphone in a stand that stood where the small band would play after the ceremony, then turned to the assembled group.

"Hi, everyone. Welcome to Jingle Valley and welcome to the wedding of April Tweed and Bill Flanagan. Please gather around as the couple takes their wedding vows." He set the mike back in place and stood to Bill's right. Carlie stepped forward to stand next to her mother. A photographer with a professional-looking camera snapped pictures from all angles.

"You look like a movie star, Mom."

"Bill's daughter Norah isn't here," April whispered.

"Don't worry about that right now. You're about to get married. I'm so happy for you." Carlie brushed her cheek against April's.

With April and Bill standing in front of the judge, and Carlie and Freddy flanking them, the judge began his speech.

Just as he said, "Let your love be an inspiration to others to reach for what is good within us all," the judge looked up and frowned at a noise coming from the other end of the barn, at the entrance. Bill and April turned to look, as did most of the guests.

Norah, dressed in black jeans and a black leather jacket, crashed in with her date, a young man who wore ripped jeans and a hooded sweatshirt. Norah's eyes were rimmed in black and the two of them stood dazed in front of curious guests. *Is she high?* April wondered to herself.

"Hey," Norah blurted in a loud voice. "Are we late?"

**

Zack had spotted Jane Nevins when she pulled up to the parking area. The photo Freddy had shown him was exactly what she looked like that afternoon, and Zack jogged over to her car as she attempting to park.

"Jane Nevins?" he boomed as she rolled down her window.

Jane surveyed Zack with a sneer. "Who's asking?"

"Ma'am, you were not invited to this wedding. I'm going to ask you to drive back out."

"You don't know that I wasn't invited to this wedding! And my own wedding is right here, in this same place, at the end of the month. I'm a paying customer and I have every right to be here!" She rolled up the window and opened her car door.

Zack put his big hand on the door and pulled it open, effectively blocking her from exiting her own car. "Ma'am, you actually do not have the right to be here. This is an invited guests only event. You were not invited. And I do know, because I was told by the owners."

Jane squeezed out of the car, brushing Zack's chest. Even in her heels, she had to look upwards to glare at him. She pressed her index finger to his chest. "The owners want my business, believe me. I am simply going into the barn to see what it looks like. Don't worry," she scoffed, "I'm not looking for free food."

"Ma'am. I will carry you out of here if I have to."

Jane took a sharp gasp in the cold air. Perhaps it was the idea of being picked up by the giant man. Perhaps it was somewhat arousing for her to consider the possibility of it. Whatever it was, Jane's face turned bright red as she looked up at Zack. "Fine," she spat. "I'm going. But Fred is going to hear from me in the morning." She slid back into her car and pulled the door shut.

As Jane Nevins backed her Range Rover out of the parking area, turned and drove back to the main road, Zack breathed a sigh of relief. And never noticed the disheveled couple that had arrived late.

THIRTY-TWO

"Let's just continue, please," Bill whispered. April stood next to him and tightened her grip on his hand. She gave Freddy a meaningful glance and he said quietly, "I'm on it." As April and Bill stood stoically in front of the justice of the peace, Freddy disappeared, but was back within a minute.

"Julie's taking care of it," he muttered. To the judge, he added, "Let's continue, please."

The couple exchanged vows and rings, were pronounced married, and shared a brief kiss before turning to face the attendees, who applauded. April scanned the back of the barn for Norah and her accomplice but didn't see either of them.

Before she could think any more about it, or even say something to Bill, Freddy picked up the microphone.

"Please remain standing if you would, everyone, for a quick toast to Bill and April."

Someone handed the couple flutes of champagne. Bill, already tense, set his glass down on the nearest table. "You have no idea how much I want to drink that. And that one. And a few more bottles."

"Honey, they're taking care of the situation. Freddy, could someone get Bill a seltzer water? Or something that's not champagne? Babe, try not to think about it."

"Seriously? How can I not think about it? My daughter nearly ruined our wedding." He craned his neck. "Where is she, anyway? And the cretin she dragged in with her?"

"I'm guessing Julie's got it. Or better yet, maybe they have Zack dealing with it. Do you want me to find out?"

"No, honey, you stay here. Most of these people are your friends, anyway. Excuse me." He pulled away from April just as her agent Karen approached.

"Sweetie! You are *stunning*. Oh, where's your husband going, I wanted to meet him."

"He'll be back. Thank you so much for coming!" She air-kissed Karen. Karen's partner (*don't call him Abner,* she reminded herself) walked up and April racked her brain to remember the name he went by. She switched into April Tweed the Celebrity mode.

"Hello! Thank you so much for coming!"

Karen, with her agent antennae, said, "April, this is Rocket."

Rocket! Of course.

Rocket gave her a too-wet kiss on the cheek. "How about that little ruckus, huh? Who the hell let those two in?"

227

April lifted her shoulders in response and took a long sip of champagne. She didn't even know where the publicity people were, but she had to leave that one to Freddy. It was his idea, after all.

**

Zack had strong-armed Norah and her friend, whose name was, unsurprisingly, Chase, and brought them around to the far side of the barn, where Julie was waiting.

"I was dealing with Jane Nevins when these two snuck in," he growled.

"What the hell is wrong with you?" Julie hissed at Norah.

"Who the hell are you?"

"I'll take them to our house," Zack offered, and was about to drag them off when Bill jogged up. His forehead was dotted with perspiration.

"Norah."

"Hey. Congratulations." She stared at him with her black raccoon eyes. Chase struggled briefly against Zack's grip, then must have realized how futile it was and relented.

"I was going to bring them to my house, wait for them to sober up."

Bill said nothing for several seconds, but when Julie touched his arm, he dragged his hand over his scalp.

"Good idea. She can stay. Not him."

"What the hell? We came together."

"And we set a room aside for you, Norah. Not for him."

Norah laughed hard. "That's hysterical. You wanna play daddy now?"

"Nope. I really don't. But I do want to go back inside and join my wife. Do whatever you want, Zack. You know what? Neither of them is staying here. I'll pay for their hotel in town." He turned to Julie. "Okay?"

"Okay. We'll take care of it, Bill." She watched as he stormed back around the barn.

Once he was gone, Julie turned to face Zack and the young couple. "I'll arrange a room for them at the hotel, or another hotel if ours is booked. If you wouldn't mind driving them there, I'd be grateful. I'll ask Luke to bring their car to the hotel."

"Sure thing."

Then she got into Norah's personal space. "You are not welcome here, is that understood? Someone thought it would be nice for you to reconnect with Bill." She held up her palm, stopping Norah from saying anything. "I don't care what your life has been like. I don't care if someone else raised you. You were invited here, to share in the happiness of two wonderful people, one of whom is your biological father. You've shown nothing but contempt for their kindness, so understand that you and your friend are now excluded from these grounds."

Zack held on to Norah and Chase by their elbows. "Let's go."

"Well, that was fun," Chase drawled. "Didn't even get a piece of cake."

**

Back inside the barn, the band had begun playing light swing music as more cocktails were poured. Julie found Luke and relayed her request that he drive the rental that Norah and Chase had arrived in and bring it to the hotel, where he'd meet up with Zack and return to the reception.

Then, she found Freddy, standing with his husband Bob and looking shaken. There was very little that could rattle Freddy. "Are you all right? You're pale."

"He'll be okay," Bob said. "That was just a bump in the road." He glanced at Freddy, who gulped and nodded.

"Where's Bill?" Julie asked and followed Bob's glance. "Thanks, guys. Freddy, can you still do emcee duties?"

"Of course. I just need a minute."

She kissed him on the cheek and headed for April and

Bill, then gently pulled them away from well-wishers standing nearby.

"Are you guys okay?" she asked.

"We will be," April said, linking her arm through Bill's. "Where are they?"

"Zack is bringing them to the hotel. I was able to get them a room for the night. I didn't think you'd want them next door to your suite. Bill, I'm so sorry."

Bill waved his hand. "It's not your fault." Cutting his eyes to April, he added, "It's not anyone's fault."

"Well, we'll be serving dinner in about ten minutes. Freddy's got the microphone. It'll be fine," she said. "And, guys? Congratulations." Julie leaned in to hug April and Bill. "If you need anything, I'm here, okay?"

"Thanks."

After Julie had left, Bill scanned the room. "I need to find Dan. I'm sure he's wondering what all that was about. He probably doesn't know it was Norah. Okay if I slip away for a minute?"

"Of course, honey." April watched Bill wander the barn in search of his brother. Her shoulders sagged under the weight of the situation. *If only I could change the past.* She accepted another glass of champagne from a young man holding a silver tray and fixed a plastic smile on her face.

"Mom."

"Hey, baby girl." April kissed her daughter, then accepted a peck from Axel.

"You okay?"

April shrugged. "Nothing a magnum of champagne can't fix," she quipped.

"Stop. Really, though, are you and Bill all right? Where are they?"

"Julie had someone take them to the hotel."

"Oh. They were supposed to stay here, right?"

"Yeah. But under the circumstances…"

"No, of course not. We could have given them our room and stayed here."

"Didn't think of that. Julie got them a room. They won't be back."

"I'm really sorry, Mom."

"But congratulations nonetheless!" Axel exclaimed. "Seriously, all the best."

April gave them both a wan smile. "Where's Gran?"

"Mom, I think she actually missed the whole thing. She had to use the bathroom just as the judge started talking, so she excused herself. At the time, I thought, *Oh no, Gran's gonna miss it*, then I thought maybe she *wanted* to miss it. And now I'm *glad* she missed it."

"Me, too. No need to fill her in, you know."

"I know, Mom. I know. Love you."

"Love you more."

**

People took their seats and dinner was served, a meal of apple sage stuffed chicken or stuffed Portobello mushrooms for the vegetarians. Freddy sparkled throughout the meal with anecdotes about April and Bill (provided to him by April and Bill), and by the time the newlyweds cut their wedding cake, no one was gossiping about the weird couple who had crashed the wedding.

On the dance floor, April whispered to Bill, "I know this is torture for you, my love."

"What, dancing with you? I couldn't ask for a better moment than this."

"No, that's not what I meant. Come on, it sucks."

"Yeah, a little. But this doesn't." He pulled her closer.

"The evening's almost over. And it ends when we say it ends. All I have to do is tell Julie or Freddy and they'll take it from there. So just let me know, okay?'

"I'm doing fine, Mrs. Flanagan." He pressed his lips to hers as other couples joined them on the dance floor.

**

Julie scurried back and forth, from the barn to the house. The kitchen staff had everything under control, keeping coffee and decaf and tea at the ready. The bar ran efficiently, and Julie's barman had a keen sense if someone had had too much. Zack and Luke had returned from the hotel but had offered to drive anyone there if they couldn't drive themselves.

When Freddy entered Julie's kitchen, she almost burst into tears.

"Oh my god, Freddy!"

"I know. I feel awful about it. Where the hell was Zack? Why couldn't he have kept them out?"

"Because he was running interference trying to keep Jane Nevins away. They got in while he was preoccupied with her."

"Oh, for crying out loud. Jane would have been easy compared to those two." Freddy opened the refrigerator and pulled out a bottle of water.

"That's true. I really feel bad for Bill. That's his daughter. Nice way to reconnect."

"Well, I'm sure there's a lot of story there that we don't know about."

"I don't doubt it. Still, she had no right to show up like that. The two of them looked really strung out."

"And that outfit! Puh-lease." He upended the bottle and gulped down half of it. "My mouth was so dry!"

"You'd better get back there. I'll be right behind you."

Freddy kissed Julie's cheek. "Just think, we get to do this all over again at the end of the month. With Jane Nevins and Edward Lack-a-shaft!"

"Lackshaft. Go." She opened the door and shooed him out, stepping outside and closing the door behind her.

THIRTY-THREE

By the time April and Bill had kissed their guests goodbye, the incident with Norah and Chase was forgotten. Or at least it wasn't mentioned. April hoped it was forgotten. Freddy told April that he had spoken privately with the photographer from the magazine, who agreed not to publish anything about the interruption, and with his friend Alison, who told him the focus of the article was the barn and its décor, not a couple of punk kids who had walked in. The whole reason for them being there was to showcase the barn, anyway, and to mention April. Finally, thankfully, no one had told her mother about it, because April knew that if they had, Ellen would be only too eager to comment about it for the rest of her life.

Norah and Chase were gone, hopefully sleeping off whatever they'd put into their bodies, but at least they were in the hotel in Pittsfield and not upstairs, next to their honeymoon suite. Ellen was in her room at the end of the hall, and Carlie and Axel, Fr. Dan, and Eileen and family were all in Pittsfield. There were two empty rooms between Ellen and April.

"Is Dan coming back for brunch tomorrow? And Eileen?" April added hastily.

"They said they would. They know it's a small

gathering. Just family." Bill looked beat. His face was drawn, there were dark patches under his eyes. April knew Billy was probably fighting his demons. She'd vowed to support him in his determination to stay sober, even in the face of such a traumatic event. But he reiterated that he was okay, and she believed him.

"Are you going to call her? Or text?" April whispered as she changed out of her dress.

"I don't see the point," he said. He undressed methodically, hanging his suit and shirt, slipping his dress shoes back into their flannel bags. He changed into a clean tee shirt and pulled on cotton pajama bottoms.

One thing April knew for sure: they wouldn't be making love on their wedding night. She opened a drawer and stared down at the red silk slip of a gown she'd purchased just days earlier. She plucked an oversized cotton tee shirt from underneath and turned her back. Dropping her underwear to the carpeted floor, she stood motionless, contemplating.

She felt him behind her and his arms slipped around her waist. She leaned back against him and closed her eyes as one of his hands went north, the other south. As she turned to face him, she stared into his eyes. "I know it's our wedding night, but if you're not in the mood, I understand."

His hands continued their exploration of her backside. "It is our wedding night, and nothing's going to get me out of the mood, Brenda Bornstein."

Whenever he called her by her given name, she had to smile. "Well, okay then," she said as he lifted her in his arms and carried her to the wide bed.

**

The following morning, Julie, with help from Sarah, set out a simple buffet brunch in the barn.

"How many are coming?" the diminutive woman asked.

Julie paused and spread her fingers as she counted. "Um, April, Bill, April's mother. Carlie and…Axel," she added. "And Father Dan, Bill's brother. Bill's sister Eileen and her family would have been six more, but she called this morning to say they had to return to Connecticut. Then Freddy and Bob, Luke and me, and of course, you and Zack are welcome."

Sarah dipped her chin. "That's very kind, but no," she said. "What about little Valentino? Does he need to be watched?"

Julie peered at Sarah. She and Zack had no children of their own, but Sarah had taken an interest in Val and frequently offered to babysit.

"Maybe. That would be helpful, Sarah, thanks. Want me to send Freddy a text?"

Sarah nodded and turned away but not before Julie caught a smile lifting the corners of her mouth.

"Anyway, there are ten of us. Let's get us all around the

bigger table, okay?"

**

At ten minutes before eleven, Father Dan drove up the long drive that led to Jingle Valley. He was followed by Bob and Freddy, who were met at the car by Sarah and Zack. As Sarah welcomed Valentino with a big smile, Zack extended his hand to Dan.

"We didn't meet yesterday, Father. I'm Zack. I work on the property." He shook Dan's hand hard.

"Ah! That's quite a grip you have there. Pleasure to meet you." Dan glanced behind him and greeted Bob and Freddy. "Am I the first to arrive?"

"Come on in where it's warm." Freddy escorted Dan into the barn, then turned back and returned to Sarah, who was squatting down low to talk to Val. Bob patted Val's head, but the boy ignored his father, entranced with Sarah.

"Hey, guys, thanks for babysitting. Should only be a couple of hours."

"Oh, we don't mind, do we, Zack? It's nice to have Valentino with us! I made pumpkin stew—do you think he'll eat it? Val, do you like pumpkin?" Her light and airy voice was hypnotic, and Val stared at Sarah as if she was the most magical being he'd ever seen.

Bob shrugged. "You never know! He's picky with us, but he loves you, Sarah. You have a special way with our boy." Bob bent down to kiss Val on the top of the head. "You want us to pick him up at your place?"

"Sure," Sarah murmured, offering her tiny hand to the boy.

Freddy nudged Zack and wiggled his eyebrows. "She's good with kids. Just saying," he added before hurrying into the barn.

**

Julie stayed close to Luke. At the table, she was seated directly across from Axel, and every time she glanced up, he seemed to be staring at her. She rested her free hand on Luke's thigh and focused her attention on everyone but him. *What a player*, she thought. *He's here with Carlie and staring at me.*

Dan cleared his throat. "If I may," he began. "A toast to Bill and April, and to a lifetime of happy memories. May every day be blessed." He raised his flute.

Everyone raised a glass. Some were filled with champagne, some with orange juice, some with both. But all murmured their best wishes.

"Are you heading off on a honeymoon?" Axel asked, winking at Julie. *What the hell?* she mouthed, looking away.

"Not right now," April said, dabbing a napkin to the corner of her mouth. "Bill has to return to teaching, and…" She paused.

"And?" Axel prompted.

"And, I've been fielding offers."

"I didn't know that!" Bill said.

"Nothing yet, but I'm always open to opportunities," she said, smiling around the table.

"We've got a honeymoon planned, actually, but not until the spring," Bill added.

"Well, don't be away for Julie and Luke's wedding!" Freddy chirped. "First of June—just six months away." He caught the hard look Julie fixed on him and smiled sheepishly.

"Six months seems a long time to wait," Luke said. "In our minds, we're already married." Julie stole a glance at Father Dan, who stared into his coffee. Then she forced herself to look at Axel, who raised his cup to her.

"Congratulations, Julie! And Luke. Wonderful news!" His black eyes teased her and Julie felt an involuntary shiver slide down the back of her neck. *Creep.*

"You're all welcome to come back up for the wedding. The farm is lovely in June," Luke said, and Julie wanted to kick him. *Axel will* not *be invited to my wedding*, she promised herself.

THIRTY-FOUR

Everyone had departed, and Julie was alone. The light faded early in December, with the sun setting before four-thirty. She turned on lamps in the house and put a casserole of chicken and rice into the oven. Luke had driven to the shop to check on things. His business wouldn't pick up again until closer to Christmas. It would be dark by the time he turned into their driveway, and Julie would see his headlights from the kitchen.

All alone in the big house, Julie tried to envision her life with children in it. Or even just one child. They were trying, even before their wedding, but so far there was no pregnancy news to fill her heart. *Should we keep trying? Should we go through the same channel as Freddy and Bob? What if we adopt and then I do get pregnant? Would that be so bad?*

She'd been mostly abstaining from wine, but she pulled a bottle of Pinot Noir from her shelf and opened it. *One glass of wine with dinner won't do any harm*, she thought. My mother drank wine every day and we all turned out fine. She pulled the cork and poured a small amount in a glass as she tossed a salad.

Luke's car headed up the long drive and Julie watched as he pulled into the open carport. *One day we'll build a real garage*, she thought. *One day, one day. Not if we have kids.*

Cold air rushed into the kitchen with Luke. "Oh, it's good to be back home!" he said. As he leaned in to kiss Julie, she kissed him back with fervor. "Well! That's a warm greeting!"

"I'm happy you're home," she murmured. "Dinner's just about ready. I'll pour wine."

"Okay, I'll change and be right back." Julie watched him walk away and felt a surge inside her abdomen. *Tonight could be the night*, she thought. Spicy *arroz con pollo*, good wine, a warm house, and a more-than-ready fiancée.

**

He was tired, she could tell, so she made it easy for him. But Julie was determined, and the calendar was on her side. She couldn't waste the opportunity.

"Twice?" he asked, chuckling. "You think I'm still a young man?"

"We're not old. And I want you so bad," she whispered.

"I want you, too, honey. Oh! Is this the time?" Julie nodded. "Well, then I'll rally for the cause. Come over here, you vixen."

**

With the Tweed-Flanagan wedding behind them, Julie

and Freddy now needed to focus on the Nevins-Lackshaft nuptials. But first, Freddy needed to schmooze Jane Nevins.

"Her feelings are very hurt, you know, because she wasn't allowed in to April's wedding," Freddy said.

"Well, she has to get over it. She wasn't invited. She can't just go where she's not invited."

"I know that, and you know that, but this is Jane Nevins, and she's our customer. Our very wealthy customer. We need to soothe her feelings and make her the princess of Jingle Valley for the rest of the month."

"Well, that's your area of expertise, Freddy."

"You're right. And I'm meeting her for lunch in Lenox."

Julie rubbed her eyes and made another pot of coffee. She and Luke had not slept much the previous night, but she wasn't going to share with Freddy.

"Just Jane?"

"Just Jane."

"Are we ever going to meet her fiancé? Or is he just going to show up here on New Year's Eve and hand over a ring?"

"Now, Julie, don't be catty. It's not becoming, even on you."

She rolled her eyes. "Whatever. Smooth things over as I know you will. She's been giving Luke a hard time about floral arrangements."

"Of course she has! I imagine her dressmaker is ready to tear the fabric in half, the baker wants to smash the entire cake in her face, and the band would like nothing more than to play the chicken dance as she walks down the aisle. Jane has that effect on everyone. But I can handle her, don't worry."

"Here, take a travel cup for the road." She poured coffee into a stainless steel cup, fastened the lid, and handed it to him. "Godspeed, Mr. Campion."

"Thanks for watching Val today," he called as he left.

Sarah's part-time job at the vegan bakery left her unable to babysit Val on Mondays, and usually Freddy just brought him to the house while they worked together. But with his appointment in Lenox with Jane, he couldn't take Val with him. Julie offered, knowing Freddy wasn't crazy about playdates at other germ-filled houses. Besides, both he and Julie knew she'd need to get up to speed with childcare.

Val sat in his highchair, the same wooden chair that all of the Tate children had used in the house. He had a green bib around his neck that said, "Future banker." *Oh Bob*, she thought. *Let's hope not.* Freddy had told her that they were trying to wean Val from the highchair to a booster seat, but Julie wasn't ready. The more tethered Val was, especially in the kitchen, the less tense Julie was.

Val lifted a spoon to his mouth and smeared chunky pureed pears on his lips and cheeks. He crowed with laughter and threw his spoon on the floor.

"Oh, you think that's funny, do you?" Julie picked up the spoon, washed it, and placed it on the tray. She bent down to wipe the floor while Val inspected the spoon, ate some more pears, and threw the spoon again. More splatters of mushy pears on the tiled floor.

"Yeah, that's not going to work," she said. "You can fool your dads, but I went to business school." She picked up the spoon, washed it, and laid it on the counter, out of Val's reach. He scrunched up his face and began howling.

"Val? Val? Look at me, Val!" She tried making funny faces, acting like a monkey, twirling in circles, but Val wouldn't let up. His screams were relentless. "You want the spoon back? Okay, okay, here's the spoon." She placed it on his tray.

This time, without using it for its purpose, he simply gave Julie a toothless grin and threw the spoon on the floor.

"Lord help me," she muttered as she picked up the spoon.

**

An hour later, Julie packed Val into her car, using the

spare car seat they kept on hand for anyone other than Freddy or Bob to use.

"Yep, we're going for a ride! Isn't that fun, Val? You love riding in the car." *Please let that be the trick.* She started out down the long driveway and drove in the direction of Lenox. *I can't crash his meeting, I know that.*

She knew the place where he was meeting Jane Nevins, and she stayed clear of it, but there was a McDonald's next door, so she pulled in. Neither Freddy nor Bob would have approved of Val eating a happy meal, but what could it hurt? If Val made noise or threw food in McDonald's, no one cared, least of all Julie.

Valentino loved his happy meal. It made him happy. *See?* Julie asked silently. She ate a cheeseburger and fries, feeling herself bloat up from the sodium. *Not like I'll be doing this again anytime soon.* From her seat by the window, she was able to see the parking lot of the café where Freddy was having lunch with Jane. There was his car, parked next to a white Range Rover.

"I hope she pays," Julie muttered.

"Good!" Val peeped, holding up a French fry.

"I know! It *is* good, Val! We just can't do this again, and you definitely can't tell your dads about our little excursion. Thank goodness you can't talk yet. And you won't have any memory of it, either." *You won't, right?*

With Val happily playing with and occasionally eating his French fries, Julie watched the lot of the café like a private detective on a surveillance watch. Ah, there they were.

Freddy and Jane walked together to Jane's Range Rover (*figures*, Julie told herself. *That's a ninety-thousand-dollar vehicle right there. She doesn't care about the environment.*). Jane threw her arms around Freddy's neck and Julie watched as Freddy pulled her in for a tight embrace. Her jaw dropped as she saw Jane lean away slightly so she could kiss him, but Freddy stopped her with his hand. Whatever he was saying to her must have worked, because she nodded, twirled a strand of hair around her finger, then pulled away. She raised a gloved hand to his cheek and left it there.

"Oh, Val, your daddy's a bad daddy. I wish I could hold this over him."

"Dada!"

"Yeah, dada. Enjoy those fries, Val."

THIRTY-FIVE

Freddy opened the door to the kitchen and made a stupid smiley face at Val, who watched his father from the highchair.

"Daddy's home!" he sang, making jazz hands in the air around his face. Val blinked.

"Come on, Val, you love this! Look, Daddy's home!"

Julie leaned a hip against the stove, where she was sautéing peppers and onions. "How was your meeting with Jane?" She avoided looking directly at him, watching Val instead.

"Great. We're right on track with everything," he said, pulling out a chair so he could face his son.

"That's good news. So she isn't still miffed about being turned away from April's wedding?"

Freddy lifted a shoulder. "She played it up. That woman needed some major ego-stroking, but she's okay now."

Julie stared down at the vegetables in the skillet. She used a wooden spoon to move them around in the pan. "Well, if anyone can stroke her ego, it's you."

"Just doing what's necessary, doll. They can meet with us next Wednesday."

"Seriously?" She whirled around. "We finally get to meet the famous fiancé?"

"So she says. Apparently he's between business trips. And he wants to see the barn."

Julie turned the burner off and sat down next to Freddy. "Should I plan dinner?"

"Maybe. She seemed to like the idea when I brought it up. But I wouldn't invite them into the house."

"Why not? Not good enough?"

"I just think we should dine in the barn. Keep it business-like. This isn't April and Bill."

"No, you're right. Okay, I'll talk to the chef about a meal. You and Bob, me and Luke?"

Freddy chewed his lower lip. "Maybe just you and me. You know, business-like."

Julie stared hard at Freddy. "Business-like? Well, that would include Luke, her florist. Freddy, do you not want Jane to meet Bob?"

"No, it's not that at all. This is strictly business, so, yes, Luke should be there as the florist, but I just think including Bob makes it more familial. I don't see our relationship with Jane and Edward that way. Do you?" He stroked Val's hair.

"Of course not. Okay, I'll let Luke know. And we'll plan for five in the barn."

"Good."

Julie returned to the stove and, with her back turned, made an exasperated face, knowing Freddy couldn't see it. "Do you want to stay for supper? It's Mexican. You could call Bob."

"Nah, thanks. I ate too much at lunch. Hey Val, what do you say? Ready to go home for supper?"

"Happy eel!"

"What? What's happy eel?"

Uh-oh. Yikes. When did Val get so good with words?

"Uh, I think it was something he saw on television this afternoon."

"Yeah, but eel? That's pretty good, Val. You got your fathers' brains."

Riiight.

**

It was a week until Christmas, and Julie and Sarah had been baking for days. Pies for the neighbors, cookie trays for the merchants in town, everyone who helped to contribute to the success of Jingle Valley over the past year. In between, Julie whipped up a chocolate and salted caramel tart for the following night's dinner with Jane and Edward, and had spoken to her chef about creating a meal around lamb, because that's what Jane had asked for. Apparently she and Edward had a thing for lamb—they wanted roasted lamb for her wedding reception, whether her guests wanted it or not. No vegetarian option, no chicken. Roasted lamb, oven-roasted potatoes, Brussels sprouts. *Because whatever Jane wants*, Julie mused.

Luke, who was swamped with orders, had brought his assistant, Libby, on for more hours and to help out in the shop while he made deliveries around town. Not surprisingly, Jane was particular about her wedding flowers, and Luke had gone to great lengths to procure the buttercup ranunculus she had demanded. Luke had pink and coral for her bouquet, and its bigger cousin, the peony for the tables.

"Is it really necessary that I'm there for this dinner tomorrow night? I've dealt with her. And Bob gets out of it."

"Bob isn't invited, and that was Freddy's idea. I get the feeling that he doesn't want Jane to meet Bob."

"What? Why in the world not?"

"Because Jane flirts with Freddy, and Freddy flirts right back. He'd deny it, he'd say it was about schmoozing with the client, but I think he enjoys her attention, and bringing Bob into the mix would change the dynamic. It might be weird, Bob not being there. And Jane might act very different with her fiancé present."

"Does she not know he's gay?"

"I don't know. But she does know he's married. He never takes his ring off."

"Oh, man."

"I know." And then Julie confessed to spying on Freddy the previous week, when he met Jane for lunch and they had a tender embrace in the parking lot.

Luke dissolved in laughter. "What?"

"Yeah."

"The funniest part of that whole story is that you fed Val French fries."

Julie smiled. "It was wicked of me, wasn't it? And that afternoon, when Freddy came to pick him up at the house, he chirped out 'Happy eel!'"

"Happy eel?"

"Happy meal. Val's a smart little kid. I have to remember that he retains things. And forms words, mostly. I must have said 'happy meal' a dozen times. Freddy didn't catch on, though."

"Well, if I could get out of this dinner with Jane Nevins, I'd take Bob to that Indian restaurant on North Street. I know Freddy hates Indian food. But I guess I'm stuck here with you." He grinned. "What are we having?"

"Lamb. Jane wants lamb. Local lamb. And roasted lamb for the reception."

"Really? Only lamb?"

"Yep."

"No other options?"

"Nope."

Luke shook his head. "Pricey."

"You got that right. She doesn't care, so neither do we."

They finished eating and Luke brought the plates to the sink.

"I've got these."

"I don't mind, really."

"I'll wash, you dry. Next year we'll get a dishwasher installed."

"Luke, honey, let that wait for a minute. Sit down."

Luke placed the plates and silverware in a sink filled with hot soapy water and took his seat back. Julie laid her hands over his and watched his expression change.

"What's wrong?"

"Nothing," she said, but the word caught in her throat. She swallowed hard and pressed her tongue to the roof of her mouth, thinking it might keep the threatening tears at bay.

"Something's wrong. Jules, what? Are you all right?"

"I haven't brought this up, because it's so hard for me." She swallowed again and forced herself to meet his penetrating gaze. "Luke, I love you so much."

"You're scaring me now."

Julie clenched his hands in hers, squeezing tight. *Tell him.*

"I don't know about having a baby."

Luke leaned back in his chair and exhaled. "I thought you were sick. I thought you were dying." His chest rose as he breathed hard.

"No, I'm fine." She let go of his hands and sat back, too.

"Was it the time you spent with Val?"

Julie nodded. "I love Val, you know that. But... I don't know, I just tried to imagine every day. At one point he wouldn't stop crying, I mean he was *screaming*, Luke. I took him to McDonald's because I didn't know what else to do. It wasn't to get back at Freddy. Well, I know the McDonald's was right across from the place where he and Jane were having lunch. But I took the easy way out. I couldn't stand to listen to him cry anymore."

"Why didn't you tell me this? You made it sound like it was fun."

"Part of it *was* fun. But I think I liked knowing I could give him back to Freddy later that day." She looked at Luke with fearful eyes. "I was afraid to tell you. We've been talking about this so much."

"Yeah. But we can't start the process of adoption if you don't want it. Julie, we both have to be on board with this."

"But you want it."

Luke flattened his palms on the table and stared at his fingers. "I only want it if *you* do. I never want you to agree to something for me. Jules, this is too big to mess around with. It's a kid. And a lot of money. And a lifetime commitment."

Julie nodded. "I know," she whispered.

"Can you tell me for sure? It's no?"

Julie dropped her chin to her chest. A rush of memories flooded her mind—days of her youth on the farm, in the loving presence of her parents, her siblings, the animals. Of standing next to her mother in the same kitchen where they now sat, watching her cook. Of cuddling with her father in front of the fireplace as the snow fell. But that was more than thirty years ago. Times were different then. She could be a great mom or the worst mom. They could adopt a foreign-born child who would treasure them forever and care for them in their old age, or have a child who grew up resentful, distant. It was a crap shoot, this thing called parenting. You could pour everything you had into it and still end up disappointed. Was it really worth the risk?

"Julie?"

"I can't." She stood up and walked away, leaving Luke alone at the table, wondering if her reply was to say she couldn't go through with it, or she couldn't promise it was definite.

THIRTY-SIX

Freddy and Bob had traveled to Maine for Christmas to visit with Bob's sister and her family—an obligation Freddy had said they couldn't refuse. Ethan Crane from up the road had offered his annual invitation to join his big family, but Julie had declined politely, offering a flimsy excuse that she was sure Ethan didn't believe.

Luke invited Zack and Sarah, probably because he didn't want to be alone with Julie, at least that's what Julie kept telling herself. Surprisingly, they'd agreed, and Sarah said she'd bring a black bean casserole and a loaf of her lovely sourdough bread.

"I'm going to roast a chicken whether they like it or not," Julie said, slamming a cupboard door.

"They accepted our invitation, honey. They know we eat meat." Luke stood just inside the entryway and shrugged out of his coat. After hanging it on a wooden peg and pulling off his boots, he stuck his feet into felt slippers that were kept by the door.

"I have a few things I need to get in town. I think I'll head out and pick them up before the shops close." Julie turned to grab her purse and keys, but Luke caught her wrist.

"Wait. Jules. Come on." He pulled her closer. "You've been avoiding me for days. We should talk more about this. Please don't go out just now."

"But—"

"It can wait. Come on." He slipped his hand into hers and led her into their living room. "Sit with me."

Julie slumped to the sofa. *I don't want to have this conversation*, she thought. *Didn't we already go through it?*

"You've had time to think about things. I have, too. Julie, I want nothing more than to have a baby with you, whether it's ours or adopted as ours. But if you feel that strongly—if you know in your heart that you don't want a child, well, then I won't ask again. The other night I didn't feel as though I had a clear answer from you." He took both of her hands in his and pivoted to face her full on. "Jules, do you want a child?"

She couldn't look away. It was true, she hadn't thought about anything but their conversation since it had transpired. *I know he wants a kid, and I love him, so I should want a kid, too. For Luke. For us.*

"Honey?"

Julie pulled air into her lungs, hoping the words would find her. It was a moment she knew she'd remember for the rest of her life. With a commitment from her, they'd move forward with the adoption paperwork. She was convinced there wouldn't be a baby any other way.

"I'm scared to death."

Luke suppressed a smile. "Of what? Of being a mom? Jules, you'd be a great mom!"

"I'm afraid of all of it. Of going through the process, of waiting. Of maybe being denied, or waiting for years. Of getting older. Of being, what sixty when he or she graduates from college? Of being too old to enjoy any of it? Of dying young, denying our child a normal life?"

"You're over-thinking. Let's back way up. The adoption process is complicated, and yes, it will take time. If we go the route that Bob and Freddy took, we're looking at a year, minimum."

Julie puffed out a big breath. *I'm too old*, she thought, but didn't say the words out loud.

Luke moved his hand to her cheek and brushed his thumb along her jawline. "We don't have to go the same route as Bob and Fred, though. Would you ever consider an older child?"

"An older child? Like a teenager?"

"Not necessarily. There are group homes full of kids whose parents can't care for them. Some are school-aged, some are mixed ethnicity. And, there's always fostering a child, Jules. There are so many kids in need. We don't have to go overseas to find the right child for us."

"So, it's a lot to think about." They sat with those words, as Luke held Julie's hand.

"It is. But I want us to keep talking about it. And once Jane's wedding is over, let's figure it out. Okay?"

"Okay."

**

With the unspoken fears about child-raising now spoken aloud, Julie slept through the night, and awoke to a snowy day. Snow for Christmas Eve, just like it was when she was a girl, living in the same farmhouse.

Luke was up and out of the house, getting floral deliveries ready for the final push of Christmas Eve.

Julie padded out to the kitchen and poured a cup of coffee. A post-it note was stuck to her mug: *"Closing at noon today. I'll pick up the wine. Call me if you need anything else. I love you"*

She smiled. It was nice of Luke to offer to pick up the wine, but she'd still head out for last-minute items. She'd already wrapped a set of Mason jars for Sarah and a solar-powered lantern for Zack, but she still needed to pick up Luke's present, a watercolor of the Bridge of Flowers at Shelburne Falls. She'd spotted the painting, by a local artist, and had already bought it, but she needed to call the gallery in Williamstown to confirm he'd be open.

When her call went to voice mail, she felt a tiny bubble of concern rise in her throat. She waited for the beep, then spoke. "Hey, Jeffrey! It's Julie Tate. I'd like to pick up the watercolor of Shelburne Falls this morning. Would you call me please and let me know what time is convenient? Thanks so much!" *There, chipper and friendly. But he'd better be there.*

She finished her coffee, tore through a corn muffin, and cleaned the entire kitchen. Fueled by a sense of urgency *(why did I wait until Christmas Eve to pick up the painting?)*, Julie made the bed and wiped down the bathroom in ten minutes. It was still snowing, but lightly. She checked the weather forecast on her phone. Light snow ending mid-afternoon, then temperatures dropping to the teens overnight. *Well, that's what everyone wants for Christmas, right? No complaining allowed around these parts.*

She pulled on her parka and headed to the barn, where she found Zack.

"Morning!" she called. He straightened up and turned his big shaggy head in her direction.

"Good morning," he said. "Everything okay?"

"Oh, everything's fine. Just taking a peek. I'm going to call Jane Nevins in a bit and let her know we're good to go for the thirty-first."

Zack nodded and turned back to whatever he had been doing. In the barn, there was always something that needed tightening or loosening, or scraping or spackling. Whatever it was, Zack would make it better. He'd constructed the wooden arch she'd requested, and it looked spectacular. Once Luke's flowers were attached, it would truly be a showpiece.

"Looking forward to seeing you both tomorrow!" she said. "Come over anytime, Zack. We'll eat around two, okay?"

He raised his paw in acknowledgment without lifting his head.

Julie sighed as she exited the barn. There wasn't going to be a lot of witty repartee at Christmas dinner.

**

In Williamstown, Julie walked up to the gallery and saw a note on the door.

CLOSED UNTIL JAN 2—HAPPY HOLIDAYS!

Stamping her boot on the sidewalk, Julie cursed under her breath. *Dammit! Why did I wait so long? And why didn't Jeffrey contact me to pick up the painting?* She'd have to print out a picture from the website and present it as an IOU to Luke. *Dammitdammitdammit.* A half-hour's drive for nothing. Frowning across the street, Julie spotted the A-Frame's sign in bright red. *Doughnuts.* That'll help. She sprinted across the road.

THIRTY-SEVEN

On Christmas Eve afternoon, Jane Nevins's voice was edged with drama. "I'm very concerned about a blizzard next Monday," she said on the phone.

"Don't even think about it, Jane," Julie said, thinking, *you're the one who wanted a wedding on New Year's Eve! Should have gone to Aruba.* "We're prepared for anything. We can get your guests from the hotel to the reception if you need us to, but I think everything will be fine."

"I am so stressed," she whined. "Edward and I aren't even going to have a real Christmas."

Julie didn't ask her what she meant, mostly because she didn't want to listen to Jane's answer. "I'm so sorry. But next week you're getting married!" *Rah! Rah!* Julie kept any tinges of mockery out of her voice.

"Honestly? I can't wait for it to be over. I am so *done* with this wedding planning." Jane let out a heavy sigh fit for a diva. *Yeah, lots of luck, Edward Lackshaft*, Julie said to herself.

"Is there anything I can do for you here, Jane?" *It's Christmas Eve and Luke's still delivering arrangements.* She wanted her to hang up and try to enjoy the holidays, but Jane Nevins was going to have a very expensive wedding reception, and Julie needed to treat her right, no matter what.

"I'm so bummed Freddy isn't around. He'd know what to do. Where is he, exactly? He was very vague with me when I asked."

Not surprising. "Um, I know he said Maine, but I don't remember if he told me where in Maine." *York. It was York. She had Bob's sister's number in her phone.*

"Ugh. And he's back when? Tomorrow?"

"No, he'll still be in Maine tomorrow. For Christmas. He's coming back on Friday. He's actually cutting his trip short so he can be back here to take care of whatever you need."

"Isn't he the best?"

"He is! So, nothing I can do for you, Jane?" *Last chance. After this, your calls will go to voice mail until Freddy comes back.*

"No, I guess not. My mother and Edward's mother are here. I couldn't take another mom!"

Julie wished she had an old-fashioned telephone so she could slam down the receiver.

"Okay, Merry Christmas!" And she disconnected the call before Jane could say another word.

**

Christmas dinner wasn't so bad after all. Sarah was sweet and gracious, and neither of them said a word, or rolled their eyes, when Julie pulled the chicken out of the oven. In deference to her vegan friends, she had Luke carve it on the counter in the kitchen, so the bird wasn't sitting on the dining room table in front of her guests. She and Luke sat across from Zack and Sarah, and Julie had discreetly set a thick cushion on the chair that would be Sarah's. The head and foot of the table stayed vacant. *We're all equal here!*

When they arrived at the house, Sarah presented Julie with a Mason jar filled with dark liquid. "This year we made our own plum wine. It should last a few weeks in your refrigerator."

"Thank you! I don't think it will last that long!" Julie took the wine from Sarah, glad she had chosen the set of Mason jars as a gift.

They all enjoyed Sarah's casserole, and as usual, her bread was perfect. After dinner, Julie put on a pot of coffee and set two pies on the table. "Both are vegan-friendly," she said proudly. "Pumpkin and chocolate."

Zack looked up at her, caught her eye. "That was very kind, thank you," he said.

Julie felt her neck grow warm. "It wasn't difficult at all."

"No, but it was thoughtful. We appreciate it."

Julie looked from Zack to Sarah, then let her eyes rest on Luke. Her Luke. She wondered why Zack and Sarah had never had children, but that wasn't a question you asked anyone.

Luke served pie, chocolate for Sarah, pumpkin for Zack (who said he'd have to try both), and pumpkin for himself.

"Jules? Pumpkin or chocolate?"

"Chocolate, please." She watched him cut a perfect wedge and slide it onto her plate. And at that moment, she saw him in a Christmas Yet to Come, a dad, smiling at his son or daughter, serving up pie. She reached across to lay her hand on his forearm and met his eyes. "Yes." He raised his eyebrows in a question and then tilted his head slightly, asking without asking. "Yes," she repeated.

He leaned over and kissed her on the mouth, in front of their guests. So unlike Luke. So unlike Julie. Things were changing.

**

One day before the wedding, on New Year's Eve eve, Freddy said he wanted to kill Jane Nevins. Strangulation, food poisoning, it didn't matter. So long as she didn't breathe air ever again.

"I can't take another day of this!" he said, sweeping his hand across his brow.

"Oh, please," Julie retorted. "Tomorrow they'll be married. We got a huge boost from this wedding."

"Jules." Freddy stood in front of her, fisted hands on his narrow hips. "Until the dysfunctional couple says 'I do' in front of Pastor What's-her-name, I cannot rest." He inhaled deeply, gearing up for more. "I mean, why us? Why did she choose us? We're not on the list. We're not Santarella or Blantyre. We're not The Red Lion. We're just a little farm in sleepy Dalton that does weddings. Maybe she wants us to fail so she can tell everyone she knows never to come here."

"You're delusional, you know that, right?"

"No I'm not. Everything is too weird."

"Freddy, stop it. Give her a call in an hour to check in. She loves to hear from you."

"She called me seven times when we were in Maine. Bob made me hand over my phone."

"Good! I dealt with her. Everything's going to be fine. We've done all the things she's asked. Luke got the little peonies, whatever they're called. She seems satisfied with the lamb and the rest of the menu, even if some of her guests won't be. For god's sake, she's got a nine-hundred-dollar wedding cake! Stop working yourself up." Julie patted his rock-hard bicep. "Is this from lifting Val, or have you been working out?"

He shimmied at the compliment. "At least someone

appreciates it." Before Julie could ask what he meant, he added, "I'll touch base with her this morning." Freddy put his hand on the doorknob and paused. "You want to hear something *really* weird?"

"What's that?"

"Yesterday I had Val in the car with me and we drove by a McDonald's. He started pointing and asking for a 'happy eel.' And then he started crying when I drove past. I'm telling you, Julie, no more play groups for my boy." He kissed her cheek. "Bye, doll."

THIRTY-EIGHT

Jane Nevins and Edward Lackshaft had a wedding to beat all weddings. Three hundred guests, three photographers, two videographers. Six bridesmaids and six ushers. A little ring bearer and a flower girl who had to be escorted down the aisle by her mother. Jane arrived in a Bentley Flying Spur (Julie wouldn't have known if Luke hadn't told her—to her it was just a nice silver car). Edward's family consisted of his very tanned father, his father's younger-than-Jane wife, his regal mother and a sister who both looked angry throughout the entire event, and his best man, a pal from grad school who hadn't brought a date, instead hoping to hook up with one of the women Jane had invited.

But Jane and Edward did look happy, Julie noted. Jane was effusive with her praise for Jingle Valley, and thanked Julie three separate times. When she approached Freddy toward the end of the evening, she threw her arms around his neck and hung on for longer than necessary, plastering his face with pink kisses. Bob, standing next to Freddy, extended his hand and introduced himself as Freddy's husband, and Julie only wished she'd been fast enough to take a picture of Jane's face. *Oh please,* she told herself, *you already knew.*

When the last guests had left the barn and climbed aboard the shuttle bus that would return them to their hotel in Pittsfield, Luke and Julie and Bob and Freddy stood in the barn as staff got to work with the post-party clean-up.

"See? Everything was fine," Julie said.

"She loved the flowers. Told me twice," Luke said.

Freddy added, "Okay, you were right, Jules. They both looked perfect, didn't they? Even when Edward flubbed his words, she kept that smile on her face. And did you see the miniature Jane and Edward on the cake?"

"An eight-layer cake!"

"Let's sit." Bob pulled out a chair for Julie, then jogged to the back and pulled a bottle of Prosecco from behind the bar. He grabbed four flutes and returned to the table. "Sit and have a drink."

"Just a tiny bit," Julie said quietly to Bob, who raised an eyebrow in her direction. She shook her head.

"What shall we drink to?"

"A successful 2018," Freddy said. "It's already 2019. Happy New Year!"

"It *was* a good year, wasn't it? Jingle Valley had its best year."

"We got Valentino."

"I got Julie back."

"And we're going ahead with adoption plans," Julie added. "But not Colombia. We're going to try to adopt a child from foster care, and an older kid is fine."

"How old?" Freddy leaned forward.

"Not a teenager, but six or seven, maybe. If it works out." She glanced at Luke, whose smile was so wide it nearly split his face in two.

"That's terrific, you two." Bob raised his glass. "To 2019."

"To 2019!"

**

With a new year and no events on the calendar for January, Julie devoted her free time to research. She contacted and made an appointment for Luke and herself to meet with Stephanie, a counselor at the agency in Hadley.

They entered an office furnished with a scratched wooden table instead of a desk and two orange plastic chairs on the visitors' side of the desk. Stephanie rose from her chair, an old high-backed desk chair with a three-inch tear in what Julie assumed was not real leather.

"Hi, come on in and have a seat," she said. "I have instant coffee and plain tea. But I don't think we have any milk."

"We're fine, but thanks," Luke said, stealing a glance at

Julie.

"Well, we operate on limited funds here, and whenever we get an infusion of money, we tend to put it toward the kids."

"That's understandable," Julie said, shifting on the uncomfortable seat.

"So, Julie, I know you mentioned an interest in adoption when we talked on the phone, but I'd like to hear from both of you what brought you here today."

Julie nodded to Luke, who began. "Julie and I would like to have a child, but we're both in our late thirties, and it hasn't happened for us yet."

"But you're trying?"

Julie nodded, feeling her neck grow warm for no apparent reason. "We are, but at the same time, we both think it's probably not going to happen. And I'm not sure either of us is prepared for an infant as we approach forty."

Stephanie sat back in her chair. Her brown hair was caught up in a messy bun, and Julie noticed about a half-inch of gray at the part in the center of her head. She looked to be in her late forties. A very tired forty-eight, Julie would say, remembering April Tweed, the same age. *We carry our joys and our frustrations on our skin,* she thought.

"But you're still trying to get pregnant. Sorry, I don't mean to sound like I'm prying into your private life, but if you were to get pregnant next month, would you scuttle plans for adoption?" She fixed her stare on Julie, not Luke, which Julie found irritating.

"No! Look, I said we're trying, meaning we're not actively trying *not* to get pregnant. But we're busy, and older…" She trailed off and looked away from Stephanie.

Luke cleared his throat. "Stephanie, we think this is the best course for us. If, by some miracle, Julie gets pregnant, we're still looking to adopt. Right, hon?"

Julie listened to an electric clock on a wall tick three seconds before she answered, "Of course."

"Okay. Well, here's the deal. We have a lot of kids in foster care right now. It's usually because the parents are unable to care for the kids. Sometimes the dad is not around, or not known. Sometimes it's that one or both parents are incarcerated. Sometimes it's because they're physically unable to parent a kid, because of addiction. If a child is in foster care for a year or more, and if the parent or parents have made insufficient progress toward being able to care for their child, that child could be ready for adoption. Generally, when that happens, the foster family is given first priority. Remember, the child has been living with a family, in a home, and is accustomed to certain people and a certain environment. It's familiar."

Julie's heart hammered in her chest. She fingered the outside seam on her jeans, tracing the line down her thigh.

"Now, if the foster parent or parents cannot adopt the child, then you might be able to. We have a class for parents looking to adopt. It runs for six weeks. There's also home study. We want to be sure you're ready." Stephanie smiled, but looked mostly at Luke. "As the process moves forward, there would be a home check as well, you know, to make sure the home is suitable."

"We did talk a little about our home," Julie said. "Jingle Valley." She breathed in deeply, picking up a scent that was neither pleasant nor awful. Just stale, she assumed.

"Yes, I'm familiar with it, actually. I remember when it was a farm."

"It's been in my family for generations. We no longer farm, but we hold weddings and special events in the barn."

"I remember my mother bought preserves there. Was it your mother who made them?"

Julie beamed. "It was! I helped her sometimes."

"I was just a girl, but I do remember special trips to get jams and jellies. I'm glad to hear you're still there. And you've had some success with it as a wedding venue?"

"We've done well," Luke said. "Julie and her business

partner have worked hard over the past three years. And I run a flower shop in town."

"Excellent." She looked down at her paperwork. "You two are not married, correct?" She looked up quickly. "Not that it matters. It used to, but not anymore."

"We're getting married in June," Julie said quietly. *Maybe we should have just gotten married before Christmas.*

"That's fine. Any other children by either of you? No, okay."

The interview continued for another twenty minutes, and by the time it was over, Julie felt like overcooked spaghetti. She and Luke shook hands with Stephanie.

"See you next week for class!" she called after them.

Once outside, Luke took Julie's hand as they walked to their car. She fell into the passenger's seat and waited until he'd closed his car door before speaking.

"Can we go somewhere? Before heading back home? Doesn't have to be anything fancy. I could eat something, though."

"Of course we can! Do you know any places around here? Oh, wait. I know a spot. It should be quiet this time of day, and I don't think we'll see anyone we know."

"Good," she whispered.

**

"Are you still okay with it? Be honest with me, Jules."

"I am okay with it. I mean, it's a lot to take in, but yes, I still want to move forward. But when she asked about what if I get pregnant, it did make me pause."

"I don't think you're going to get pregnant."

"But I might. And, Luke, I'd never abandon a plan to adopt once we set it in motion. I wouldn't. But do you think we should maybe stop trying?"

He poked a French fry with his fork and held it at eye level, then slid his gaze over to Julie, meeting her questioning eyes. "I'll take care of it. I don't want you on pills."

Julie forced a laugh. "What the hell? Who thought we'd be dealing with this now?"

"Or we could pretend to be in high school."

She looked at him, saw a sparkle in his dark eyes. "Let's go home."

THIRTY-NINE

February brought more snow, and there were four-foot-high drifts outside the barn. Nothing was scheduled except for the monthly book club meeting and a retirement party for one of Bob's friends, so Freddy offered to shoulder the retirement party if Julie would coordinate the book club.

"You get the easy one, doll."

"Really? Book club women are high-maintenance. They want specialty teas, fancy nibbles. They're very intelligent. You've got an old geezer retiring. And bankers. Come on, Freddy, you got the easy one."

"Think again. Bob said this woman is in her early sixties and the life of the party. Apparently she wants a little spice in her send-off."

"Meaning what? A male stripper?"

Freddy nodded. "Afraid so. And a karaoke machine. And a scavenger hunt. And a fortune teller."

"Oh, good grief."

"She can't have it all."

"Why not?"

Freddy stared at her.

"I'm just saying, you get to charge for all of it. And it's all we've got booked this month. She's paying, right?"

"No, her sister and two brothers are paying."

"Fine. So draw it all up, let them know. If it's too much for them, they can decide what to do without. Like a menu. Poor thing worked in a bank all her life, she deserves a little fun."

Freddy stood up, his hands on his hips. "Bankers are fun, Julie, and you know it."

"*Your* banker is fun, Freddy. He's one in a million."

"He sure is."

**

Julie and Luke had training for three hours in the evening, from six to nine, twice a week. Low season at Jingle Valley worked in Julie's favor, but poor Luke. He had Valentine's Day the day after the first training class, and his assistant Libby came down with the flu. When class ended at nine, they crunched over crusty snow to their car. The air was crisp and the sky was filled with stars. Julie tilted her head back, thinking how lucky they were.

"I'll drop you off at the house, but I need to go back in

to the shop. Too much to do tonight, and massive deliveries tomorrow."

"Oh, honey," she said. "Let me help you."

"No, it's okay. You go on home."

"Luke, I'm coming with you. I know enough that I can help you out. And if you need me to make deliveries tomorrow, I can do that, too. Freddy might even be able to help. Want me to text him?"

"No, don't bother him. I have a guy who can do deliveries for me tomorrow, I just need to set everything up tonight."

"Okay, let's go then." She turned on the radio as he started the engine. The car filled with sounds of an angry man ranting at the world. She shut it off.

Luke began to sing softly, one of her favorite songs about finding love in the nick of time. Julie leaned back and smiled. *He can't sing. But who cares?*

**

By the time Luke arrived home on Valentine's Day, it was nearly eight. Julie watched his headlights as he drove up the long driveway and swung the car into the carport. She opened a bottle of Pinot Bianco and poured wine into his glass. *And just a drop for me.*

She opened the door for him and he stumbled in, exhausted. "Happy Valentine's Day." He held out a bouquet of red roses. "I sold out. Good thing I'd set these aside earlier in the day."

"Here, let me take your coat, honey." She helped him out of his heavy parka and made him sit while she pulled off his boots. She pushed a glass of wine across the table.

"Why aren't we wintering in the Caribbean?" he moaned.

"Because we're hardy New Englanders?"

He shook his head. "Nope, that can't be it. I don't feel hardy at all." He took a long swig of wine and Julie topped off his glass.

"Hungry?"

"I am, but I'm too tired to enjoy it."

"Well, I didn't start anything, because I knew you'd be home late. But I can make a quick omelet."

"Yes, please." He got up slowly. "Okay if I shower first?" He'd already left the kitchen when she turned around to say yes.

**

With the frenzy of Valentine's Day behind him, Luke was more available for the twice-weekly sessions in Hadley. Stephanie, joined by another facilitator, guided the attendees through topics such as communication, positive discipline, child guidance, and building self-esteem. Their social worker, Kyle, visited the house.

"So, your bedroom is on the first floor and the other bedrooms are all upstairs," he remarked, making notes on his tablet.

"Yes, but we're willing to move our room upstairs if that's necessary," Julie said.

"Or we could turn the den downstairs into a bedroom," Luke added.

Kyle looked up from his typing, glancing at each of them. He smiled, then resumed typing.

"I've got your tax returns, thank you," he murmured. "And your physician reports. Check. Your clearances have come back, all clear," he added, looking up again. At her puzzled expression, Kyle softened. "You'd be surprised. Sometimes we get a rap sheet that's pages long."

"Wow. I'm surprised someone would apply to adopt if they had a criminal record."

Kyle gave Julie a look and she could almost hear Freddy saying, *Puh-leeze. I've been doing this for a long time. I've seen everything.*

"Now, you're interested in a school-aged child, so we don't need a gate for the stairs," he tapped his finger on his table, "or covers for the electrical outlets. But your upstairs windows need locks."

"Uh, okay." Luke pulled out his phone and tapped.

"And let's get your emergency numbers posted by the telephone in the kitchen. That's your only landline?"

"Our office phone is in the den, which is our office. It's a separate number."

"Mmm-hmm." Tap tap tap. Finally Kyle turned off the tablet, set it down, and turned his full attention to Julie and Luke.

"Shall we sit?" he asked. Once situated, Kyle leaned forward, resting his forearms on long denim-covered legs. "We have a little girl, Mishell. She's five."

Julie drew in a breath. *A five-year-old girl!* She took Luke's hand in hers and squeezed hard.

"I want you to hear me out, okay? Listen to all of what I have to say."

Julie nodded and waited.

"Mishell is bi-racial. An African-American father and a Filipino mother. She's an alert, bright little girl, physically fine, but very shy."

"Okay. She sounds wonderful," Luke said.

"She is! She's a sweet little girl." Kyle leaned back and crossed one leg over the other. "Mishell has a brother. Efren. He's seven, and from the same parents. Now, I know you've learned a little bit about keeping siblings together during your training sessions. But in case you didn't know, all research available suggests that when siblings are placed together, they have a better chance of success. There are, of course, the emotional benefits of keeping a brother and sister together—they feel more secure and they're able to help each other adjust to their new lives." He uncrossed his legs and leaned forward again. "What would you say to the possibility of adopting both Mishell and Efren together? Would you be open to that?"

Julie couldn't answer at first. She loosened her grip on Luke's hand and let it drop in her lap. *Two? Two little kids at the same time?* She'd been so hoping for one, she'd never thought about two, even though they'd touched on the topics during one of their training sessions.

"It would be an instant family, wouldn't it?" Luke said. He turned to Julie. "Jules, what do you think? Two for one?"

Julie blinked hard. She wasn't ready to wrap her head around the idea of having two children in their house. *Could I handle it? Could we?*

"It's daunting," she whispered. "I was thinking, how lucky if we're able to adopt one. Now you're telling us there are two."

"There are two available for adoption, yes. We're adamant about keeping siblings together whenever possible. You and Luke meet all of our standards, Julie. But if you'd rather wait for one single child, we'll go back to trying to make that happen." Kyle kept his eyes on Julie.

Julie stared back at him. Kyle's light brown eyes were almond-shaped, his skin like cappuccino. *He's bi-racial, I'll bet.* He was a good-looking man, with close-cropped tight curls on his head, broad shoulders, fine hands.

"You don't have to decide right now, of course. Just something for you to think about."

Julie turned to Luke. "Mishell and Efren. I like those names." She blinked fast against the building emotion behind her eyes. *These kids have had the bond with their mother broken once already. If I become their mother, that bond will never be broken.*

"I think we'd like to meet them," Julie said, and as she heard the words, it was as if her heart filled with helium and lift her to the ceiling. From that height, she watched as Luke stood. Kyle stood as well, but when Kyle offered his hand to Luke, he was embraced in a bear hug.

"Looks like you're on the way," Kyle said. "I'll get back to the office so I can fill out the beginnings of what will be a lot of paperwork."

"Thank you, Kyle," Julie said, holding out her arms for a hug. "Thank you for bringing these children to us."

As he pulled back, Kyle looked again deep into Julie's

eyes. "These are terrific kids. You'll see."

FORTY

With the adoption process officially underway, Julie had a more pressing problem.

"I think we should get married sooner," she said to Luke one morning. "It's nearly March, and I don't want to wait until June."

Luke raised his eyebrows over his coffee cup. "You know I'm ready today if you want."

"Well, not today. But do you think we could get married in April? Early April?"

"Of course, honey, whatever you want. Call Freddy. He'll be more than happy to pull together a wedding in a month. He's already elated over the prospect of this adoption."

"I don't know if my sister and brothers would be able to come on such short notice."

"Well, let them know and hopefully they can." Luke slathered apricot preserves on a slice of wheat toast.

Julie nodded, lost in thought. *So much to do, so little time.* Mishell and Efren would have their bedrooms upstairs, in the two rooms that the Tate boys used to share. Those rooms were connected by a door, and Julie was glad she'd never walled off the connector. But Luke was also installing a monitoring system that would allow either Julie or Luke to hear if one of them cried at night. She checked her calendar. April 6 was a Saturday, about five weeks away. Her wedding wasn't going to be grand, anyway—Freddy could help pull it together in five weeks. Kyle had said the process could be completed as early as September, or as late as next year. Either way, she and Luke would be married when Kyle brought Mishell and Efren for their first visit. It might not matter to Stephanie, or Kyle, or the agency, or the kids, but it mattered to Julie.

"I want to start saying 'our kids' now!"

Luke looked up and smiled. "Get used to it, honey." He wiped his mouth. "Okay, I'm off. See you tonight. I love you."

"Love you, too."

As soon as Luke's car was headed down the long driveway to the road, Julie called Freddy. The notorious late-sleeper had had to change his ways, ever since Val came into their lives. Julie knew Bob left for work around seven-thirty. It was nearly nine-thirty, and Freddy answered on the first ring.

"Hi, Mommy," he sang. Julie could hear Val babbling in the background. It made her heart do cartwheels.

"Hi, yourself," she said. "Listen. I've got big news."

"Oh my god, you're pregnant!"

"Shut your mouth. Can you even imagine? No, here's the thing. Luke and I want to move up the wedding date. If things work out, the kids will come for a visit in late April, and I want us to be married. I know they don't care, they won't even know, but, you know. I mean, can I get married on April 6?"

"I don't know, can you?" he teased.

"Freddy, you know what I mean. Can we pull together a wedding by then? It's five weeks away."

"Of course we can, doll. We're us, that's what we do."

"I just want to be married sooner. In case."

"You're adorable. Yes, my sweet traditional girl, we can. What else is on our schedule?"

"Nothing, I checked. Well, except for little events—a baby shower, book club, fiftieth birthday party. The next wedding we have booked isn't until the end of May."

"Fine, then it's no problem. I'll be over in about thirty minutes or so." Freddy made kissing noises into the phone before clicking off.

**

Julie held a bedsheet in her arms. "Come on, I need you for this." Freddy extended his arm, took two corners and stepped backwards, away from her, until the sheet was spread out between them. "I'm going to invite my family, even if they can't—or won't—make the trip out east." They folded lengthwise once, and once more, before Freddy walked his corners to Julie and handed the sheet back.

"Wow, I get to meet the Tates. The old Tates."

"Haha. Well, you already know Tommy."

"And who are the others again?"

"My brother Eric is the oldest. He's 58, lives in Austin."

"The millionaire, right?"

"Yeah. Then there's my sister Ella. She's 55, lives in San Diego."

"Oh, right, with her wife."

Julie nodded. She hoped Ella could come, with Jeanine. "Then there's Don in Phoenix. He's 50, he's the one Tommy lived with when he first went out west."

"Yep, I remember. Don and his wife Linda. Don was Air Force?"

"Correct! See, you know them all. Then Tommy, of course. And his wife Maria."

"Great. So, first thing is let's get an email to them. We can do a quick save-the-date, then get something in the mail. This way they can make plans if they decide to come out."

"I would love it if they could come, Freddy. I haven't seen them—well, except for Tommy—in so long."

Freddy opened his laptop. "I know, sweetie. Which is why I'm sending this email out pronto." He paused. "Or should you text them? Or call them? Or maybe do all of the above?"

Julie laughed. "Let's start with the email and go from there."

Twenty minutes later, Valentino was hungry and making noise. Julie headed into the kitchen to make Val's favorite yogurt bowl. "You want a snack, too, Freddy?" Freddy had never learned that she was the culprit of the McDonald's Happy Meal caper, but now that she was thinking about having two children of her own, she understood the fixation with what kids ate. She had no idea what Mishell and Efren had been eating in their foster home, but she hoped to get them on track to healthy eating once they were in Tate/Plante house.

As they all took a break in the kitchen, Julie ruminated about how much, how fast, life could change.

"When I think about it, Fred, I'm still overwhelmed. Last fall, I wasn't even sure Luke and I would get back together."

"Well, that was a classic case of miscommunication."

"I know, and we try to never let that happen again. But then everything—him moving in, us trying to get pregnant, the disappointment every month, then turning to adoption, and having this happen so fast, it seems. Now I'm about to get married, and if things go right, we'll be a complete family within a year!"

"Then we'd better get cracking, doll."

FORTY-ONE

March refused to loosen her grip on winter, and Julie worried that her rescheduled wedding date of April 6 might prove to be an error. Would the snow melt? Would it ever be warmer? What about all the mud? No wonder they had no weddings booked. But she'd sent the "Save the Date" emails to her siblings, followed up by real cards, and she anxiously awaited their replies.

Ella was the first to phone her.

"Little sister!" she crowed. "What wonderful news!"

"Thanks, El. We'd planned for June originally, but circumstances had us move the date earlier."

"Oh! You're expecting?"

Julie laughed. "No, I'm not. Well, in a way, I am. Luke and I are hoping to adopt a brother and sister, and we decided we wanted to be married before we meet them. The process is in motion, and we're very hopeful about the outcome." She crossed the fingers of her left hand.

"That's so great, Julie, really. We're so happy for you both."

"I can't wait to see you and Jeanine!"

"So listen, Jeanine and I talked it over…"

"I know you're busy, it's okay," Julie said, unable to mask her disappointment.

"Let me finish! We can't both fly out, but I want to be there, and Jeanine wants me to be there. I'm going to fly in on Friday, but I have to leave early on Sunday, okay? It's the best I can do."

"Okay! I'm thrilled! Oh, Ella, it'll be so good to see you. We'll put you up in one of our rooms. Wait until you see it! And I can have someone pick you up at the airport, and drive you back."

"No need. I'll rent a car. Listen, I'll call you later tonight. Right now I've gotta run, but I'll see you soon!"

Julie disconnected the call with a surge of happiness. *Wouldn't it be great if they could all be here?* she thought.

**

Kyle arranged for the first meeting to take place at a neutral location. When he suggested McDonald's, Julie nixed it immediately.

"I know kids like burgers and fries, and I'm not about to force health food on them, but how about the place next to your agency? Would that be all right?"

"Sure, Julie," Kyle said with a chuckle. "We just want the first meeting to take place away from the foster home and not in your house. The second meeting will be at Jingle Valley."

"As long as they don't hate us, right?"

Kyle looked at her with kind, compassionate eyes. "It'll be fine. These kids are sweet. They're social and mannered, and they will not hate you. Trust me."

So the following Thursday, Luke and Julie arrived early at the sandwich shop next to the agency in Hadley. When Julie asked about bringing gifts, Kyle had advised against it. It was nearly three o'clock and the restaurant was empty, except for an elderly couple.

"Here they are," Luke whispered as Julie turned. They stood up as Kyle ushered in a seven-year-old boy with milk-chocolate skin, a head of russet corkscrew curls, and a toothy smile. He was followed by a five-year-old girl with the same hair, just more of it, and large brown eyes with long lashes. She held Kyle's hand and looked away when she caught Julie's eye.

Luke offered a hand to Efren, who shook it solemnly. He crouched down to Efren's height. "I'm very happy to meet you, Efren. I'm Luke."

"I know your name already. Kyle told me. I'm seven."

As they conversed, Julie turned her attention to Kyle and Mishell. Taking a cue from Luke, she knelt down in front of the shy girl. "Hi, Mishell," she whispered. "I love your hair." A tiny smile escaped the girl's lips.

"Let's sit, shall we?" Kyle helped the children into their chairs and continued to guide the conversation effortlessly, drawing out responses from Efren, which wasn't difficult, and from Mishell, whose shyness dissipated over the forty minutes they were together.

Later, as Julie sat with the children, Kyle pulled Luke aside. "This went very well, especially with Mishell. I think we'll set up a visit to your house for next month. I'll bring them, but I'll make sure you have plenty of time without me hovering. Maybe we could have lunch or dinner there."

"Julie and I are getting married on April sixth," he said.

"Oh! That's great, congratulations. I'll make a note of that in your paperwork. Luke, this all looks good. You know, nothing moves at warp speed, and we do want to be sure, as we want you and Julie to be sure, too. But the way I'm seeing it, if everything goes as well as this first meeting did, we could be looking at late summer, early fall. If there's a way to place kids before a new school year begins, we try to do that. But no guarantees, you know that."

They shook hands, and both Efren and Mishell gave Julie and Luke hugs before leaving.

**

Luke spent his free time painting the bedrooms upstairs. Kyle had told them that Mishell loved everything blue, so Luke used shades from 'Summer Rain' to 'Deep Blue

Sea.'

"Look, we were going to paint these rooms anyway, right?" he asked one morning.

"I know, I just don't want to jinx anything. I was looking online at IKEA furniture. I just don't know if it's too early. They haven't even come to the house yet."

"Jules, make a list for now, okay? Kyle said Mishell likes elephants, Efren likes fish. Work with that."

"I'm so tired!" Julie said one morning a week later as they lingered over breakfast. "I know you are, too, honey."

"It just seems like there's a lot to do. Preparing for children is a lot different from preparing for a wedding, or a book club. I guess I'm glad it's a slower time at the shop right now."

"I heard from my brother Don yesterday. He and Linda are coming to the wedding!" Julie shook her head when Luke lifted the coffeepot.

"Well, that's good news about your brother. And your sister, and Tommy. What about Eric?"

She chewed a bagel and swallowed. "Haven't heard yet." She shrugged. "Could be traveling. I never know with him."

"He's the oldest, right? How many years between you

two?"

"Nineteen. My mother was twenty-one when Eric was born, and forty when I came along. Eric was already at college by then, so I never really spent any time with him."

"Well, it's great that the others are coming."

"I offered Ella one of the rooms in the barn. She's coming in late on Friday and has to leave early on Sunday. She's going to rent a car, as I imagine everyone else will, too."

"What else is a pressing need right now?"

"I need a wedding dress. When I can find the time."

"Jules. Find time. This is important."

"Maybe I'll take Freddy with me."

Luke chuckled. "He's probably your best bet. Well, I'm off." He kissed Julie, turned away and put his hand on the doorknob, then turned back to kiss her again, longer. She held the back of his neck as Luke dropped to his knees, encircling her waist and pressing his cheek to her belly.

"Oh, now I don't want you to leave," she breathed.

He checked his watch. "I could be a little late," he said, lifting her off the floor and carrying her into their bedroom.

**

When Freddy called later that morning, Julie had just stepped out of the shower.

"Good morning!"

"Ooh, I can hear that grin through the fiber-optic cable. You must have woken up on the sunny side this morning. Wait. Never mind, I don't need to know."

"I'm a blushing bride-to-be, Freddy. And I need a wedding dress."

"Are you telling me, or asking for my help?"

"You know I'm asking for your help."

"What else is on our schedule today?"

"Nothing. What about Val?"

Freddy let out a dramatic sigh. "I'm giving the playgroup another chance. Both Anya and Paige swore up and down they did not feed Valentino a Happy Meal. He must have seen it on TV."

Julie tapped her toe on the floor. "Let it go already, and come pick me up after you drop him off. I have a few places I want us to visit."

**

Four hours later, Julie was frustrated and hungry, Freddy was unenthused and also hungry, and they both decided to stop for lunch in Lenox.

"Is it me? Why is nothing right?" Julie picked at lettuce in her salad.

"It's partly you," Freddy said, sticking a sweet potato fry in his mouth. "You're picky, which is good. None of those dresses is right because they're not you."

She rested her chin in her hand. "I should just wear a dress I have."

"Nope," Freddy said. "That's not how it's going to be. This is your wedding, doll. Hopefully your one and only." He pulled out his phone, then glanced up at her. "I know, I know, our rule. No phones at meals. But let me make this one call." He tapped his phone and lifted it to his ear.

"Who are you calling?"

Freddy held up a finger. "Vienne? *Salut! Comment ça va?*"

Whatever else Freddy said next was lost on Julie, who couldn't understand his rapid French. She heard her name spoken once, but Freddy had turned sideways in his chair to speak and Julie couldn't catch his eye. He'd say, "*Oui oui*" multiple times, then laughed and said "*à bientôt*" before disconnecting and turning back to face her.

Julie spread her palms. "What was all that?"

Freddy wiped his mouth. "Either finish your salad or get a box. We have to leave." He raised his arm to signal their server, and when she approached their table, he handed her his credit card. "We need to leave." He cast his eyes at Julie's salad and added, "She doesn't need a box."

FORTY-TWO

"Where are we going?"

"To my friend Vienne's house."

"What friend Vienne? I've never heard of her. And why? Does she have an extra wedding dress?"

"No," Freddy said, keeping his eyes on the road. "She's going to make you one."

"What? Freddy, there isn't time!"

He made a sharp right turn down a side street and braked hard in front of a Victorian house painted pale green with dark violet trim. Lace curtains filigreed large windows and there was a wreath of shiny green shamrocks on the front door. It shimmered in the midday sun. Freddy jumped out of the car and opened Julie's door before she could undo her seat belt.

"Come *on*!" he urged.

Julie hustled from the car and trotted after Freddy's long strides up a concrete walk to the front porch. He pressed the doorbell and in the quiet neighborhood, Julie could hear chimes inside the house. Within seconds, a short woman with dark furrowed skin and snow-white hair opened the door.

"Fred-dee!" she chirped, hugging him. Her head was no higher than his chest.

"Vienne, Julie. Julie, Vienne." To Julie, he whispered, "She is the best."

"Joo-lee!" She hugged Julie as well. Julie could have rested her chin on Vienne's head, but she made sure not to.

"Hello, Vienne, it's nice to meet you." Julie glanced at Freddy again but he was already stepping inside the house. *Why am I just hearing about this woman now?*

"*Entrez, entrez,*" she said, welcoming them into her home.

Julie looked around. The double parlor, typical in Victorian homes, was covered with bolts of cloth, mannequins, tape measures. Toward the back, there were two sewing machines and two ironing boards, plus a long table where Julie assumed Vienne cut her fabric.

"Vienne, as I mentioned on the phone, we've been looking for the perfect dress for Julie's wedding, but we've had no luck."

"*Non,* they are not good. I make you a dress you will love!"

"Well..." Again Julie glanced at Freddy. "How did I not

know about this lovely woman, Freddy? We've been working together for years, but you've never mentioned her." She stared hard at her friend. *Well, it's true*, she thought, *who is she and why am I just hearing about her now? I know nothing about her credentials, her expertise. It's as if she materialized out of thin air.*

"Actually, I learned about Vienne from Jane Nevins. You remember Jane, don't you, Julie?" He turned to Vienne. "*Nous avons coordonné son mariage.*"

"Ah *oui*, Jane Nevins," Vienne said. Her lips pinched together and she looked like one of those dried-apple dolls. "Difficult."

"*Oui*," Julie said, laughing. "But her dress was…*magnifique.*"

Vienne nodded. She looked at Freddy and spoke again in rapid French.

"Jules, Vienne has a tough time with English, so I'm going to be her interpreter. She needs you to strip down." He pointed to a windowless corner of the room where a flimsy curtain hung.

"Oh. How stripped down are we talking? All the way? Because you need to leave for that."

"Even though I've seen you naked."

"I'm engaged. You don't get to see me naked anymore."

"Point taken. Leave your little thong on. I'll be in the kitchen drinking coffee." He said something to Vienne, who cackled and waved him off.

Julie stepped behind the curtain and removed her clothes, leaving on her bra and, unfortunately, the oldest pair of cotton panties she owned, chosen because everything else needed washing. When she emerged, Vienne was ready for her, holding a tape measure in her small hands.

"*Alors.*" She was quick with the measure, speaking aloud the measurements of Julie's bust, waist, and hips. Then she measured the length from her neck to her waist, from her shoulder to her wrist, and on and on, until Vienne had recorded a list of Julie's vitals.

"Fred-dee!" she called. Julie grabbed her shirt and struggled into it before Freddy entered the back room.

After she'd spoken, Freddy gave Julie an approving smile. "She said you've got a great figure. Now, what shade and what fabric?"

"And what style? Isn't that important?"

"Yeah, yeah. Sleeves? Please don't say you want sleeves."

"Don't roll your eyes at me. I'm modest. But no, I think sleeveless is nice. I'm pale, but so what?"

"Pale is the new tan. Lace? Silk? Satin?"

Vienne had no pictures, no bridal magazines. Julie knew what she didn't want, but how to describe what she envisioned?

"You know I'm simple with my taste. But I want elegant." She pulled out her phone and scrolled through her photos. "See this? I kept it because I saw it online and really liked it, but I didn't have any information about who had made it. And I didn't see anything like it when we were shopping."

Vienne peered at the small photo for minutes. She didn't say a word, but Julie felt that Vienne was memorizing it. Finally she handed the phone back to Julie and ran her small hands down Julie's sides to her hips. She cupped her palms under Julie's breasts and patted Julie's behind.

With a furtive glance at Freddy, Julie whispered, "This had better be good."

"Hey, I should ask her to make something for me. I haven't been felt up like that in months."

"Shut up."

"You think I'm kidding. I'm not. It's like having a roommate, not a husband."

"Why didn't you tell me?"

Freddy brushed it aside. "I don't know. I guess I was hoping it would change."

"Fred." Julie reached for his hand.

"Yeah, I know." The smile he gave her broke Julie's heart. "Let's get this dress made, okay?"

Vienne promised it would be ready by the first of April, and Julie hoped it wouldn't end up being a cruel April Fool's prank. She agreed to return on the nineteenth for a fitting and shook hands with tiny Vienne.

On the drive back to Dalton, Freddy was quiet. "I'm sorry I told you. It's nothing, really. He works hard, he's tired."

Julie thought about how tired Luke had been lately, but not so tired that he'd ignore her. Never that tired.

"Maybe you guys need a getaway. Without Val. Just the two of you. Would you like us to take Val for a long weekend?"

"I don't know if Bob wants to."

"Well then, ask him. Plan something and tell him. Maybe he just wants it planned out, you know?"

Freddy gripped the steering wheel like a newly-licensed driver. Ten and two. "Everything will be fine."

FORTY-THREE

Eric had emailed his regrets. *Not even a phone call?* He wrote that he had a business trip planned for early April and would be in Hong Kong. Couldn't be helped, he wrote, and wished her all the best. *Of course.*

The brother she barely knew wouldn't be at her wedding, but the rest of her family was going to fly across the country. For that Julie was grateful. Her dress was being created by the mysterious but delightful Vienne, and Freddy had promised to talk to Bob about his concerns.

"And of course now I'm getting sick," she muttered to herself. "All winter long I'm fine. I hate these late winter colds." She'd gotten a flu shot back in November, but she still felt like crap.

"Freddy, I'm going back to bed. I'm achy and tired and if I'm getting sick, I don't want you anywhere near me."

"What can I do for you? Chicken soup? I'll bring it by."

"No, nothing. I'm going to have Luke reschedule the social worker. I just need to sleep."

"Okay, doll. Feel better."

Julie pulled the shades and turned off her phone. She put

on her softest pajamas and fuzzy socks and crawled back into bed. And as soon as she did, she heard someone knocking on the front door. *Shit*. Had she locked the door? Would they go away?

She heard the door open. *Dammit!* She got out of bed. "Who is it?" she called in a wobbly voice.

"Julie? It's me, Sarah." The diminutive girl did have free access to her kitchen, but still.

"Hey, Sarah." Julie leaned against the doorway, arms folded across her chest.

"Oh! Are you sick?" Sarah eyes grew big in her small face as she took a step back toward the door.

"I dunno. I feel crappy, probably the start of a cold. I figured I'd go back to bed for a little while. You need the kitchen? Help yourself."

"I was hoping to do some baking, but I don't want to disturb you."

"You won't, don't worry. I'll close my door."

"Julie!"

Julie turned back. "Yes?"

Sarah stared at her for a moment, a look of concern etched on her face. Then her features softened. "Nothing. Everything is good."

Julie frowned, but that was Sarah. Hard to figure out. She padded back to her bedroom.

**

Hours later, Julie awoke to the smell of cinnamon. She stretched and slid out of bed. The house was quiet and Sarah was gone, but there were freshly-baked cinnamon muffins in a covered basket on the counter. And a loaf of lemon bread in the refrigerator. *Oh, Sarah, I love you.*

She felt better after having slept, and half-filled the empty coffeemaker with water. She pulled a bag of dark roast from a shelf and opened it. But as soon as she took a whiff of the ground beans, her stomach lurched in protest. *Coffee never bothered me before*, she told herself.

Julie paused and stood motionless in the kitchen. *Oh no. Am I?*

Ten minutes later, she had her answer. Julie stared down at the stick in her hand and took slow, measured breaths as her mind tried to catch up.

"Two children and a baby." She stood alone in her kitchen, then picked up the basket of cinnamon muffins and sat down hard at the table. She lifted the cloth covering the basket and took out two muffins. *Luke. How am I going to tell Luke?*

**

By noon, Julie was showered and dressed and driving to

Luke. She ignored the calls from Freddy, but managed to sneak a text in while she was waiting at a stop light.

I'm fine driving now later

She found a parking spot just down from the flower shop, but her feet moved as though she was wearing leaden boots. The little bell tinkled as she entered. One woman was browsing, so Julie stood back, out of the way. When Luke looked up and caught her eye, he waved. She waved back and smiled.

The woman placed an order and paid, then smiled at Julie on her way out.

"This is a surprise! Did you come to take me to lunch?"

"If you can get away, otherwise I'll skip down to the deli and bring sandwiches back."

"Libby's in the back. Hang on." Luke disappeared into the back room and when he came back out, Libby, the twentyish assistant he'd hired, accompanied him.

"Hey, Julie." Libby was a quiet girl, with perennially red cheeks and a dimpled smile. She wore eyeglasses with green frames, a cute contrast to her long strawberry-blond hair. Luke said she loved working in the shop and wanted to study botany.

"Hey, Libby. We're just going to the deli for lunch. Want me to bring anything back for you?"

"No, thanks. I brought mine."

"Okay, back soon," Luke called as they exited the shop.

**

Once they'd secured a tiny table in the deli, Julie wished she'd thought of a quieter place. It was the height of lunch hour, and this was the best deal in town for hungry workers. Luke stood at the counter to order a pastrami on rye for himself, and a turkey on wheat for her. He came back to the table with two bottles of water and a ticket.

"What's your number?"

He glanced down at the scrap of paper. "Seventeen."

"Lucky number," she murmured.

"Is it?"

Julie looked up and into his eyes. "I hope so. I'm pregnant."

In the seconds that followed, it was as if the cacophony of the crowded deli had dissipated into the ceiling. Julie waited for Luke's reaction.

He walked his fingers over to her hand and grasped it. "For real?"

"For real. Well, those sticks are pretty accurate. I took two tests. Both of them said yes."

"Holy cow, Jules," he whispered.

"I know. We wanted one, and we're about to have three."

"You don't know how far along?"

Julie shook her head. "I've been tired, you know? But we're both tired, trying to get everything ready in the house, planning the wedding. This morning I went back to bed, and when I got up, I started to make coffee. I couldn't even bear the smell of it and I wondered. So I took a test. And then another. And then I drove here."

"Julie Tate." Luke's voice caught and Julie squeezed his hand.

"I know. But you're happy, right?" *Please be happy.*

"Are you kidding? I'm ecstatic." He pulled her hand to his lips as a piercing voice called out, "NUMBER SEVENTEEN!"

FORTY-FOUR

After lunch, Julie decided to drive straight to Freddy's house. This wasn't the kind of news to deliver over the phone. She remembered the conversation they'd had when he and Bob had decided to adopt little Valentino. Freddy and Bob had come together to Julie's house. She was scrubbing out the bathtub and was not prepared for guests, but Freddy said it didn't matter. She'd pulled off the rubber gloves and put on a pot of coffee and screamed with joy when they told her.

As she turned down their road, Julie saw Freddy's car in the driveway, and another vehicle, unfamiliar, parked behind it. *I should have let him know I was coming*, she said to herself.

Pulling to the curb, she sent him a text:

Hey, I'm right outside your house! But it looks like you have company. Bad time?

She lowered the car window for some fresh air and waited for a reply.

Ding! Wish you'd let me know. Not the best time, doll.

She wrote back.

OK, sorry I didn't c all first. Heading home. Call me when you can. xxx

**

Julie walked into the downstairs den/office and looked around. While it made sense to turn it into a nursery, would Mishell and Efren feel weird about it? Being upstairs, separated from their new parents and a new baby? They were coming to the house next month, and both Julie and Luke wanted to have their rooms ready. *I can't separate the kids.*

She stood in the middle of the office/nursey and talked to herself. "Hold on, Julie, it's early. The baby's not coming for months." *How many months? Six? Seven?* She knew she needed to call her doctor and make an appointment. Add another thing to the list.

Freddy was handling the fiftieth birthday party scheduled for the following weekend, and Julie had the book club meeting on Thursday at six. They always wanted 'pickies,' as they called them, but 'pickies' usually meant heavy hors d'oeuvres. At cheese-and-cracker prices. She'd ask Sarah to make mini quiches and cookies. The book club members were told they could bring their own wine if they wanted, otherwise Julie set out coffee and tea.

There was something else scheduled, she thought. *What was it? Dammit, where's Freddy?*

As if on cue, he drove up. Julie watched him exit his car and noted the slump of his shoulders, the way he dragged his feet. She opened the door to the kitchen.

"Hey, you! Sorry about earlier. I never just show up, and I should have let you know."

He kissed her cheeks. "It's okay."

"No, I should have texted you before I was parked in front of your house."

He blew out a breath and pulled a chair away from the table. He stared at his feet before dropping heavily into the chair.

"Hey, what's going on?"

"I met with a lawyer this afternoon."

Julie's hand flew to her mouth. "What? Why?"

He shook his head. "Bob doesn't know. I just want to find out what my options are." He looked up at Julie, who was still standing in front of him. "Come on, sit with me. Things aren't any better. And now I think he might be seeing someone." Freddy took an angry swipe at his eyes. "We have a child together!"

"Hang on for a minute. Let me catch up. So, you haven't had a talk with him and now you think Bob's *seeing* someone? For real?"

"I don't know. I'm just trying to stay ahead of things, you know, just in case."

"You *have* to talk to Bob. Freddy, you still love him, don't you?"

"Very much," he said quietly. "I don't want to lose him. And I don't know what to do to keep him."

"Okay, honey." Julie scootched her chair up next to his so she could wrap her arms around him. "So the first thing you do is tell him. Tell him you're worried. Tell him you love him. Tell him you and Val need him. And if you need a professional counselor, do that, too."

Freddy nodded but kept his eyes lowered. After a beat, he looked up.

"What about you? You never come over without calling. What's going on?"

"Nothing really."

"Stop it. You came over for a reason. Is everything okay with *you two*?"

"I'm pregnant."

Freddy's jaw dropped. "Get out! Seriously, Jules? Oh. Em. Gee."

"Yep."

"Luke knows, right? Of course he knows."

"Yes, I did tell Luke before I told you, Freddy."

"Good. Wow. Julie, three kids! What's the name for an Octomom with only three?"

"Don't even start," she laughed. "I might need you to speak with Vienne. Probably going to need a looser waist."

"Ha, yeah." He paused and looked deep into her eyes. "You're such a good friend, you know that?"

"Right back at you."

**

Freddy took care of the birthday party and told Julie to take the evening off. But she couldn't, she had to check on decorations and food.

"Will you give me some credit, doll? I've been at this game as long as you have. I know what I'm doing."

"I know, I just like being involved. Hey, did you talk with Bob?"

"After two failed attempts, yes. We had a long talk last night. I drank too much, but I told him I was worried about us."

"Did you tell him about the lawyer?"

"Good lord, no! And I think we'll be okay. We're going to have a real vacation, right after your wedding. Paige is going to take Val."

"Good! Where are you going?"

Freddy rubbed his palms together. "Islamorada, in the Keys. April can be busy, so I found a place that won't be as crowded."

"I'm happy for you, Freddy. Really."

"Me too. Bob acknowledged that he'd been distant. He said it's like we lead two separate lives sometimes, and I know what he means. We interact with completely different people during the day, so there's no common thread to discuss at night. I talk about Val, but we need to be adults sometimes. Do you get it? Of course you don't. But you will, Jules. You'll see. Valentino is everything to us, but our lives can't always revolve around him. I think this little getaway will be perfect."

"Well, if Paige needs help, make sure you give her my number. We can't take a honeymoon, anyway, but it's fine. We're having the kids come to the house next month, probably for an overnight. Unless they go ballistic."

"Stop it, they're going to love it here. The first meeting went well, didn't it?"

"It did. I was so nervous! But they need to come here, get a feel for the place. If it goes well, we'll try to have them come once a week or so. Our social worker is very optimistic. We still don't have a definite date, but it's probably sooner than we think. Once they're here, I won't be as available for Val."

"Yeah, but I'm going to bring him over all the time anyway. What's one more kid, right?"

"Shut up," she said, smiling. "I've got the book club covered tonight, and what did you say was going on this weekend?"

Freddy waved his hand in the air, swatting an imaginary fly. "Baby shower. Brittany Davis, remember her mom Lorraine? They used to live way up on Tower Road. The girl is nineteen and the father was sent off to army training in Georgia. Mom's planned it down to everything. We're just supposed to stand there and watch, I guess."

"What's she having?"

"No idea. I asked Lorraine. Apparently they're doing a 'gender reveal' at the shower. Sarah's been tasked with baking the cake, and she's the only one who knows what color to make the inside. Big secret." He rolled his eyes.

"I don't know, that's kind of cute. Maybe I'll do something like that, when the time comes."

"We'll think of something better for you, doll."

FORTY-FIVE

Julie headed back to Vienne's seamstress shop, this time
without Freddy, who was busy getting the baby shower
ready. She'd asked him to call ahead and explain things
to Vienne, as she knew they had difficulty
communicating. As she parked in front of the grand
Victorian, she wondered if she should have waited until
he was free.

"She just needs to adjust a little," Julie muttered,
slamming the car door and walking up the concrete path
to the front porch. She rang the bell and waited. And
waited. Frustrated, she pressed the button next to the
door again, this time holding her finger there while she
counted to four. After what seemed like minutes, Vienne
opened the door.

"Oui, oui, j'arrive." Vienne opened the door and stepped
aside as Julie walked in.

"So. Hi. Freddy? He told you? *Je suis enceinte?*"
Cupping her hands around her belly, Julie thought, *some
words I remember.*

"Oui. Come please." She picked up her tape measure and
gestured to Julie to remove her sweater. Then she
wrapped the tape around Julie's waist and squinted at the
number. Julie bent forward to look as well. *Twenty-nine?*

Really?

"*Vingt-neuf,*" Vienne said quietly, then lifted the tape to encircle Julie's chest. With a wink, she added, "*Trente-sept, très bien.*" Julie pulled her sweater back over her breasts. From a thirty-four to a thirty-seven practically overnight. No wonder Luke was always smiling.

To get the bigger boobs, I have to take the bigger stomach, too, she reminded herself.

"It's okay?"

Vienne rested her hand on Julie's belly. She appeared to go into a trance and swayed slightly, and when she opened her raisin eyes, her cheeks pleated in merriment before she clucked, "*Oui*, okay. *Un fils*. A boy for you."

A son? Was that a prediction? How could she know that? And, Julie thought, *she's got a fifty-fifty chance of being right.*

She slipped into the still-unfinished dress and stood statue-like as Vienne muttered. The waist of the cream silk dress would be lifted to Empire style, and the cap sleeves would be embellished with tiny rhinestones. A little bit of bling for the relatively modest bride.

"I'll be back on the second for the final fitting." Julie paused. "*Avril le deux.*" She held up two fingers.

"Okay, Joo-lee!" Vienne grasped Julie's hands in hers, and Julie bent down to kiss both of her cheeks, in the

French custom.

As she waved goodbye and walked back to her car, Julie said a silent prayer that this woman knew what she was doing.

**

On Saturday, Julie peeked into the barn as Zack and two assistants worked on decorations. Everywhere she looked there was pink and baby blue, as well as pale yellow and green. A sea of pastels, like the M&Ms that came out at Easter, or those Jordan almonds that were fashionable years ago. Her sister Ella had come home from a wedding with a little net bag of them, and Julie remembered cracking a tooth on the hard-shelled nut. No Jordan almonds at her wedding!

"Hi, Zack," she called to him. The big man stepped down from a ladder, where he'd been fastening crepe paper streamers from the chandelier to the corners of the room. Brittany Davis's mom had gone to town on this one. "Is Sarah baking the cake?"

Zack nodded, his dark shaggy hair falling over his broad forehead. "I can't go home until she says so," he deadpanned, but Julie noticed the corners of his mouth turn upwards.

"Oh, that's right. The gender reveal. Do you think she'll let me see it?"

"Not a chance, Julie. Don't even try. Actually, she likes

peace and quiet when she bakes."

"That's true. She could have used my kitchen, you know."

"Nope. Said she wanted to do this one in her own home. No peeking." He raised a long finger and waved it ominously, but Zack's dark eyes glittered with mirth.

Julie laughed. "Fine. The place looks great. What time does this happen? Four?"

"Five. And it ends by nine sharp. Freddy's orders."

"Okay. Well, maybe after dinner Luke and I will stop by. You can always call me if you need anything."

Zack smiled again, a rarity for him. He looked much less threatening when he smiled.

**

Luke arrived home earlier than usual, and Julie hadn't even started dinner.

"You closed up early?" she said as he shrugged off his jacket. It wasn't warm yet—they were lucky if the temperature reached fifty during the day, but Luke refused to wear his winter parka any longer.

"Yep, all done." He wrapped his arms around her. "How are you feeling?"

"I'm fine! Freddy's got a baby shower in the barn soon.

I told him we'd stop by after supper. But I haven't even started yet." She opened the freezer. "Tortellini? Or veggie burgers?"

"It can wait, babe. Don't worry about it."

"Aren't you hungry?"

Luke smiled. "I'm not starving. Are you?"

Julie felt her cheeks turn warm. "I've been snacking all afternoon. But I'll cook if you're hungry."

"Let's go next door and see if they need anything."

"Oh! I thought we'd head over later."

"If we go now, we won't have to go later."

"Smart man. That's why I'm going to marry you."

"I thought it was because I knocked you up." His arm around her waist made her remember her wedding dress. Vienne had assured her that it would be beautiful.

"Well, that, too. Come on then." She pulled him with her as they left the warm house and trekked across the yard to the barn.

The double doors were open and Julie could see inside. The pastel streamers looked a lot better than she thought they would. Not high school prom-like at all. With tons of white twinkling lights, the effect was actually chic and festive. *Leave it to Freddy*, she thought.

There were people gathered at the far end of the room, near the bar. *For a baby shower?* But as she and Luke stepped inside, the group turned around and shouted, "Surprise!"

Julie turned to look behind her. Where was Brittany Davis? Where was her mom, Lorraine, a girl Julie remembered from high school who was a few years ahead of her? Luke, whose arm hadn't left Julie's waist, leaned in close and whispered in her ear, "We got you, Jules. Welcome to your bridal shower!"

"What? My shower? This is for me?"

Freddy took his usual long strides to meet her at the entrance. "We had to do pastels, doll. Otherwise you would have caught on."

"I love the pastels! Very spring-like. I just can't believe it. How did I not know?" She looked past him to see so many friends from town, vendors, suppliers, even some of the women from the book club! There was Bob, looking handsome in a dark button-down shirt and slim slacks. He looked like he'd lost weight.

"Hi, honey," he crooned. "And surprise!" He kissed her cheek and she thought how good he smelled.

"Were you in on this, too?" She gave Bob a playful poke in the chest.

"Only as needed. Freddy is the genius behind this." He slung his arm around Freddy's shoulders and Julie beamed. *They're good*, she thought. *They're fine.*

"Come on, hon." Luke kept a grip on her hand as they walked into the main room, where tables were set with pastel floral arrangements. Along the long side wall, there was a buffet table that echoed the colorful theme. *Freddy!* she thought. Bowls of cut-up fruit: yellow peaches, green kiwi, orange slices, red strawberries. Yellow, orange, and red pepper strips, celery, carrots, and a dip that was actually pink. As she turned questioning eyes to her friend, he laughed.

"Goat cheese and sun-dried tomatoes, doll. I made sure it was pink."

"Wow. I'm speechless." A protective hand rested on her belly, now a barely-noticeable curve.

For the next three hours, Julie laughed and chatted with her guests. Out of the corner of her eye, she spied a ribbon-festooned basket full of envelopes. *Whatever cash is in there, we'll put aside for the kids,* she promised silently. *For all of them.*

"Julie!" The voice was familiar, as was the face, but it took Julie too long to smile, and Mary Jo Browning made a face. "It's me, Mary Jo!" Her yellow hair was cut short and she must have gotten contact lenses. Or that corrective surgery. She looked great.

"Of course, I know! I'm just so overwhelmed tonight, my brain isn't operating at normal speed." *She has a daughter. What's the kid's name, dammit? Wait.* "And how is Taylor?" *Whew.*

Mary Jo's face split into a wide grin. "She's great, thanks for asking! She's almost ten, you know. Such a good girl."

"And how about you, Mary Jo? How are *you* doing?"

"I'm good. Still single, but all of my effort goes to Taylor." She looked away for a moment, to a place behind Julie's head. "But you found yourself a hottie! Good for you, Julie. And did I hear that you're going to adopt?"

Ah, nothing stays secret in this little town, Julie said to herself.

"Thanks, and yes. A brother and sister. They're wonderful. It's not finalized yet, so I haven't said anything (*and still you knew about it*), but we're very close. Hopefully this summer." She took a step closer to Mary Jo and lowered her voice. "And I'll let you in on a secret. I'm expecting."

The word was barely out of her mouth when Mary Jo screamed, loud enough for most of the guests to stop and turn in her direction. *Wonderful, Julie. Might as well grab the microphone and make the announcement.* Mary Jo had covered her mouth with her hand, but the curiosity hadn't gone away.

"What's going on?" Pauline Crane, from the farmhouse up the road, approached. "Are you all right, MJ?"

"Oh, *I'm* fine. But you should be asking the bride-to-be here."

Oh, for crying out loud. Julie forced a smile. "I suppose it won't be a secret for long," she said, casting her eyes on Mary Jo, who was oblivious to the silent rebuke. "Luke and I are expecting."

Pauline threw her arms around Julie and whispered into her hair. "Wonderful news, honey. But now that you told Mary Jo, the entire town will know before long. Maybe you and Luke would rather tell them yourselves, before she does."

Julie nodded and patted her friend on the shoulder. "Excuse me."

She found Luke and pulled him away from his group. "We need to announce my pregnancy," she said.

"Why? This is your wedding shower, honey."

"Because I slipped and told Mary Jo Browning, and if we don't tell our guests, I guarantee she will before this evening is over."

Luke grimaced and rolled his eyes. "You told the town crier."

"I know, I know. Come on, let's do this. I'd rather they hear it from us."

FORTY-SIX

Julie had never been as tired as she was on the day before her wedding. She struggled to get out of bed, even though the list of things to do was a mile long. *I can't wait to go back on caffeine*, she thought.

Five of her relatives were flying in from out west—Ella coming from San Diego, Tommy and Maria and Don and Linda all on the same flight from Phoenix. No one needed to be picked up at the airport, thankfully. Judge Snow was confirmed. Freddy was handling everything—food, music, RSVPs, and Julie tried not to think about anything except looking her best. *It would help if I could sleep*, she told herself.

"Do you know what I want to do today?" Luke asked, handing her a steaming mug of herbal tea.

"I'm afraid to guess," she said. She pushed the mug away and pulled apart a blueberry scone.

"Tomorrow is going to be chaotic, even with Freddy taking care of the details. People coming and going constantly. Even our house here will be full of people."

"You want to elope?"

Luke chuckled. "Don't think it hasn't crossed my mind,

you know." He plucked a muffin from the plate and peeled off the paper liner, setting is aside before taking a gentle bite. Julie noticed her scone was gone and she desperately wanted a second.

"What is it then?"

"I think we should take the day and go somewhere. Tell Freddy we need to be away from the house and the barn. Come back at night."

"What about the rehearsal dinner?"

"We'll be back in time. It's not until six."

"Where should we go?"

"I'd like to surprise you, but if I tell you there's a body of water involved, would that be enough to satisfy your curiosity?"

"Probably not," she laughed. "Are we driving or flying?"

"Driving. Unfortunately, we can't fly to the Bahamas and be back in time for the rehearsal dinner."

"That's a shame."

"Jules, life is about to change for us. And I don't mean just being married. In most ways I feel as though we're already married. But once Mishell and Efren arrive, and then with our own baby on the way, we're not going to have much time alone together. I want us to have this one day."

Julie nodded. He was right. "Is it a long drive?"

Luke glanced at his watch. "Long enough that we should head out now. I sent Freddy a text. He'll take care of everything."

It wasn't just that Luke loved her, it was that he understood her. He knew that she tolerated some surprises, as long as they were thought out and reasonable. He understood that her wedding day would be filled with emotion, that she'd be missing her parents, but that traveling to another place would be a welcome distraction. He was confident that Freddy would handle whatever might come up and not call or text while they were away.

"I'll get my jacket."

**

The surprise turned out to be Lake George, a two-hour drive north and east from Dalton. They crossed into New York at Lebanon Springs, named for the once-famous thermal waters, and continued west toward the capital of Albany, where traffic increased and Julie felt herself tense.

Thirty years earlier, on a drive into Albany, her father's Dodge Omni was hit by a sixteen-year-old driving a massive Buick Riviera. Everyone survived, but the teenager denied responsibility and her father suffered a fractured femur that never healed properly. Julie hated driving through Albany.

Once they'd passed the worst of it, Julie allowed herself to relax. They neared Troy, the home of Rensselaer Polytechnic Institute, where Eric had gone to school, and the all-women's Russell Sage College, where Ella had studied childhood education. By the time Julie was three, Eric had graduated and Ella was a junior, and she rarely saw either of them.

"It's too bad Eric can't be at the wedding," she murmured.

"I know, honey. What did he say again? He's traveling?"

"Hong Kong. Couldn't be helped. He did send us a very generous check. Still, I'll be glad to see the others. And your family, of course."

"It's just my sister and her husband, and a couple of friends who live in Florida." He stole a quick look at her while driving. "Are you disappointed?"

"No! Of course not! I didn't want a *big* wedding, Luke. I think there are going to be more people there than I'm comfortable with, but I left it up to Freddy, and, you know…"

"I know." He laughed and navigated around a construction site at Saratoga Springs.

**

By eleven o'clock, they had arrived at the lake. Still early in the season, most of the smaller shops were still closed. **See you in May!** was posted on the doors. Only the larger chain stores and supermarkets were open daily.

"One request, though," Luke said. "Can we please leave the phones turned off? Maybe even put them in the glovebox?"

"Good idea," Julie said, taking both of them and locking them away. "No distractions today."

They walked hand-in-hand down Beach Road, and stopped for lunch in a rustic-looking taproom. Dark paneling inside lent a cozy, if dim, atmosphere, and they slid into an empty booth along one wall. Black-and-white photographs of vintage Lake George adorned the walls. As hungry as she was, Julie opted for a salad. Vienne hadn't let her dress out *that* much, after all.

"You have a lot of events booked for spring and summer, don't you?" Luke asked, eating a burger like he had no worries about fitting into his suit. Because he actually had no worries about fitting into his suit. Luke stayed slim no matter what he ate.

"Mmm," Julie replied, chewing lettuce and cucumber. She eyed his French fries with lust, but wouldn't permit herself to snatch even one, fearing it would open the Pandora's box of her ravenous appetite. *Steady, Jules.*

"Is Freddy willing to take on the bulk of the work?"

"Why would he?"

"Julie, our family needs are going to shift dramatically. Mishell and Efren come for an overnight in two weeks, but we'll probably have them every week until they're ours forever. Kyle said it could even happen by the end of June. Everything's about to change. For both of us."

She used her fork to swirl salad around in her large wooden bowl. "But you get to go to work away from home every day, and I don't."

"They're going to need a lot of attention. I can take some time away whenever it's possible, and I will, of course. But it's not just Mishell and Efren. You need to take care of yourself, too. You can't work at a frenetic pace. It's all different, honey."

"Like I don't know that?" She set down her fork. "Sorry. I didn't mean for it to sound so sharp."

"Jules, I know this is a bad time to bring it up, but Freddy's going to have to take on the bulk of the work. Or you're going to have to hire someone who can help him."

"You're right, it is a bad time to bring it up. I thought you brought me here to de-stress."

"Point taken. We'll let it go today. Just something to think about."

"They have cheesecake. I want some. Two bites."

**

They were quieter on the ride back. Luke concentrated on driving, and Julie closed her eyes, feigning a nap. But all she could do was toss his words around in her already-crammed-full mind. *What is he asking? I can't quit my job. Summertime is always busy, and if we do get the kids at the end of June, they won't be in school. It would give me more time to bond with them. I could do more work at night, after they're in bed. Kids that age still go to bed early, right? We'll deal with it.*

But Julie knew that Luke was right. They'd agreed to take two small children into their home, into their lives, and there was no turning back. Everything would change, as Luke had said. And if she wasn't ready, she'd better get ready. Preparing to welcome adopted children into their home was more than just painting the bedrooms and putting together IKEA furniture. They'd finished the preparatory classes, they'd found a pediatrician and a children's dentist.

It's not as if I expect it all to go perfectly, Julie thought. *There will be adjustment issues, but we'll love these kids so much. We'll do whatever it takes to help them adjust.*

"Am I being naïve?" Julie asked aloud.

"What?"

"I mean, am I not prepared for them? Do I expect too much?" And the real question: "Are we making a mistake, Luke?"

There was a rest stop ahead, and Luke pulled over. He parked the car and switched it off, giving the engine a chance to rest. Turning to Julie, he cupped her face in his warm hands. "We're definitely not making a mistake, honey. It's normal to feel this way. One step at a time. I want more than anything to be married to you. Do you feel the same way?"

"I do!" In spite of her worries, she laughed.

"See? Who needs a rehearsal dinner? We know our lines." He turned on the ignition. "Everything will be fine, trust me. We need to get back if we're going to make this rehearsal dinner."

"Okay. Don't get a speeding ticket."

FORTY-SEVEN

They made it back to Jingle Valley with ten minutes to spare.

"But it was worth it, wasn't it?" Luke asked with a grin as he unbuckled his seat belt.

"It was a wonderful day," Julie said. "Is everyone here?"

"Probably. Come on, let's go in."

Julie fished their phones from the glovebox and clicked hers back on. Thirty-seven messages. *Uh-oh, that can't be good*, she thought. "Luke, hold up." She scrolled quickly through the texts as he walked back to her.

"What is it?"

She lifted a finger. "Oh, shit," she muttered, grasping his arm with her free hand. "Bob's been in an accident. All of these messages are from Freddy. He's at the hospital with him."

As Luke took his turned-off phone from her trembling hand, he gave Julie a guilty look. "One of us should have had ours turned on, I guess. I'm sorry, honey."

"I am, too. We need to find out what's going on." They

ran from the car into the barn.

**

Julie's brother Tommy met them at the door. "What happened, Jules? Freddy finally got a hold of me, after he couldn't reach you."

"I know. We were out all day and had our phones off. Is Bob all right?"

"Far as I know. You should call Fred. Hey, he asked me if I could stand up with Luke. You know I'll do it, Jules," Tommy said.

"Thanks," she said, her eyes glued to her phone. She dialed Freddy's number but it went straight to voice mail. Catching her breath, she scrolled through his messages.

Call me. ASAP

Where are you? I need you to call me!

Bob's in the hospital. Accident. PLEASE call me.

WTF Jules

"Do you know what happened?" Julie searched Tommy's face for a clue. Would anyone know?

He shook his head. "Car accident is all I heard. Try Judge Snow."

She made a beeline for the justice of the peace, whose

face changed when he spotted her.

"Julie! We were all so worried! First Freddy, er, well, Bob…"

"Do you know what happened?"

Judge Snow ran a meaty hand through a thick shock of white hair—*snowy white*, Julie said to herself—and puffed out his jowly cheeks.

"He was driving home from work and got sideswiped by a kid. It pushed his car off the road near Berkshire Crossing, and another car hit him."

"Oh no. Is he going to be okay?"

The judge nodded. "Looks like it. He was awake when they transported him. Freddy's there with him."

"And Valentino? Their son? Where is he?" *I should have been here.*

"One of his friends has him. Freddy felt awful about missing this. He probably won't be here for the wedding tomorrow."

Julie nodded. "Of course not." She turned to Luke. "Should we postpone it?"

"We can't, honey. Everyone flew in for this."

Julie looked around the great room of the barn. Freddy had done such a beautiful job of decorating. And now he wouldn't even be able to be here.

"Julie!" Her brother Don, sister-in-law Linda, and her big sister Ella were walking toward her and Luke. Quickly, she shifted gears and pasted a big smile on her face. Don was first to embrace her.

"It's been too long, sis. Congratulations, and the place looks amazing."

"That's my partner Freddy's doing," she choked out. "He's the genius of our business."

"I'm so sorry about his friend," Linda said. "But from what we heard, he'll be okay."

"Bob's his husband, Linda."

She turned to her sister Ella, who enveloped her into a warm hug and whispered in her ear, "Why don't you do a quick run-through here and get to the hospital? We're all settled in, and we'll spend time tomorrow. These are your friends, Jules."

Julie looked straight into her sister's eyes. For as long as she could remember, Ella was a good three inches taller, but now they stood level with each other. Had Ella shrunk? There were fine lines around the corners of her eyes and mouth. She no longer colored her hair, which was silvery gray and spiky. Earrings of turquoise and silver dangled against her neck, a neck that had seen a lot of sun out in sunny San Diego.

"Thanks. I'll let Judge Snow know that we'll just quickly go through the ceremony." She said the same to Luke, who transmitted it to the judge.

Judge Snow cleared his throat, then let the assembled guests know.

**

Julie rushed through the rehearsal, anxious to speak with Freddy. "Look, we know what to do. Don is going to walk me in. Luke, you'll be there, standing with Tommy. When I get to you, Judge Snow begins. Right?"

"Er, yes," the judge replied.

"We have the rings." She cast a quick glance to Luke, who nodded. "And we didn't write vows. There just wasn't time, but we're willing to say 'I do' to whatever you ask of us," Julie joked, but no one laughed.

Luke pulled her to one side. "Honey, I know you want to talk to Fred. But everyone is here and we're all going to have dinner. All right? You can't do anything for Bob right now. He's being taken care of and he has Fred with him." Luke's fingers circled her wrist, and she lifted her eyes to his.

"I know. You're right." She turned around to face her family members.

"Sorry, everyone. I'm really excited you're all here!" She conveniently omitted mentioning Eric's absence. "Why don't we all sit down and eat? Judge Snow, please stay."

"Thank you, but I'm unable to stay. I'll see you back here tomorrow at three." He waved and left the barn.

Julie sighed. "I can't believe this," she said. Then, realizing she sounded as self-absorbed as Jane Nevins, she added, "Everyone, let's have dinner." She pivoted and lowered her voice. "Should I call him, Luke?"

"Send him a text, let him know you're here. He'll call if he can."

He's probably so mad at me right now, Julie thought.

**

Once the rehearsal dinner, which was really just dinner, was over, Julie made her excuses and grabbed Luke's arm. "Come on, we have to go to the hospital."

"It's an hour's drive, Julie."

"What? Isn't he at Berkshire Medical?"

"No, they took him to Great Barrington. Did you text him? I don't think we should visit unless we're invited."

"Really? This is Freddy!"

"Yes, and Bob's the one who was hurt. Go ahead, try to call him. I'll leave you in peace. Give them both our love." Luke kissed her and walked back to their house.

Her siblings and in-laws had all left, all gone upstairs to the rooms in the barn or back to their hotel. Julie didn't know whether Don and Linda or Tommy and Maria had taken the bridal suite. She knew Ella would be in her room, probably telling Jeanine about the disastrous day. Julie shook her head to clear the thought. Well, it was true—the day had been a disaster, even if it hadn't started out that way.

She called Freddy. When he answered, his voice was ragged.

"Hey, doll."

"Freddy. Oh my god, Freddy, I'm just sick over this. How is Bob?"

"He'll be okay. Broken foot and they're watching him for concussion. He was lucky."

"He was," she breathed. "Freddy, I'm sorry I wasn't there for you. I turned my phone off."

"It's okay. You had good reason not to want to be bothered. We're all so dependent on knowing everything immediately. I was panicked, and I'm sorry about all the messages."

"I feel awful. Luke and I went to Lake George for the day and just needed some quiet time."

"Everything all right with you two?"

"Yes. We're fine. But when we came back and I turned on my phone, oh, Freddy. I let you down. And you've never ever let me down."

"Oh, sure I have, Jules. Don't worry about anything. And don't cry! Come on, you're getting married tomorrow! I'm just sorry I can't be there, but I have to be here with Bob."

"Of course you do. I wouldn't have it any other way. Is Val okay?"

"He's fine. He's with Brooklynn having a sleepover. Funny, a couple of months ago he'd wail when I left him, and today he seemed thrilled."

"He's growing up."

"Stop. You'll know this feeling soon enough. Hey, how are you feeling?"

"Other than being worried about Bob and you? I'm fine."

"And the fam? Everyone is in town?"

"They're here. Well, not Eric. Don's going to walk me in."

"Everything will be splendid, Jules. Luke's got the flowers all set, the food will be great, the music…oh, crap. The band."

"What?"

"Oh, Julie. I forgot to confirm the band. Shit. I'm so sorry."

Shit. Julie took a breath. "Um, maybe I can call them in the morning? They might be available."

"I'm really sorry. I dropped the ball."

"Stop it. It doesn't matter. I'll give them a call." She racked her brain for anything else before she let him go. "Was anyone else invited that said no? I know we talked about it a few days ago."

He groaned. "Yes. April and Bill let me know this morning that they wouldn't be able to make it. I think she has a job out of state somewhere. She was so sorry to miss out. Bill, too."

"Oh. That is too bad. I was hoping to see them again. Well, maybe they'll come for a visit sometime. Meet my new family."

"Listen, doll, I need to go."

"Sure, Freddy. Hey, thanks for everything. I love you."

"I love you, too. Next time I see you you'll be married."

FORTY-EIGHT

How does one feel on their wedding day? Excited? Nervous? Julie felt sick. Not because of marrying Luke, of course not. She was just as good as married to him, anyway. They'd been living under the same roof for months. She washed his dirty underwear.

But that morning, she woke with waves of nausea. *I thought I was finished with morning sickness*, she fumed silently. Dry heaves took over her body and she knelt on the cool tiled floor of their downstairs bathroom, waiting for the next regurgitation.

Luke was already up and out of the house. He had managed to get two experienced florists to come in and run the shop for the day, but they couldn't work on Sunday, so he'd be closed. He'd lettered a sign for the front door: **CLOSED today as I celebrate my marriage! Back in business Monday (very understanding wife)**

Julie heaved again, her stomach muscles protesting against the contractions. *I should call Dr. Wilde, just to be safe.* She had no idea what time it was, but, craning her neck to look past the bathroom door to the bedroom, she noticed some light at the curtained window. She hoisted herself to her feet and checked to make sure she wasn't bleeding. Then she moved slowly to her telephone and called her doctor.

"You're at fourteen weeks, Julie. This is still normal. Don't worry, the morning sickness should be over soon."

"I'm getting married this afternoon."

"Ah, congratulations! Have some dry toast and ginger ale, and keep some hard candies close by. Julie, you'll be fine. Take it easy this morning—rest if you can. And I hope you have a wonderful day."

"Thanks." She hung up and poured a glass of ginger ale.

**

Julie woke when she heard the door. It was nearly noon—she'd slept for three hours.

"Honey, are you all right?" Luke rushed to the bed.

"Just felt sick this morning. I called the doctor, but she said it was still normal. I went back to bed."

"Has anyone come by?"

"I have no idea. I was out."

"Okay. Well, maybe it's time to get up. We're getting married in a few hours."

"Isn't it bad luck for you to see me before the wedding?"

"We've been living in this house together for months,

MARTHA REYNOLDS

hon. I wouldn't worry about that." He sat down on the edge of the bed. "You sure you're okay?"

"Yeah. I'll take a shower and I'll be great."

"The flowers are all set. The cooks are in the kitchen. Sarah's bossing people around, even the chef, so that's a good sign," he said with a laugh.

"Oh, the band." Her hand flew to her forehead. "I was supposed to call them this morning."

"I called, Jules. They took a gig. I'm sorry. I even called a few others, but no luck with such short notice."

"What are we going to do?"

Luke traced his finger along her cheek. "I'll hook my phone up to speakers. Don't roll your eyes! I'll make it work. I can download whatever songs we want. I probably have most of them already."

"Really?"

"Yep. I'll do it now." He kissed her again and stood. "Come on, take your shower. I'll make you tea. And you need to eat. Sarah left a round loaf on the kitchen counter. It's got sunflower seeds on top, in the shape of a heart."

**

By two o'clock, Julie was feeling better. Her hair was washed, and Ella had come over to fix it. That was

349

something Freddy was going to do, but it was nice having her big sister around.

"It's weird to be back in the house," Ella said, twisting Julie's long honey-colored hair into an expert French knot. "I had such a visceral reaction when I saw the dining room. So many memories."

"Good memories, right?" She handed her sister a hair clip adorned with tiny white flowers.

"Mostly, sure. Okay if I take a peek upstairs?"

"Of course it's okay! We haven't done much with your old room. My old room. Funny, we both shared the same bedroom but by the time it was mine, you'd moved away."

"Julie, I think it's wonderful that you saved the place. Because you did, you saved it. None of the rest of us wanted it. Once I'd moved to the west coast, I couldn't imagine returning."

Julie sat in front of the mirror, watching Ella's hands, thinking of her mother's hands. The French knot look pretty. "When I was in New York, I couldn't imagine living here again, either. But when Tommy said he was selling, I don't know, I just couldn't let him do it. This place—" Julie paused as emotions caught up to her. "It holds a sacred spot in my heart. And now that Luke and I will have a family, it means even more to me. Something I can pass down to them."

"Don't cry now. Waterproof mascara or not." Ella bent at the waist to touch her cheek to Julie's. "You look gorgeous. A proper bride. Okay if I go upstairs by myself?"

"Of course. Will you tell Don to come over at five minutes to three?"

Ella waved her understanding before walking out of the house.

Tommy and Maria were staying in the bridal suite, so Luke dressed upstairs in the guest room next door. When Don walked through the door and entered the room that had been his parents' bedroom, Julie saw his face. Just like Ella, so many emotions written there. He paused long enough to look around at the four walls, but Julie and Luke's bedroom looked very different from what her parents had had. Julie had made sure of it. Don turned his gaze to Julie, who stood before him in her wedding dress. She had to admit, Vienne was the best. The dress fit perfectly.

"Wow," he said. "You look stunning." He pretended to be interested in a painting on the wall as he swiped a finger under his eye.

"Does it feel weird to you? Being in the house? In this room?"

"Sort of. It's been so long, and I hadn't thought much about the house for years. Being out west, so far away from the farm, you kind of pack away those memories as new ones take over. But then walking in here, seeing the old table, the clock, this room. Yeah, it's overwhelming."

"Ella had a similar reaction. Do you want to go upstairs? Check out the bedrooms? We turned the one that you and Eric shared into a room for Efren. And Tommy's old room will be for Mishell."

"Is the door still there?"

"Yeah, we kept it. In case they need to talk to each other. They're going to see the house for the first time in a couple of weeks. We want them to get used to it gradually. It'll still be a big adjustment. And we'll be downstairs."

"You know I still think of you as my kid sister? I know, I know, Julie, you're all grown up. Maybe it's being in this house, but I look at you and can still see you with dirt on your face, a skinned knee. Climbing the big oak tree behind the barn." He touched a finger to the corner of his eye. "Amazing how fast time goes by."

"You'll always be my favorite brother. Don't tell Tommy." She stood in front of Don, the brother she looked up to most. Eric was absent, and had never really felt like a big brother. Tommy was closer in age, but drove her crazy while they were growing up. His wife Maria was the stabilizing factor in his life now. Don was her handsome brother, the retired Air Force captain, still fit and trim at fifty. The one who had always looked out for her. The one who became a father figure after Ben

Tate died. Of course it should be Don who escorted her to Luke.

"Your secret's safe with me, Julie. Now let's get you married." He bent his elbow and held out his arm. Julie slipped her hand into the crook and let him lead her out of the family farmhouse.

**

Luke was waiting, with Tommy by his side. He looked like a matinee idol in his dark suit, crisp white shirt, and tie. The tie was hand-printed with a floral pattern (of course) of purples and blues.

Julie glanced at the assembled guests as Don walked her into the barn. Ella, Don's wife Linda, Tommy's wife Maria. Mary Jo and Taylor. The Cranes, the Robinsons, the Turners, and the Riveras, neighbors and friends all. Vendors and suppliers, Harmony from her old job in Manhattan, standing with a man who kept his arm around her shoulders.

The traditional Wedding March began and Julie caught a glimpse of its source—Luke's phone hooked up to a Bose Wave system.

She took her place next to Luke and stole a glance at him. Her guy, the one. Finally, the one. Tommy winked at her from the side and Judge Snow cleared his throat.

**

As music that Luke had chosen specifically for their

wedding played from the Bose Wave in a corner of the great room, Julie and Luke mingled with their guests. She passed up champagne in favor of ginger ale, but didn't feel any of the nausea that had plagued her that morning.

As they were about to sit for dinner, she felt a cool gust of air as the barn door opened. Turning around, a person was silhouetted against the brightness from outside. He was tall, slender…

"Freddy!" He rushed to her and swept her off her feet, lifting her just inches off the wooden floor.

"I'm sorry I missed the ceremony, doll," he said, kissing her on the mouth. "Congratulations!" Letting her go, he shook Luke's hand, then pulled him into a bear hug. "So happy for you both."

"I can't believe you're here. How is Bob?"

"He's good. Sends his love and best wishes." Freddy cocked his head. "Hey, did you get a band?"

"Nope," Luke chuckled. "But we have music. Plenty of it." He clapped Freddy on the back. "Good to see you, man, and thanks for all you did on this."

"Ah, it's what we do, right?"

"Can you stay?"

"Just long enough to toast the happy couple. Then I need

to get back. I'm going to pick up Val before heading back to the hospital. If he stays with Paige's family any longer, he'll forget who his dads are."

"I don't think so. But thanks, Freddy. I'm so glad you're here."

**

Luke leaned in to whisper a few words to Freddy, then picked up a microphone. He pushed back in his chair and stood, grazing Julie's shoulder with his fingers as he did. Julie looked down and blinked rapidly, willing herself to keep her emotions in check.

"Hi, everyone, and thanks for being here. As most of you know, Fred Campion, who's partners with Julie in this magical venture at Jingle Valley, was slated to be my best man. He actually *is* my best man, but circumstances have kept him away from most of the ceremony this afternoon. I'm glad to say that his husband Bob will be fine." He paused for murmurs of relief from the guests and a smattering of applause. "But he does need to get back to the hospital. So I'm going to hand the microphone over to Freddy, so he can say a few words. Fred."

As Luke took his seat and coupled Julie's hand in his, Freddy grasped the microphone and walked around to the front of their table, facing the assembled guests.

"I'm the kind of guy who always crammed at the last minute, so I did not memorize my speech," he began, pulling a folded sheet of paper from his inside breast pocket. "But I did write it, Julie! I did do that." He glanced down at the paper for a few seconds before folding it back up and returning it to its place. "Forget it," he said. "Everything is different after today."

He walked a few steps and turned his eyes upwards, perhaps finding his words from above. "When Julie Tate called me, back in 2015, and told me she wanted to buy her family's farm, I thought she was nuts. Tommy, I think you said so, too, right?" Julie's brother laughed and nodded. "And maybe the rest of you Tate kids felt the same way. Your little sister, who'd made it big in Manhattan, was ready to escape the city, and she didn't want the family farm to disappear. You've got to give the girl credit."

Julie sat quietly as he told the story of their beginning, but she wanted to correct him. Yes, it was true she didn't want her brother to sell the farm, to have someone not connected to the Tate family take it over and turn it into a condo development or an office park. But it was Freddy who had come up with the idea of turning Jingle Valley into a wedding destination. He was giving her credit for an idea that wasn't hers.

"Look, we knew we couldn't manage cows and chickens, but isn't this a gorgeous space?" He looked up to the high beamed ceiling again. "Together we saw potential and turned Jingle Valley into a premier destination for events. We hosted April Tweed and her husband Bill's wedding just a few months ago. Along the way, we've bickered—yes, Julie, I can be difficult sometimes—but we've always made up."

Freddy walked around to each table as he spoke. "A few years ago, we tried to fix each other up. I ran into a bank manager who I thought might be a nice match for Julie. And unbeknownst to me, she had walked into a flower shop and thought the new guy running things would be good for me. Because, you know, a florist…" He waited for the laughter to subside. "But surprise! The florist wasn't gay. And the banker was! I married that banker…" As Freddy's voice caught with thick emotion, Julie felt her eyes fill. *Come on, sweetie, you can do this.* He cleared his throat and continued.

"And today Julie married the florist. Luke, you're like a brother to me. I wish the two of you nothing but happiness from this day onward. In the coming months, your hearts and your home will open up to children, and…" He turned to Julie with a question in his eyes. *Do they know?* He mouthed. She nodded and lifted her shoulders. *Go ahead*, she thought.

"An instant family, filled with love. Efren and Mishell are lucky, but so are you. So are we all." He stepped back to his place and stood, raising his glass. "So, a toast to Luke and Julie. I wish I had written this myself, but I acknowledge Kahlil Gibran, who said, 'Marriage is the golden ring in a chain whose beginning is a glance and whose ending is Eternity.' Cheers!"

"Cheers!" everyone responded, before sipping champagne. Julie kissed Luke and was aware of applause, but focused only on her true love.

"Okay, guys, I really do have to go." Freddy crouched between them, one hand on each of their shoulders. "I wish I could stay."

"Freddy, you're the best. Please give Bob all our love." Julie kissed him, then wiped away the lipstick trace left below his lip.

"Will do. You guys staying here tonight?"

"Yeah. We might try to get away before the kids arrive for their first overnight, if we can. But we'll be here as long as you need us. Try not to worry about anything, Freddy. Just go be with Bob."

He kissed Julie again before making his exit.

"Let's go be social with our guests," Luke suggested. "How are you feeling?"

"Better," Julie said.

Only Ella noticed Julie wasn't drinking. "Either you're on a special diet," she began, her eyes drifting down to the raised waist on Julie's dress, "or you have something to tell me." Ella's eyes twinkled, and Julie took her hand.

"I let it slip at my bridal shower, to the one woman in town who loves to spread news. If you were here for any length of time, you'd have heard it from someone other than me. But yes, we're expecting. In early October."

"That's wonderful news," Ella said. "You really will

have an instant family! And the brother and sister you're adopting? Do they know?"

"Not yet. We want them to know how much we want them in our family."

"I admire you, Julie. I thought about adopting, back when I was single, then I thought I couldn't raise a child on my own. I could have, I suppose, and now that I have Jeanine…" Her eyes traveled to a distant place, miles and miles away. "But I'm fifty-five years old. Too late for me." She smiled. "I'll have to be everyone's favorite auntie."

"Absolutely, El. But you'll have to visit more often. And we'll come to see you and Jeanine, too."

"We'd love that," she said softly, hugging Julie hard.

**

Three hours later, the barn was emptied of guests. Julie had told her brothers Don and Tommy about her pregnancy (*let one of them tell Eric*, she thought). She'd danced with her husband (*my husband!*) and eaten everything. No more nausea. As the staff Freddy had hired was busy cleaning up, she and Luke walked hand in hand back to the farmhouse, their home.

"I'm exhausted," she said, instantly regretting it. "Wait, no I'm not. I'm great!"

Luke laughed out loud. "Stop. It's all right."

"No, it's our wedding night."

"I'm tired, too, honey. It was a very long day. Can I make you a cup of tea?"

"Yes. Can I put on my pajamas?"

He gave her a pointed look. "See? We're already an old married couple."

"I guess you're right. I'll be back in a minute."

While Julie changed out of her clothes, Luke opened one of the upper cupboards that she was unable to reach and took down a small box. He laid it on the table next to her teacup.

When she came back into the kitchen, it was the first thing she spotted. "Did you buy me something? Was I supposed to buy you something? Oh, Luke."

"No! I wasn't expecting anything. This is just something I found that I thought you'd like."

Julie unwrapped the box and lifted the lid. Inside was a necklace, a gold chain with two gold interlocking rings. She lifted it out. "It's lovely," she whispered.

"Those are for us. When Efren and Mishell come to live with us forever, I'll add two more. And when our baby is born, we'll add another."

He slipped it over her head. "What Freddy said about the

golden ring in a chain? I had no idea he was going to say that, and I almost lost it when he did."

"Oh, Luke. Life is good, isn't it? It's difficult and beautiful and unexpected and strange and wonderful. And I can't wait for the rest of it."

The End

Acknowledgments

All's Well in Jingle Valley, my ninth novel, could not have been written without the support of many wonderful people. At the top of my list, as always, is my husband Jim, the sunshine of my life, my biggest fan, my kindest critique reader.

Thank you to Sharyn O'Leary of Frey Florist in Providence, for consultations about all things floral.

Barbara Ann Whitman, author of *Have Mercy*, and my go-to reader Pauline Wiles, author of the *Saffron Sweeting* series of novels, provided valuable feedback on all aspects of this book. Thank you both so much.

Sean McConway was exceptionally helpful when I had questions about Fr. Dan.

Fabiola Dreyer-Abbet, who was so brilliant in correcting the Italian words and phrases in *Villa del Sol*, came through again to be sure I got it right in French this time. *Merci, mon amie.*

Laurie Dumas, my favorite librarian, at my favorite library, always welcomes me with a cheery attitude. I'm glad we're friends! And I love my library, for quiet time editing and rewriting.

Jingle Valley is a fictional place, but it was and has been inspired by the very real Holiday Brook Farm in Dalton, Massachusetts. If you're ever in the vicinity, please stop by and say hello.

I am a proud member of the Association of Rhode Island Authors (ARIA), a 300+-member non-profit organization of local published writers committed to raising awareness of the written works crafted by Rhode Islanders. They provide a wealth of opportunities for new and established writers.

Brea Brown, a wonderful author of over a dozen novels, knows how technical issues make me want to pull my hair out—she keeps me from going bald.

Heather McCoubrey and Carol Wise, of Wise Element, created this gorgeous cover.

If you read this book and enjoyed it, please consider leaving a review online at Amazon and Goodreads. It does mean a lot to an author. You're the reason I write, and I couldn't be happier to be doing this thing I love so much.

Made in the USA
Lexington, KY
30 October 2019

56196390R00226